NIKOLAS

Stone Society Book 5

By Faith Gibson

The following is a fictional story set in a post-apocalyptic world. While some of the historical names, places, and events are real, the author created events for the book. It is intended to be read for entertainment purposes only.

Published by Faith Gibson
Editor: Jagged Rose Wordsmithing
First print edition: November 2015
Cover design by: Elm Street Design Studio
Photography: 123RF
ISBN: 978-1518836978

This book is intended for mature audiences only.

DEDICATION

To my family, whether by blood or by choice - because family really is everything. To my adoptive parents who chose me when no one else did - thank you for giving me a great life.

ACKNOWLEDGEMENTS

My writing posse: Alex, Kendall, Jen, and Nikki – thank you for continually swimming both downstream and up river with me. You are my oars, my lifejackets, and my anchors.

My beta readers: Sharon B, Shannon P, Tanya R, and Lita T

The ladies at TaSTy WordGasms, and all the bloggers out there helping to get not just my books, but all the author's books out to the readers.

To everyone who pimps for an author. Thank you. You give us time to do what we love to do… write.

To those faithful readers who leave reviews – every.single.book… You are precious.

PROLOGUE

2035

THE dirty man's cold eyes never left Sophia. He was sitting with his back against the window, turned so he could watch her. Why hadn't she sat behind the bus driver instead of toward the rear? She was going to move closer to the front, but the seats remained occupied for most of the trip. She had planned on sleeping since they were traveling at night, but with the looks she was getting from the man, there was no way she was closing her eyes. The bus rolled up to one of the sketchier stops, and the woman sitting directly across from her exited the bus. The man took the vacated seat and once again placed himself so his body was turned towards hers. Sophia faced forward, keeping him in her peripheral vision. Instead of focusing on the waves of discomfort, she returned her mind to the future and the note she left for her mom.

Tired of being coddled by an overprotective mother, Sophia decided to take matters into her own hands. Her father was out of the country, checking on one of his siblings who had yet to transition from human to half-blood Gargoyle. She waited until her mother was asleep and slipped quietly out of the house, keeping to the shadows of the neighbors' yards as she made her way to the bus terminal.

The conversation with her mother earlier that evening replayed in her mind. *"You are only sixteen. You need to wait a couple more years, Sophia. I'm not going to lose you, too."*

"What do you mean, lose me too? Who did you lose?"

"Nobody. You're father's gone all the time. That's all I meant. Now, stop asking. You're not going."

"But, Mom! Tessa started her training with Grandpa when she was younger than I am." Sophia jumped up on the kitchen island where her mother was looking at a map.

"Yes, she did. But you are not Tessa, no matter how much you idolize your cousin." Monica sighed as she did every time her daughter brought up the subject of moving to New Atlanta.

"No, I'm Sophia Brooks, daughter of Samuel Brooks, the greatest Watcher ever to live. How can I follow in his footsteps if I don't learn from the best, too?" Ever since Sophia found out her grandparents were moving south, she had begged her mother to let her go with them. She loved her parents. Really loved her father, but it was time for her mother to finally cut the umbilical cord.

Her grandfather, Jonas Montague, was an infamous doctor and scientist, one the world thought was dead. More importantly than that, he was a shapeshifter from the original line of Gargouille. He had taken Tessa under his wing and taught her the ways of their kind. Now it was Sophia's turn to learn, but she couldn't do that if JoJo, as she affectionately called Jonas, was almost a thousand miles away.

"We will discuss this more when your father gets home. Now get off the island. I need to look at something."

Before she got down, Sophia glanced at the map her mother was studying so intently. Ancient Egypt? Maybe she wanted to visit the Pyramids of Giza. When her mother caught her looking, she folded up the map and glared at her daughter.

"Fine, I'm going." Sophia slid off the cabinet. I'm going

all right, and you can't stop me, *she thought to herself. It didn't take Sophia long to write the note. It was a message she had rehearsed in her head numerous times in her own defense:*

Mom,

I know you have my best interest at heart, but this is something I have to do. If I am going to follow in Dad's footsteps, I need to learn all I can about our family, about Gargoyles. I'm going to live with JoJo. I'll call you when I get there. I love you.

If Sophia couldn't make this trip successfully, her mother would insist she had been correct and demand Sophia return to New York. Movement to her left brought her attention back to the dirty man. The intermittent flash of street lamps every thirty seconds was the only light on the bus. Regardless, Sophia was well aware of what was going on across the aisle. As inconspicuously as possible, she looked around at the other passengers, only to find them all asleep. She looked in the wide rearview mirror, hoping to get the driver's attention. The older man was focused on the road ahead of him and not those seated behind him.

The dirty man had his pants unzipped, his cock in his hand. Sophia wasn't a prude. She and her friends had looked at porn online, so she knew all about masturbation. When it was directed at her, it was an entirely different matter. She didn't dare look his way, but Sophia could see the movement of his hand, hear his heavy breathing over the hum of the diesel engine. When he shot his load, he didn't bother covering himself. He allowed the white ejaculate to shoot onto the seat toward her. He tucked his dick back into his pants and licked his hand.

Sophia sat stone still. She made no indication she had observed his lewdness. There was no way she was staying on the bus a minute longer than she had to, though. At the next major stop, she would exit the bus and take a taxi the rest of the way to New Atlanta. She felt as though she held her breath the twenty minutes or so it took them to reach the next stop. As soon as the driver began slowing down, she stood from her seat. A hand reached out and grabbed her, preventing her from walking.

Sophia glanced down at the hand circling her wrist then looked into the eyes of the man she would never forget as long as she lived. "Let go of me," she told him, barely above a whisper. When he tightened his grip, she found her voice. "I said, let go."

"Is there a problem back there?" The driver was standing in the aisle, hands on his hips. The other passengers were now stirring, her voice waking them from their sleep. The man scowled at Sophia and released her arm. She grabbed her bag and practically ran to the front of the bus. "I need my luggage," she told the driver. He followed her to the side of the bus and opened the outside compartment where baggage was stored. Once she had her suitcases, Sophia didn't hesitate to go inside where it was well lit. Not wanting to take a chance on getting a taxi driver who would possibly take advantage of a young girl, Sophia called her grandfather to come get her.

An hour later, Jonas walked into the bus stop. Sophia smiled and ran to him. Her happiness was short lived when she felt JoJo tense in her arms. She glanced up to see him looking over her shoulder. She turned around to see the creep from the bus standing in the corner of the room, eyes hooded. Sophia shivered.

Jonas asked, "What's wrong?"

"Nothing. Let's get out of here," she lied.

Her grandfather wasn't having it. "Sophia, I just drove an hour to pick you up and am going to have to deal with your mother when we get home. Do not lie to me."

Sophia turned her back on the man and whispered, "That dirty man standing in the corner behind me was creeping me out on the bus. I didn't realize he had gotten off at this stop. That's all. Now, can we go?"

Jonas released his cell phone from its holder and snapped a picture of the man.

"What are you doing?" Sophia whispered.

"Taking his picture, just in case. Now, let's get you home." Jonas grabbed one suitcase while she took the other. She gave the man in the corner one last look, but he was nowhere to be seen.

An hour later, they arrived at Jonas and Caroline's new home where Sophia would start the next chapter of her life. She had made it those hundreds of miles on that bus, coming away mostly unscathed. She thanked the gods for that huge favor. Her mother had been scared until Sophia arrived safely. Then she'd been livid. After Jonas made sure she was okay, he was ecstatic. With Tessa off doing the family's business, he now had someone else to teach. Her father was caught between a rock and a hard place. He loved his wife, yet he knew Sophia would not be deterred. When Sam wasn't out of the country, he split his time between

New York and New Atlanta, aiding his father in her training.

Sophia graduated valedictorian from New Atlanta High School and went on to study at UGA. Athens, Georgia, had been one of the cities that refused to change its name after the world fell apart and began rebuilding. The people of Athens prided themselves in maintaining somewhat of a status quo during the last thirty years. Sophia was certain they just didn't want their mascot's name to be Ugna. While at the university, she majored in history and minored in anthropology. Most of what she learned, however, came from her grandfather. She worked part-time at the library so she could study on the job, and she continued to work there after she graduated college. What better job to have than being surrounded by knowledge when she herself was the keeper of knowledge for her kind?

As long as she could remember, Sophia had studied all she could about the half-blood shapeshifters in her family as well as the full-blood Gargoyles who lived in the States. When she moved to New Atlanta, she focused on those who lived in and around the city. Sophia knew they would someday be one big Clan whether JoJo wanted them to be or not. She knew this, because one of them was her mate. She loved her family and was loyal to them as much as she could be, but as soon as she figured out the reason she had transitioned to a half-blood, Sophia made it her mission to bring them all together.

Since she had hidden cameras in Tessa's home, Sophia knew when her cousin transitioned, as well as the cause of her changing to a half-blood. Tessa unknowingly confessed the one secret her grandfather had withheld during her studies. Like Tessa, when Sophia phased for the first time, she had been alone. She knew what to expect after watching her cousin writhe around on her kitchen floor. As soon as Sophia had her inner shifter under control, she searched the city for members of the Stone Clan until she found the one who made her want to drag him into a dark alley and screw him senseless.

Sophia pilfered one of her grandfather's journals and "hid" it in the library among his published works, anticipating the day her mate figured it all out. Until then, she waited for others of his family to begin finding their mates. She knew it was only a matter of time until he found her. The day he did, her shifter rejoiced. The day Nikolas Stone came into the library and she touched him, Sophia knew her life was going to change irrevocably.

Chapter One

Present Day 2047

SOPHIA felt someone's eyes on her when she entered the airport. She wanted to chalk the feeling up to nerves since this was her first international trip, alone or otherwise. Sophia knew better, though. Having Original Gargoyle blood flowing through her veins gave her an advantage over most humans. The fact that she was a half-blood shifter herself? That intensified her gut feeling, and she knew not to dismiss it. Considering she was traveling to Egypt at the behest of an anonymous note to locate her missing parents, why wouldn't someone be watching?

New Atlanta International was still a busy hub thirty years after her grandfather brought the city, as well as the world, to its knees. The chairs outside the departure gate were mostly full. Sophia didn't want to squeeze in between strangers who might strike up a conversation. Instead, she opted to wait in one of the restaurants located on the concourse. She kept her back to the wall and her senses aware. She had almost an hour before her flight began boarding, so she pretended to read a book while sipping on a cocktail. What she was really doing was regretting having to leave the country now that Nikolas had found her. If he'd only found her sooner, they could be taking this trip together. She knew if they were truly mated, Nikolas Stone would never let her make such a dangerous journey alone.

When it was almost time to board the flight, Sophia

made a quick call to Tessa, letting her know she was on her way to Egypt. If her cousin didn't have her hands full with her watcher duties, Sophia would have welcomed the company. However, Tessa was juggling her time between the still-human siblings and was needed in the States. The first class passengers were called to the gate, and Sophia grabbed her carry-on bag, making her way through the throngs of people headed to their own area. While sitting in the restaurant, she hadn't felt the twinge of being watched again, but that didn't mean someone wasn't. Sitting in first class gave Sophia the advantage of observing those who got on the plane after she did. Almost everyone had boarded when goosebumps pimpled on her arms. She tried desperately not to look, but she failed.

The last group of passengers consisted of several men and only one woman. The female was late twenties, about five-ten, had long blonde hair, and wore cowboy boots and a denim jacket. She could have been a model she was so stunning. Most of the men were forgettable. There was one man, though, who demanded attention. He was broad and tall, reminding Sophia of one of the Stone Clan. If she didn't know better, she'd say he was a Goyle.

As the flight attendants prepared the cabin for takeoff, Sophia's mind drifted back to the last time she'd taken an impromptu trip alone. She hadn't thought about the bus ride in a long time, nor the way she left home. Thinking back to that night reminded Sophia of the map her mother had been studying. Egypt. The note she received regarding her parents' whereabouts instructed her to travel to Giza. Could it possibly be a coincidence? She thought not. If there was one thing life had taught her so far, it was there were no coincidences.

During her three-hour layover in France, she figured out which one of the passengers was following her. When she first thought it was the woman, Sophia ducked into the nearest restroom as soon as she was in the terminal. The woman entered the restroom at the same time Sophia was exiting. Her spine tingled at that moment, but she had to sidestep to miss one of the men. She didn't have to make eye contact to know which one it was. The testosterone seeping from his pores was a dead giveaway. Thankfully, there was a restaurant a short distance from the restroom. Sophia pretended to look around at her options, making sure the man wasn't waiting on the woman. The woman exited the restroom and walked down the concourse. The large man never looked her way. He did, however, look Sophia's. It was amazing to her how obvious the man was being. Whoever was in charge of this kidnapping, abduction, whatever this was called, should have hired someone a little stealthier to follow her.

Now, they had landed in Cairo. While Sophia had been waiting in line to get her tourist visa, she didn't feel anyone else's presence, but now she was waiting for her luggage at the carousel, and the nagging tingle had returned. Both the woman and one of the regular guys were also waiting on their baggage; however, the large man was nowhere to be seen. Sophia could feel him, though. As soon as she tapped into his energy in

France, she was able to continue monitoring his presence with her shifter senses.

Once she retrieved her suitcases, Sophia made her way to the taxi stand. She waited while the driver put her bags in the trunk, and when he got in and closed his door, she told him *where to.* If there was anything to be thankful for, it was the fact that whoever had her parents had brought them to an English-speaking country. Her Spanish was good, her French decent, her Italian passable. She had only started studying Italian when she figured out Nikolas Stone was her mate. She couldn't think of the gorgeous male now. She had to keep her mind sharp and worry about getting her parents home safely. Once she'd accomplished that, only then would she think about a future with the hot Gargoyle.

The note Sophia received instructing her to travel to Egypt had listed an address for a hotel in Giza. She made a reservation there under her name, but instead of actually staying in Giza, Sophia made another reservation in Cairo using an alias, Clara Fort. She would use the size of the Nile Grand Hotel as well as its busy location to her advantage. She had also made a reservation at a bed and breakfast downtown under a false name. The people following her would probably continue to tail her for a while, but eventually she would give them the slip. That was the plan, anyway.

Sophia might be new to traveling abroad, but she was not a novice when it came to hiding out. She learned from the best. JoJo had told her his story – from the time he met Caroline and was ostracized, to cloning Tessa, to the present. He taught her as much as she could learn about chemistry and physics. She secretly watched Tessa. She followed her cousin when she went out in New Atlanta. She sneaked into Tessa's home when she was out of town. The feisty redhead wasn't the only one who could bypass an alarm, pick a lock, or install hidden cameras. Sophia might not be experienced, but she wasn't scared. Not really. She was ready to put her knowledge to the test.

Sophia checked into the large, posh hotel. The bellman aided her with her luggage since she had several pieces. When she packed, she had no idea how long she would be away or what equipment she would need. She had brought only the basic electronics, fearing the larger pieces would cause her to be detained by customs.

As soon as she tipped the bellman, Sophia turned and took in her room. She had wanted to book a suite, but she figured most of her time would be spent at the bed and breakfast. The room was large, even if standard size. It was nicely furnished and would suit her needs for the little time she would be there. She tossed her bags on one of the double beds and began unzipping the one containing her disguises. A scratching noise came from outside her door. "What the hell?" she asked herself as a piece of paper appeared underneath. So much for not going to the hotel as they instructed.

Since she didn't have a gun on her, Sophia reached out with her shifter senses to detect footsteps running down the hall. When she found no sign of life outside her door, she walked over and picked up the note. It was typewritten, same as the previous one had been.

Travel by ferry to the Giza Zoo. Have a seat across from the leopard.

Her original note told her to go to Giza. Now she understood why. It surprised Sophia that the zoo was open. As with most of the world, the near apocalypse brought social devastation to Egypt but not to Cairo. The larger cities waned for a bit, but most bounced back quicker than their smaller, sister cities. Giza, once a booming tourist attraction, was still trying to find its way back on the map.

The fact that she received another clue at a hotel she wasn't supposed to be staying in meant they knew where she was. No date or time was listed on the note telling her when to be there. Normally, Sophia liked puzzles. When her parents' lives were on the line? Not so much.

She pulled out her laptop and turned it on. While waiting on her computer to boot up, Sophia unpacked her clothes, separating them into two stacks: those she would wear as herself and the ones she would don as her alter egos. Having watched her grandfather these last few years had taught her so much more than sitting in a class at the university had. Tessa had been a teacher of a different sort, only she hadn't been aware of her younger cousin's presence. If she ever found out how Sophia had repeatedly duped her, she'd probably be one pissed-off redhead. Sophia would worry about that if and when it happened. Now, she needed more information on the Giza Zoo.

The zoo was not as thriving as it once had been,

but it still had a goodly number of animals. *This ought to be fun.* Animals didn't like shifters because they sensed the beast inside the human body. No puppy or kitten for her when she was little. It wasn't nearly as bad with half-bloods as it was with Gargoyles. They may look human, but they were truly all shifter. She had once asked JoJo why the Gargoyles looked human when they weren't, and he said the only explanation he could come up with was so they would fit in the human world undetected.

The note specifically said to take a boat to Giza. That seemed odd considering she could take a taxi and be there a lot quicker. Sophia searched the internet for ferries traveling the Nile. She found one that left early the next morning, so she booked it. Since the note didn't specify when, Sophia made the choice for the next day so she would have the rest of the afternoon to check into the bed and breakfast and store the majority of her equipment at the smaller inn.

Closing down her computer, Sophia was ready to do a little recon. Using the prosthetics, she transformed herself from the twenty-something young lady she was, to an older, grandmother type she would never be.

After calling for a taxi, Sophia grabbed two suitcases and rolled them to the door. She reached out with her shifter senses. Not hearing anyone in the vicinity, she eased into the hallway. She needed to be certain whoever followed her didn't see an old lady leaving her room. When she reached the front of the hotel, she made her way to the cab waiting for her at the curb. She allowed the driver to stow her luggage in the trunk as she got into the back seat. She gave him directions to another hotel. Once there, he removed her bags, and she paid him. She then hailed a different taxi and rode the seven blocks to the bed and breakfast.

Her second temporary residence was a small, two-story building. It was within walking distance of The Nile Grand, but she'd taken the taxis just in case. She entered the small hotel and admired the few Halloween decorations adorning the lobby. She checked in using the name Beatrice Nightingale and made her way to the assigned room on the second floor overlooking the park across the street. Sophia requested the second floor for safety reasons. Should someone try to get into her room through an exterior window, they would have a harder time if her room was higher up. With only two suitcases, Sophia rolled her own luggage to her room. Unlike the hotel's opulence, this room was small and quaint. That suited Beatrice just fine.

Once inside, Sophia unpacked the clothes from one suitcase, hanging the grandmother-style clothes in the closet so they could unwrinkle. There were also items someone like Tessa might wear. She hung those up as well. The bag containing half of the gadgets and disguises she left intact. She would remove the items as she needed them and store the unneeded ones under the bed. Keeping her current persona in place, Sophia grabbed a few things out of her case and deposited them into her large handbag. Checking her reflection in the mirror, Sophia was pleased with what she saw. She hauled the purse over her shoulder, and Beatrice headed out to do some sightseeing.

There were plenty of people walking on the crowded sidewalks, so Sophia decided against another taxi. She kept her senses open to anyone who might be following. Someone had followed her to the new hotel, and it was possible he might be somewhere close by. She was certain she had lost him when she left the hotel as Beatrice, but she would remain on high alert, just in case.

Beatrice ambled through several shops as a tourist would do. She was about to step back out onto the sidewalk when she caught sight of the blonde woman from her flight. She was not alone. Walking beside her was the same man from the luggage carousel as well as the large one Sophia could sense. All three of them were scanning the area. Sophia had a feeling she knew who they were searching for.

CHAPTER TWO

NIKOLAS was getting desperate. When he asked the other librarians for Sophia's schedule, neither one would give him the information he sought. The look on both their faces when they refused his request had been one of pity rather than disdain. Why wouldn't they tell him the truth? If they thought they were protecting Sophia, he could accept that. If it wasn't that… Was it possible she had a boyfriend? Nik hoped not. He'd hate to have to kick a human's ass.

Even though he felt bad about invading her privacy, he attempted to run a background check on her. Nik wasn't as adept at hacking as Julian, but he was no slouch. His research on the girl had come up with the bare minimum. He didn't want his brother to know what he was up to, but at this point, he was getting desperate. Nik had a decision to make. Would he involve Julian, or would he wait it out? He wanted to know more about the cute librarian. He decided to give it one more try before getting Jules involved.

Nik drove downtown and parked outside the library. As soon as he reached the inside of the tall building, he knew Sophia wasn't there. He couldn't sense honeysuckle anywhere. Still, he climbed the three flights of steps to the area where she usually worked. When he reached the information desk, a young girl looked up from the computer. "Can I help you?" she asked with a bright smile.

"I'm looking for Sophia. Is she here?" he asked, already knowing the answer.

The girl shook her head. "No, I'm afraid not. She's

taken a leave of absence."

"What? When?" Nikolas was happy to get more information from the girl than the other women had offered, but it wasn't the information he wanted to hear.

"A couple days ago."

Nik began pacing the room. He ran his hands through his hair but stopped when the girl said his name. "Mr. Stone." When he looked at her, she continued. "I have something for you." She held out an envelope. It wasn't your basic, everyday number ten. It was fine linen stationery in a pale shade of peach. His name was written in beautiful cursive on the outside.

Nikolas muttered, "Thank you," and took off down the stairs. He would read her words in private. He opened the door to his Audi and slid into the driver's seat. Nik's heart was tapping out a beat that did not match his usual calm. He didn't use his Gargoyle abilities to slow it down, either. He relished the feeling of adrenaline coursing through his five-hundred-year-old body. Even flying and taking down Unholy didn't give him the jolt this envelope did. Allowing the claw on his index finger to elongate, he carefully sliced open the paper. He retracted the sharp nail before pulling the letter out. Inhaling deeply, he unfolded the peach paper and scanned the short message:

Nikolas, I am so sorry to have to leave just when you found me. Yours, Sophia

Nik turned the paper over, looking for more writing on the back. When he found none, he reread the note. What the fuck did that even mean? *Just when he found her*. And she signed it *yours*. If she was his, why the fuck had she disappeared on him? Why would she take a leave of absence now? He had too many questions and not enough answers. Fuck invading her privacy. He was going to confront her at home.

WALKING around dressed as Beatrice allowed Sophia to follow the blonde and her companions. She couldn't believe she'd been wrong about them. When the three of them split up, Sophia decided to follow the woman. After a few blocks, the blonde hailed a taxi, so Sophia did the same. "Where to?" the man asked in a thick Egyptian accent.

"Follow that taxi, please." If the driver was suspicious, he didn't let on. They rode for almost twenty minutes before arriving at the zoo. Sophia pretended to fumble around in her purse for money, giving the other woman time to get out of her own taxi. When she was almost out of sight, Sophia shoved the money in the driver's hand. She hurried to the entrance and arrived just in time to see the woman paying for her ticket. Sophia ducked behind a small family, purchased her own ticket, and headed in the direction the blonde had gone. Considering the woman had been in New Atlanta, Sophia had no doubt she had misjudged who was following her. Now that she knew all three passengers had been together, she would have to be more cautious. If the blonde was in bed with whoever was holding her parents captive, more than likely, she was headed to the leopard enclosure.

Before she reached the area, Sophia hid behind a clump of bushes, watching the other woman to see what she was up to. The blonde sat on the same bench Sophia had been instructed to sit on. The woman glanced around before removing something from her pocket. She then leaned forward and placed her hand underneath the bench. When she sat up, her hand was empty. The woman didn't immediately stand up. She pretended to be a tourist, enjoying the view of the large cat in front of her. She glanced around the area before rising and walking off, headed straight toward Sophia. As she passed by, Sophia put her camera in front of her face and clicked.

Once the blonde left the area, Beatrice walked toward the bench, curious as to what was placed beneath. Was it a bomb? If so, it would need to be detonated by hand or else anyone who sat down would be a victim. Were they watching now? Was someone waiting for Sophia Brooks to sit on the bench so she could be killed? She walked closer to the bench and listened. She didn't hear ticking, so she sat her somewhat heavy bag on the seat where the blonde had been. Again, she reached out and didn't hear anything out of the ordinary.

Sophia decided to take a chance, as stupid as it was. Sitting down, she placed her purse in her lap and dug around. She pulled out a pack of gum and *accidentally* dropped it on the ground. As she bent over to retrieve the gum, Sophia felt under the bench for whatever had been placed there. If they wanted her dead, surely they would have killed her somewhere less public. Her fingers touched a cold, metal object. This is what they wanted her to find. She pulled a round disk off the underside of the bench and palmed it. She placed it in her lap while she unwrapped a piece of gum and stuck it in her mouth.

Instead of standing immediately, Sophia decided to enjoy the scenery for a while longer. Sensing the shifter inside her, the big cat hissed and kept its distance. Sophia raised her camera and snapped a picture of the gorgeous animal. So as not to torment it any longer, she stood and left the area, dropping the disk in her bag before walking off. As curious as she was to find out what the object was, she continued her visit around the zoo, not wanting to draw attention to herself by leaving too soon.

After a couple of hours, Sophia made her way back to the bed and breakfast. If JoJo knew she had walked around that long with an unknown object in her possession, he'd probably revoke her watcher card. Not that there was an actual card she received, but still… Once in the privacy of her small room, Sophia removed the gold disk from her bag and studied it. It was larger in diameter than any American coin, but not heavier. One side contained miniscule hieroglyphs. The other side was smooth. The outer edge contained a groove that ran the circumference. She placed her thumbnail into the groove and pulled, but it didn't come apart.

When her stomach rumbled, letting her know it was dinner time, Sophia placed the disk inside the room safe and locked it up. She checked Beatrice's reflection to make sure the prosthetic needed no adjustment. When she was pleased with her appearance, Beatrice headed down to the dining room. There were two couples, one older and one younger, seated at the table when she arrived. She smiled at them all as the older woman introduced them. "We're the Waterfords. I'm Yvonne, and this is my husband, Fred, our son, Garrett, and his wife, Millicent."

"It's a pleasure to meet you. I'm Beatrice Nightingale," she said through the transmitter at her throat. The voice coming out of her mouth belonged to a sweet little lady who visited the library once a week with her grandchildren. She understood the mechanics behind the transmitter, having watched her grandfather design the device. Still, she was amazed how something so small could be so powerful.

"So, what brings you to Egypt? And alone I might add," Yvonne asked.

Sophia didn't appreciate the other woman's judgmental tone. "Oh, my dear, I'm not alone. The pyramids were on my bucket list, so my daughter and her husband brought me here on vacation. They love the fast-paced life and are staying at one of those large, posh resorts. I prefer something smaller, quieter," she said while she waved her arm, indicating the room. "Are you on vacation as well?"

"Yes, Garrett and Millicent are on a belated honeymoon," Yvonne said with a frown.

"That explains why the kids are here. Why are *you* here?" Sophia asked, not holding back a smirk. She'd bet her last pound the woman had yet to untie the apron strings. Millicent did her best to hide her amusement. Garrett rolled his eyes. Fred looked at the ceiling. Yep, Sophia was right.

Yvonne huffed. "I'm here because they are too young to travel so far alone. I don't know why they couldn't have gone to the beach like a normal couple. It would have been so much cheaper."

Sophia turned her attention to the "kids". "Too young? What are you, late twenties? Why, you're my age."

Millicent raised her eyebrows. "Your age?"

"Oh, silly me. I meant my daughter's age. Heaven knows I'm not young. But you two, you're definitely old enough to travel without a chaperone." Sophia winked at the young woman as Yvonne gasped beside her.

"Now listen here!" Yvonne started to speak her mind, but she was cut off as dinner was carted into the dining room.

After the servers left the room, Millicent grinned and asked, "So, Beatrice, what else is on your bucket list?"

Oh shit. She hadn't thought about what she would like to do besides Nikolas Stone. "Well, let's see. I would love to fly through the air like a bird, so jumping out of a plane is on the list." *I want to fly with Nikolas, see his massive Gargoyle wings spread out.* "I collect books, and I want to go to the British library one day." *I want to see Nik's personal library.* "I think riding a camel in the desert is something I definitely want to try while I'm here." *I want to ride Nikolas Stone, in the desert, at the beach, in the shower...* Sophia mentally chastised herself. *Get a grip, woman.* She had to get her mind off her mate. "So, Garrett, what do you do for a living?"

The conversation stayed on the younger couple for the rest of the meal. If Yvonne tried to interrupt, Sophia managed to steer talk back their way. She felt sorry for them. Having an overprotective mother-in-law couldn't be easy. That's one thing she'd never have to worry about. At least she didn't think so. Having studied the Stone Society for many years, Sophia knew Nik's father, Roberto, was no longer living. It only made sense that his mother wouldn't be, either. Her own mother might not be ecstatic when she found out Nikolas was Sophia's mate, especially since she'd kept her transitioning from her parents, but Monica would get over it. Her relationship with her mom was much better now that Sophia was grown. Sighing, she remembered the disk and the real reason she was in Egypt.

"If you'll excuse me. It was a pleasure meeting you all, and I'm sure we'll dine together again." Sophia pushed her chair away from the table and stood. Everyone stood with her except Yvonne. She was obviously miffed at being dismissed during dinner.

Millicent squeezed her hand. "Beatrice, you are a peach. I hope you have the opportunity to complete your bucket list."

"Thank you. I don't plan on leaving this world anytime soon. I plan on adding to my list," she told her with a wink. Sophia patted the young woman's hand and headed upstairs. There was some arguing at the table regarding Fred not taking up for Yvonne. Sophia shook her head. It took all kinds.

Once in her room, she stripped out of her disguise.

The prosthetic was light, but it still itched after several hours. Sophia washed her face and changed into pajamas before opening her laptop and settling in to do some research.

"THE disk is in place. Now we wait for Miss Brooks to show up," the blonde told her partner on the phone. "Sergei, do you have eyes on the ferries?"

"Yes, Kallisto. I have men set up at each port, and they all have a photo of the woman."

"Good. Drago has a team ready at the zoo. Remember, we do not want to capture her. We only want to ensure she complies with our demands. We need to keep her on this, as the Americans say, 'wild goose chase' as long as possible."

"What is the purpose of this charade if not to kill the woman?"

"I am merely following my father's orders. Now, don't stay away too long. I might get lonely."

"I will see you soon," Sergei promised before disconnecting.

Kallisto Verga was the adopted daughter of one of the most powerful males in all of Greece. She had no idea why her father was targeting this American family. He had the power to take them out discreetly, yet he was toying with them. She hated these cat-and-mouse games. Kallisto would rather shoot the girl and get it over with.

CHAPTER THREE

AS a watcher for the family, Ezekiel was in New Mexico putting out a fire when he got a phone call from Elizabeth Flanagan. His cousin's mate would not be calling unless it was an emergency, and emergency it was. Zeke's brother, Sam, and his wife had been kidnapped. Sam's daughter, Sophia, had already left for Egypt after receiving a note from the kidnappers. While Sophia was training to be a watcher, she was still young and inexperienced. Tessa, Elizabeth's daughter, was another watcher, and she was planning on going after Sophia. Elizabeth was intervening, as mothers often do, begging Zeke to go look for Sam and Monica so Tessa wouldn't head off to Egypt alone.

Zeke was currently listening to his sister, Cordelia, rant and rave about being a half-blood shifter with no prior knowledge or warning. It was a complaint Zeke was used to as well as tired of. Cordelia had transitioned, and he was helping her come to terms with what she now was and why the family had kept the truth from her. This wasn't the first time he'd gone to check on a sibling only to find they had already met their mate. Cordelia was pissed off, to say the least. She didn't have a boyfriend, so she had no idea who her mate was.

All of the older brothers and sisters had already transitioned. There were only a couple of the younger ones who were still unaware. Tessa had recently helped Dane through his initial change. She had also talked to Lilly almost immediately after she went through hers. Tessa had confided in both him and Sam what caused the transition. Why Jonas wanted to keep the trigger a secret was a mystery.

Zeke had no idea who his own mate was. He had transitioned almost thirty years ago and had spent those same years without a woman by his side. When Tessa told him the trigger, he went through a myriad of emotions - anger, betrayal, and sadness were on top of the list. How could he have been so close to his mate only to lose her? Since they didn't make the bond official, his mate had continued to age while he looked to be in his thirties.

Zeke decided right then that after he helped Sophia get Sam and Monica home, he was having a long talk with his father. It was selfish to keep the truth from the remaining siblings who were in the dark, and he was going to inform them of their bloodline and what could happen. For now, though, he had to hop a plane to Egypt.

NIKOLAS sat in the corner of Rafael's dining room as Dante erupted in fury. His cousin phased, knocking shit off the sideboard. Dante and Isabelle weren't mated yet, and he was already losing his mind. It was utter chaos. Nik thought of his own mate and the note in his pocket. Nikolas wanted to talk to Julian, but his brother was arguing with the new half-blood, Dane. The maelstrom continued all around him. Rafael roared at Dante to stand down. Gregor walked into the room looking about as low as Nik felt.

Kaya let out a loud whistle and chastised them for their behavior. Nik had to grin inwardly at Rafael's mate. The former chief of police was making a fine Queen to Rafael's King. When the mood abated somewhat, Rafael ordered them all outside to continue their meeting.

The conversation turned to Gregor's and Dante's newly found mates and why the half-bloods were afraid of mating with the Gargoyles. When Gregor spoke to Nik, he raised his head. "Nikolas, you look like someone kicked your puppy. What's wrong?"

Nikolas closed his eyes and sighed. "I have been to the library several times to see Sophia, but she hasn't been there. Yesterday when I went, someone gave me a note. All it said was she was sorry to leave now that I had found her."

"Did you say Sophia?" Gregor and Dante asked at the same time.

Nikolas straightened up, staring at both his cousins. "Yes."

"Hang on a second." Gregor pulled out his cell phone. He didn't announce himself, just cut off whoever was speaking on the other end. "Listen, you mentioned someone named Sophia. She wouldn't happen to be a librarian, would she? Just curious. Gotta go." He thumbed the phone off and told Nikolas, "I know where your woman is - Egypt."

"Egypt? Why the fuck is she in Egypt?" Nikolas couldn't help but raise his voice.

Gregor filled him in. "Her parents are missing. From what I gather, Tessa and two others in their family are called watchers. One of those others is

Sophia's father. They look after the half-bloods who haven't transitioned yet. Sophia's parents have allegedly been abducted. Tessa planned on going after them, but her mother called and wanted me to intervene."

Nikolas didn't hear the rest of the conversation. His head was spinning with this new information. His mate knew what he was. She *knew* he was a shifter! Her parents had been abducted, and now she had gone to find them. He had to go after her. *Fuck!* He looked over at his King.

Rafael didn't hesitate when he nodded at Nik and said, "Do what you have to do."

Nikolas didn't need any more permission than that. He took off running toward his car. He had no idea where to look for Sophia in Egypt, but by the gods, he would find her.

Since Sophia had at least a twenty-four hour head start on him, he didn't wait on a commercial plane. Instead, Nikolas took the Stone Society jet. He needed all the help he could get finding his mate in such a large country.

Nik should be furious at Sophia. She fucking knew what he was. He thought back to their conversation at the library.

"Are you one of those romantics who wishes she would be swept away by a creature of the night?" Nik asked.

"Creature of the night? Oh my, no! I prefer shifters." Sophia had blushed. Not because she was shy, but because she was telling him the fucking truth!

"Shifters, huh? So if I told you I was a shifter and wanted to steal you away, you'd be okay with that?" Sophia

had given him a sideways glance. Had she known then they were mates? Of course she had. That's what she meant in her note about him finding her. Godsdamn, woman! When he found Sophia, he was going to spank her ass. Then kiss her. Then fuck her senseless. *Then* he would help her find her parents. He just had to find her first.

Nikolas checked in at the Sitela West Hotel in Cairo. Before he'd flown blindly across the pond, he hacked into the flight logs at New Atlanta International and found Sophia's name. Even though she flew into Cairo, she could have landed and driven somewhere else. She could be staying in the same hotel he was. His first order of business was to set up his computer and check the local hotels to see if he could find her that way. He didn't want to go door to door, but if he had to, that's what he'd do to find his mate. Nik also hoped to be able to connect with other Gargoyles.

Nikolas tipped the bellman and began unpacking his equipment. He set up his computer on the desk in the living room of his suite. While it was booting up, he tossed his clothes in the drawers of the dresser and put his toiletries in the bathroom. He ordered room service so he could concentrate on finding his woman instead of going out for food. His computer was online, but he needed Julian's help in setting up the new encryption program. He called his brother but got no answer. "Jules, give me a call when you get this." He knew Julian would still be at the lab. There was too much going on for him to leave early.

Nik had scarfed down all the food he ordered and was checking the third hotel for any listing that might be Sophia when Julian returned his call. "Nikolas, you're not going to believe this shit."

"Whoa, you sound out of breath. You chasing your girl on the TV screen again?" Nik really shouldn't give Julian shit about his mate. He had a feeling the fates were going to make it hard on all of them when it came to the women in their lives.

"No, asshole. Tessa was in a car chase with the Redhead Killer. They both wrecked, and now she's in a coma."

"Oh, gods. What the hell happened after I left?"

"Gregor got a call from Tessa. She was at the fair when she ran into the killer. He followed her, and get this - Gordon Flanagan was in on it. He was in a helicopter chasing her the same time the killer was following behind. After both cars crashed, Frey got into a firefight with the other helo and shot it down. Kaya's in trouble with the locals for being out of her jurisdiction and not calling for back-up."

"Holy hell. How's Gregor holding up?" Nik couldn't imagine what his cousin was going through. Well, he sort of could. Here he was in the middle of Egypt with no idea where his mate was or if she was okay.

"As well as you'd expect."

"So, he's about to tear the hospital apart?"

"Pretty much. Now, what can I do for you? You said something about the encryption program."

Nik had to admire his baby brother. Next to Rafael, Julian had the most important job in the Clan. "Yes. I want you to remote in and install that new program you've been working on. I want to be able to run searches without being traced."

"I'm glad you're taking extra precautions. If Alistair is behind our troubles, we cannot be too careful. Okay, I sent you a request to remote in. Click the yes button."

"Can't you hack into my computer without asking permission?"

"Of course I can, but this way is faster." Julian could probably hack the world's most complex systems if he took the time to try. It was another reason Nikolas admired him. Not because he could be a criminal, but because he was so smart. "Okay, I'm in. Give me a few minutes, and the program will be installed."

"Thanks, Brother. I doubt if Sophia checked in under her own name. If she's anything like Tessa, I have a feeling she's going to be hard to find. Dammit! I wish she'd have confided in me before she left. She knows I'm her mate, yet she didn't trust me to come with her and help her."

"More than likely, she didn't tell you for the same reason Tessa didn't tell Gregor. She's protecting you."

Nikolas knew Julian was probably right, but it still didn't soothe the sting. "Maybe." When Nik heard Julian yawn, he did the math in his head. It was almost two in the morning back home. "Shit, Jules, I'm sorry it's so late."

"You know that doesn't matter. I'd rather be there with you." Julian yawned again as he tapped away at the keys on his computer. Damn, if his brother was yawning, he was way past the point of exhaustion, considering Goyles didn't require much sleep.

"I have a feeling you're going to be needed at

home. I'll be fine as long as I can call you." Nikolas didn't say he wished Julian was there with him, too. He didn't want his brother to feel any more conflicted than he already did. It wasn't often the two of them were separated. Julian was younger by twelve years, but being over five hundred years old, that small gap stopped mattering a long time ago.

"And you can, anytime, night or day. Please, Nik, don't worry about the time difference. If you need me, I'm here for you. Promise me, Brother."

"I promise." Nik just hoped he could find Sophia quickly and help her find her parents.

"Okay. The encryption is running. Even if you turn your computer off, it will automatically run when you boot back up. I'm going to try to locate some Goyles in Cairo and vet them for you. You never know who's loyal to whom. We don't need you running into a Clan that is in Alistair's back pocket."

"Thank you. That will allow me more time to hunt for my mate. Please give Gregor my love and keep me posted on Tessa. You, dear brother, go get some rest. I will talk to you soon."

"Be well, Nikolas. I love you."

"And I love you." Nikolas disconnected before his emotions got the better of him. He and Julian joked with each other all the time, but their bond was as strong as any in the Clan. Before he started his search for his mate, he sent up a prayer to the gods for Tessa and Gregor.

"Okay, my little bunny, where are you?"

CHAPTER FOUR

SOPHIA spent half the night researching Egyptian hieroglyphics. Singularly, the glyphs on the disk made sense. Grouped together, they were nothing more than a mishmash of symbols. When jet lag finally won out, she had put away her computer and lain down to sleep. As the early morning sun shone through her second-floor window, Sophia stretched and planned her day. Since she already had the disk, she argued with herself about going back to the zoo. If there was to be another clue, would they not give it to her since they didn't see her actually grab the disk? Or was that the only clue she was supposed to get? Too many decisions and not enough coffee. She didn't want to bother becoming Beatrice, yet she really needed breakfast.

The bedside clock told her it was already eleven a.m. Her internal clock was still adjusting to the time difference. Taking a risk that no one else would be roaming the halls, she dressed in jeans and a sweatshirt before making her way downstairs. She heard voices as she reached the kitchen door. Sophia paused and listened. When she only heard the cooks speaking about the lunch menu, she continued. Sophia knocked on the doorframe. "Good morning. Could I get some coffee, please?"

The two women smiled back, and one asked, "Would you like a cup or a carafe?"

"A carafe would be wonderful, thank you. I know it's late, but is there anything left over from breakfast? A muffin would do if you have one."

The kitchen was large, decked out with new

appliances that would rival most restaurants. A tray loaded with coffee, creamer, sweeteners, and an assortment of pastries was presented to Sophia. She took it, thanking the woman. When she turned to go back to her room, footsteps sounded in the hallway. Sophia waited until the person either passed by or came into the doorway in order to avoid dumping the items off her tray. She was greeted with the sight of a grumpy Fred. Sophia smiled and said, "Good morning, Fred."

He furrowed his brows and responded, "Good morning, Miss." He took in the carafe on her tray and asked the women in the room, "May I have a pot of coffee, too?"

Sophia remembered she wasn't Beatrice, so she didn't make any further small talk. Hopefully, Fred wouldn't think any more about her. This spy shit was harder than she thought it would be. She had to remember not to be quite so friendly in the future. Back in her room, she poured a cup of coffee and sat down in the oversized chair that faced the window. She wanted to go out on the balcony, but she didn't want to risk anyone else seeing Sophia and not her "grandmother".

As she sipped her coffee, Sophia turned the gold disk over in her free hand. She needed to find a local to tell her what the inscription meant, yet she didn't trust anyone with the object. For all she knew, it could be a stolen priceless artifact, and showing it around could land her in jail. Sophia set her cup down and pulled her computer onto her lap. She opened the files that listed her father's siblings. One of her aunts lived in

South Africa. At forty-seven, Xenia Carmichael was the oldest of her aunts and uncles who had yet to transition. If it were up to Sophia, she would tell every last one of them what they had hidden inside and warn them about their mates.

When Sophia did a search on her aunt, she found the woman was no longer living in South Africa, but Alexandria. How fortuitous. She should have already known that, but her mind had been preoccupied as of late with one tall, handsome Gargoyle. Sometimes she felt like a teenager with her first crush. She might as well be. Sophia hadn't dated much and was still a virgin. Hopefully, Nikolas wouldn't be too rough their first time. Then again…

Dammit, she really needed to focus. Tessa had been to Africa several times over the last decade watching over Xenia. According to her documentation, she had never actually met with the woman, only observed her from a distance. Sophia would need to come up with a good excuse to visit her, especially if she was going to entrust her with the disk. She would probably trust Beatrice at first glance more than a young woman traveling alone, but Sophia didn't want to chance getting mugged dressed as the older woman. She also didn't want to risk being noticed as herself, so she chose to become Clara Fort.

She checked the train schedule from Cairo to Alexandria. Even though she already had her first clue, Sophia was tempted to get on the ferry to see if she was still being followed. She definitely wouldn't take a chance on going back to the zoo. At least, not as Beatrice. When she decided against the ferry, she called and canceled her reservation.

Even though she'd had a couple of pastries, Sophia was still hungry. She blamed it on her shifter metabolism. She ordered a hummus and pita plate from room service and in less than twenty minutes, there was a knock on the door. Since she wasn't Beatrice, she called out, "Please leave it." Sophia reached out with her senses. When the footsteps retreated, she opened the door and picked up the tray.

While she was eating, a ping sounded from her computer. The only one who had this particular email address was Tiffany, her friend at the library. There was only one reason she would be emailing - to let her know Nikolas had received her note. Her fingers hit the wrong keys several times before she typed in the correct password. *Calm your ass down. It's not like he even knows where you are.* Sure enough, Tiffany relayed what transpired: "I told him you had taken a leave of absence, as you instructed. The man was not happy." Sophia couldn't help but smile. She closed out of the email without responding. Knowing her mate had come calling again lightened her heart a fraction.

After putting on the Clara prosthetic, Sophia gathered everything she thought she might need and dropped it in her bag. Not taking a chance with the disk, she slid it into the pocket of the black slacks she was wearing. She French-braided her long hair before wrapping a scarf around her head. Being lighter skinned than Egyptian women, she dressed conservatively, not wanting to draw unwanted attention to herself. She locked her room and snuck downstairs to hail a taxi. While she would love to take the ferry to Giza, she wanted to decipher the clues that were on the disk more. Maybe when she had her parents back safely, she could enjoy the scenery.

The express train ride took a little over three hours. The scenery had been less than spectacular, so Sophia used the time to devise a plan when she met her aunt. As she made her way to the platform, she shrugged her bag higher on her shoulder. She had brought a different disguise as well as a change of clothing, just in case. Being prepared for anything couldn't hurt.

It was early afternoon, and she was hungry again, so she decided to find something light to eat. Spotting a small restaurant, she ordered Samak Mashwi with a side of Kushari. *It's a good thing I don't have a weak stomach.* The fish had a wonderful, spicy flavor she enjoyed, even if it was served whole. Ignoring the eyeball staring back at her, Sophia dug the flesh out of the center and ate it with the rice and lentil side dish.

Xenia's home was located in a neighborhood containing the railway station. Even though the house was close, Sophia had no desire to walk the few blocks by herself. She hailed a taxi, and a few minutes later, sat in front of her aunt's small home. Sophia paid the cab driver and got out onto the sidewalk. As she was walking toward the house, she heard a crash coming from inside. "Get out! You can't see me like this!" a woman shouted.

Something else shattered, and a man yelled, "Fuck, Xenia. Stop this. What is wrong with you?"

Sophia hurried into the house and found a good-looking man dodging flying objects. Whoever was flinging those objects was nowhere to be seen. When a crystal vase was thrown around the corner, the man yelled, "Xenia, seriously, cut the shit!"

Sophia took a big chance and walked into the kitchen where her aunt was hiding. Even if the man hadn't spoken her aunt's name, she'd have known it was her. Xenia was the spitting image of Caroline, or would be if her grandmother hadn't stopped aging and if her grandmother had fangs.

"Oh, shit!" Sophia ducked as another glass item flew through the air, this one headed her way. "Xenia, calm down," she scolded her aunt.

"Calm down? Calm down, she says. She, who I don't even know who the fuck she is, is telling me to calm down! Do you fucking see this shit?" she asked, holding her clawed hands out to her sides.

Before she could say any more, Sophia returned to the man and blocked his view. "I think it would be best if you go. I've got this." Using her shifter strength, she ushered him toward the door.

"But she said she doesn't know you. I'm not letting some stranger in here without—" He was cut off as another object grazed the side of his head.

"Out, now!" she said as she shoved him out the door. Sophia flipped the locks and turned to face her aunt. This was what she had been training for. The man banged on the door, yelling to be let back in, but she ignored him.

"I have fangs. And I have claws. Fucking claws!" Xenia looked around, probably for something else to throw. Blood was running down her chin.

"Xenia, I can explain," Sophia replied with her hands up in the defensive.

The woman whirled around and shrieked, "Really? You can explain to me why after almost fifty years I suddenly sprout fucking fangs?"

Instead of answering, Sophia allowed her own fangs and claws to come forth. "I know what you're going through, so like I said, calm down."

Xenia's eyes widened, but she did calm down enough to whisper, "What the fuck are you? What am I?"

Sophia took a chance and slowly closed the distance between them. Holding her hands in front of her, Sophia retracted her claws and allowed her fangs to retreat into her gums. "I will tell you everything, but first, I want you to close your eyes and imagine your fangs receding into your gums." Xenia did as she said, and after a few seconds, her mouth was back to normal. "Now, do the same thing with your hands." Sophia waited until her aunt's hands were clawless. "Good. Very good."

Sophia moved toward the sofa and asked, "Would you like to sit down? This is a long story."

"Yeah, but first I need a drink. Would you like one?" Xenia walked to a cabinet on the far side of the room and poured a tall glass of what looked like whiskey. Xenia downed the glassful of liquor and poured herself another.

"No, thank you. Xenia, you aren't going to believe what I tell you at first. But please, just hear me out. In the end, it will make sense. Sort of."

Xenia brought the glass with her and sat across from Sophia. When she was settled, Sophia removed the scarf from her head before she continued. "I'm sorry you had to find out this way about who and what you are. I am your niece." When Xenia started to interrupt her, Sophia held up her hand. "Yes, I know, you were adopted and don't have any siblings. Actually, you have sixteen, well fifteen now. One is recently deceased." Sophia stood and went to the kitchen, wetting a paper towel. She handed it to her aunt and sat back down. "You have a little blood on your chin." Xenia wiped the blood as Sophia continued. "You were put up for adoption by your biological parents to protect you."

"Protect me from what?"

"From those of our kind who are prejudiced against the less than pure of our kind. Have you ever read a book about a shapeshifter, you know, like a werewolf?"

Xenia's eyes were huge. "You mean we're—"

"No." Sophia cut her off. "Not exactly. But we do come from a line of shapeshifters. The earliest Gargouille date back millennia. They were created to protect humans. The name has been modernized over the years to Gargoyle. Your father is a full-blood who is from the original line of shifters. Your mother is human; therefore, you are what is considered a half-blood. My father, one of your brothers, is also a half-blood. I guess that would make me a quarter-blood, but that doesn't have the same ring to it. Anyway, what you have seen, the claws and fangs, is a small part of being a shifter. Females of our kind have enhanced strength, vision, and hearing. Once we meet our mate, we go through our initial transition into our shifter side.

"Phasing is what we call it when our extra parts show up," Sophia said, using air quotes. "Now, the males, they are special. The Gargoyles have an awesome set of wings as well as special skin that is impenetrable. And yes, before you ask, they can fly. The half-blood males get wings upon their transition, but not the thick skin. It develops over time. I know this is a lot to throw at you at once, but honestly, the worst part is over." Sophia spent the next hour filling Xenia in on all things Goyle and answering her many questions. It was a lot to take in, especially the feeling of betrayal by parents who kept some of their children and not the others.

"So, what you're saying is even though I've been seeing Keene for the last few months, anyone I've come in contact with could be my mate?"

"Yes, but you will know whether it's him or not by the feelings you get when he's near. I'm surprised it took you so long to transition, though. Most of us phase for the first time pretty quickly after meeting our mate."

"I've had fangs for months now. I just didn't know what to do about them. I've taken a sabbatical from work to come to terms with the new me."

"That makes more sense. Have you not been around Keene since you transitioned?"

"No, and as you can see, he got tired of waiting on me. I've been putting him off, telling him I was sick. When I'm around him, my body does its own thing."

Sophia couldn't help but think about her own body's reaction to Nik.

"Where did you go just then?" Xenia asked with

the first smile she'd formed since Sophia walked into the house.

"I was thinking about my mate and how he makes me feel. When he's near, I absolutely have to touch him. It's as if part of my soul leaves me and takes up residence with him. Until I'm in his presence again, part of me feels gone. You might look at others and think they're attractive, but no one else will do it for you ever again."

Xenia sighed. "Then Keene is definitely my mate. But how do I explain all of this to him? We haven't known each other that long, and I really thought he was the one."

"If he is the reason for your transition, he is the one. You should tell him the truth. He will feel the mate pull to you as well, and he won't really have a choice but to be around you. I have yet to see a mate who ran for the hills at seeing the shifter side. While most of the shifters have mates who are also shifters, it isn't unheard of for the mates to be fully human, like your mother and my mother."

"My mother… what's she like? I lost both my adoptive parents about a year ago to a home invasion." Xenia paused as she took a sip of her drink. "That's when I moved up here to Alexandria."

"I'm so sorry for your loss. Your biological mother, Caroline, is great. You look a lot like her, except older."

"Older? How is that possible?"

"When a human woman mates with a shifter then has a child, her body stops aging. Caroline had her first baby when she was in her late twenties."

Xenia frowned. "How old is she exactly?"

Sophia didn't hesitate to tell her, "Two hundred forty-five."

"You're shitting me!" Xenia exclaimed. The slang term sounded funny said with her accent.

"I shit you not," Sophia said, trying to lighten the moment.

Xenia downed the rest of her drink. "I'm too old to have a kid."

"You're the shifter, not the human. You will look the way you do now for the rest of your life. What you need to be concerned with is phasing and getting your shifter side under control before you go out into public. We're not ready for the world to know we exist."

"Yeah, I can understand that. By the way, why exactly are you here?" Xenia stood and poured herself another drink.

"It's a long story, but if I want you to trust me, I'm going to trust you." Sophia told her aunt everything she knew about her parents' abduction, which wasn't much. When Xenia asked what she could do to help, Sophia pulled the disk from her pocket. "You can help me decipher these glyphs."

CHAPTER FIVE

"WHAT do you mean the disk is gone?" Kallisto would have choked the huge man on the other end of the line had he been standing in front of her.

"Just what I said, Boss. We watched the bench until lunchtime. When we never saw the woman, we checked to be sure. It's not there."

Kallisto didn't bother saying goodbye. She disconnected and yelled, "Sergei, get in here!" When her faithful companion strode into the living room of their hotel suite, she threw her phone at him. "Get on your computer and hack into the video surveillance at the zoo. Find out who took the fucking disk," she seethed.

Sergei's men had kept an eye on the ferries, but none had reported seeing the young woman. Either she was waiting until later afternoon to retrieve her clue, or she had not followed their instructions and had found alternate transportation. The fact that the disk was missing meant she either showed up when they weren't looking, or someone else had found it. Neither scenario was acceptable. If Miss Brooks already had the disk, Kallisto needed eyes on the woman so she could eventually retrieve it back. If someone else had the disk... Kallisto didn't want to think about that scenario.

Her father would not find this acceptable. He didn't appreciate failure of any kind, and in his eyes, this minor setback would be considered failure. Her father wouldn't raise a hand to her, but he wouldn't hesitate to raise one to Sergei. He would give her that disappointed look only a parent could give their child.

Kallisto had no wish to see that look on her father's face. She saw it often enough directed at her brother.

Kallisto stood behind Sergei and placed her hands on his shoulders as he frantically searched the video feed from the zoo. He was her best friend, her confidante. Were he someone else, she would allow herself to fall in love with him. Make love to him. Since he was not, she kept their relationship platonic. Her father kept a constant eye on her. Never would she be allowed to engage in a relationship with someone beneath their station. She found that ironic considering who her mother had been.

"I've gone back to before the gates opened this morning. Nobody sat on the bench, and none of the workers stopped anywhere near it," Sergei said as he continued typing, searching.

"Go all the way back to the point when I put the disk under the bench." She squeezed his shoulder then began pacing. There had to be something there showing who took the disk. Kallisto had no idea how her father had obtained such a priceless artifact or why he would allow her to use it as a clue. Whoever discovered the disk would hold in their possession an item so rare it could land them in prison, or worse yet, in the media's eye. The Cleopatra Disk was created in 29 B.C., a year after the pharaoh's death. It disappeared one hundred years later and had been missing ever since. It wasn't the only rare artifact her father held in his private collection.

The rarity of the coin was kept a secret from all the men on her crew, including Sergei. She loved her friend, but she trusted no one. Only because she was already wealthy beyond measure did her father entrust her with the object. If it were to be discovered where the disk had been all those centuries…

"Here!" Sergei pointed to the monitor. "It was an old lady."

Kallisto couldn't believe what she was seeing. The same old lady who had snapped a picture of the leopard as Kallisto walked past was clearly the one to take the disk. "Fuck! How could I have been so careless?" She had not seen the woman until after she hid the artifact under the bench. Even then she had waited to make certain no one was in the vicinity. "This is bad. We have to find this woman and get the disk back."

Sergei stood from his chair and pulled Kallisto into a tight embrace. She allowed him to offer her strength. She had screwed up, and it would take a miracle to find an old woman in such a large city. Sergei pulled away and said, "I'm on it, Sweetheart. I will not let you down."

"HOLY mother of Horus! Do you know what this is?" Xenia turned the coin over and over, studying it closely.

"No, but I'm assuming you do?" Sophia asked.

"Yes, I do. This is the Cleopatra Disk. My father was an archaeologist. This object eluded him his whole life, and someone just handed it over to you as if it wasn't one of the most sought-after artifacts of all time." Xenia handed the disk back to Sophia.

"*If* it's the original. I'm not up on all things ancient, but this item looks to be in pristine condition. Wouldn't something that dates back thousands of years be a little more, I don't know, fragile?"

Xenia walked over to a bookcase and pulled down what appeared to be a photo album. "If it was buried under rubble for thousands of years, out in the elements, yes. If it has been kept in a private collection, *in the dark,* so to speak, then no. Take a look at this." Xenia placed the album on the coffee table and pointed at a picture. "This is a Tutankhamun Disk. It was buried along with the King. The detail is perfect, same as the Cleopatra Disk. This one here belonged to Ramesses the Great. It was found in a dig back in 1922. That is what your artifact would look like had it not been locked up tight."

"So why give me an ancient artifact that belonged to Cleopatra? Are the kidnappers telling me my parents are buried along with the ancient Queen?" Sophia started pacing. Her parents couldn't be dead. Why would the kidnappers bring her all this way if they'd already murdered her mom and dad?

"Don't get ahead of yourself. Until you have proof, you need to assume they are still alive. As for Cleopatra's burial site, no one knows where it is."

Sophia sighed. "Great. I'm no closer than I was. Why give me a useless clue? That doesn't make sense."

"You said someone was watching you. Maybe they wanted to see if you would follow their directions. Or maybe they wanted you to have the disk, and then they would contact the authorities. That would tie you up for months. Do you know anyone who would want to do this to your family?"

Sophia wasn't sure how much to tell her aunt. Did she explain how JoJo was ostracized for mating with a human? How he cloned the first human baby and disappeared from society afterwards? Or did she explain what a brilliant man he was, creating all sorts of technology that was used around the world? "If it were only my dad, I'd say no. Since he's the son of a full-blooded Gargoyle who comes from the original line? It's possible. Jonas, your father, is sort of a rebel. As far as we know, he was the first of his kind to mate with a human. This didn't go over well with some of the purists, and he was banished for it. That was over two hundred years ago. If he is being targeted, I'm not sure why his enemy would wait this long."

"What are you going to do now?" Xenia asked.

"I don't know. I guess I could go back to the zoo and pretend to look for the disk. Maybe that will appease the kidnappers, and they'll give me another clue."

"Won't they suspect you going a second time? I mean, if they wanted you to have it, I would think they would have been watching. I know I would."

"I'm impressed, Xenia. You think like they do. Are you sure you're really a history professor?" Sophia joked with her aunt.

Xenia waved her hand in the air. "I watch a lot of movies. Back to my question, won't they recognize you?"

"No. I didn't exactly look like myself when I went. As a matter of fact, I don't look like myself now.

Remember I told you your father is brilliant? He is an expert in the art of disguise." Sophia removed the prosthetic from her face allowing her aunt to see the real her.

"Oh my god. That's amazing. Now I see the family resemblance. You must take after your father."

"I do. And I have to get him back. Is it okay if I leave the disk here with you? If I don't have it on me, they can't accuse me of taking it."

"I can't believe I'm saying this, but yes. I will put it in my safe, that way nobody will know of its whereabouts. But Sophia, what are you going to do with it when this is all over?"

"I will turn it over to the authorities. Anonymously. Unless you would like the honors? You can give your father credit posthumously."

"I will think on it. Right now, I have more pressing matters, like controlling these stupid new appendages." Xenia looked down at her hands. Within a few seconds, her claws extended.

"You seem to be getting the hang of it. The hardest part is controlling the phase when you're excited. Scratching your nails down Keene's back just took on a whole new meaning," Sophia said and winked.

"Yeah, well, I doubt he'll want me when he finds out what I am." Xenia sighed and retracted the claws.

"Don't sell him short, but only tell him the truth if you trust him implicitly. Now, I've got to find my parents. Thank you, Auntie."

"I guess I should be thanking you. If you hadn't come along when you did, I'd think I was going insane."

Sophia took a pen and paper out of her bag. After writing a few lines, she handed it to her aunt. "Here is my number as well as Caroline's, should you ever wish to contact her."

"Thank you, little dove. I will consider it. Please be careful out there, and if you need a place to hide out, my door is open." Her aunt pulled her into a surprising embrace.

While waiting for a taxi to arrive, Sophia replaced the disguise. After saying goodbye to her aunt, she headed for the train station. On the ride back, Sophia considered her options. She could stay in her disguise and attempt to locate those who were following her, or she could go to the zoo as herself. Either way, she would probably run into the couple who had been on the flight with her.

Once she was back in Cairo, Sophia had the taxi driver drop her off a couple of blocks down the street from the bed and breakfast. She had to walk past her hotel as well as a couple of others before she arrived at the small inn. Sophia wanted to get some fresh air before making her decision. As she passed one of the larger hotels, a chill ran up her spine. She did not quicken her pace, but she did casually look around the area. She didn't recognize anyone, but then again, why would she? The couple probably had a team of spies keeping an eye on her. Since she was dressed as Clara, she shouldn't be recognized. To be on the safe side, Sophia circled around behind the B&B and entered through the side door. The feeling passed, and she chalked it up to nerves.

It was closing in on supper time, and Sophia was

getting hungry. If she changed disguises now, she would barely have time to take a ferry to the zoo before it closed. That might not be a bad option, but it would also have her returning after dark. Her growling stomach made her mind up for her. She would become Beatrice, join the others for supper, and visit the zoo the next day.

Chapter Six

NIKOLAS spent the rest of the day searching all over Cairo for traces of Sophia. When he failed to find her in any of the local hotels, he expanded his search to the neighboring cities. He also checked the airlines on the off chance she'd left. When he found nothing, he decided to get out of his hotel and walk around. It had been years since he had traveled outside of the States, and he'd never ventured to Egypt. There were several eateries and shops within walking distance of his hotel. He would find something for supper while enjoying the scenery.

As he walked along the sidewalk, a familiar scent floated on the air. He knew Sophia wasn't the only one who wore honeysuckle, but his heart beat a little faster at the possibility of her being so near. As he got closer to the Nile Grand, the scent increased. He had checked the large hotel's registry and found no listing for Sophia. It was entirely possible she was using an alias. It was what Tessa would have done, and they were cousins after all. Nikolas entered the hotel and headed to the bank of elevators. The scent was still in the air, so he decided to search the floors. He opted to take the stairs so he could stop on each floor without drawing too much attention to himself. He was still going to be picked up on hotel security cameras, but he would worry about that later.

When he reached the tenth floor, Nik got lucky. The fourth door he came to was strong with the honeysuckle fragrance. He reached out with his shifter hearing before knocking on the door. If someone was in the room, they were asleep, because there was no movement at all coming from inside. Right as he was about to walk away, arguing sounded from the room next door.

"I'm telling you, Princess, it's like the woman has disappeared."

"And I'm telling you, Drago, to find her!" A glass shattered, and an inner door slammed. Before Nikolas could escape, the door opened, and a large man exited. If Nik hadn't been paying attention, he'd have been plowed down. He pressed his back to the door he had been interested in, and the man sneered his way. Nik was pretty sure the man was a Gargoyle. His inner beast riled up when the man looked at him in a less than friendly manner. Thankfully, the stranger headed in the opposite direction of the stairs. Nik didn't hesitate to make a hasty retreat. He didn't want someone complaining to security that a man was spying on doors or eavesdropping on private conversations, no matter how interesting they were.

Nikolas made his way down the ten flights of stairs and exited through a side door. He wanted to get back to his computer and find out who currently occupied room ten seventeen. While he was at it, he'd also check on the room next door. Nik had his hands full with Sophia, but his curious nature wouldn't allow him to dismiss the intriguing conversation. As he continued toward the restaurants, he was overwhelmed with another blast of honeysuckle. This one was much more potent than the last. It led him to a small bed and breakfast. He was certain he'd checked all manners of hotel, motel, and inn, so asking if Sophia was there would be a moot point. He did, however, step inside the small inn. Someone was definitely staying there who smelled as sweet as his mate. He added it to his mental list of places to double-check once he returned to his hotel.

The odds of Sophia staying at either place were astronomical. Julian would be able to calculate those odds almost instantly were Nikolas to ask him to. He was okay with not knowing the exact percentage since it would only make him depressed. After leaving the inn, Nik entered the first restaurant he came to. While he was waiting, he sat at the bar and ordered a beer. He had finished his first and ordered a second when his name was called. He paid the bartender and made his way to a small table in the back of the restaurant. Nik had become so accustomed to the southern cuisine of New Atlanta that he wasn't sure what he would enjoy. He ordered three entrees off the menu and prayed he would find one to his liking.

As he sat sipping his beer, a text came in from Julian letting him know Tessa's condition. He texted back telling him he was at supper and would call as soon as he returned to his hotel. When his three plates arrived, Nik snapped a photo of the food and sent it to Julian. How he wished his brother was there with him. He would have some smartass comment about the amount of food on the table, but Nik would welcome it. He wondered what Sophia was doing and if she was feeling as alone as he was. He ordered another beer and dug into his food.

Nikolas was pleasantly surprised at how much he enjoyed two of the three dishes. He made a mental note of the one he didn't care for so he wouldn't order it again. He declined dessert and headed back to his hotel. As he passed a small boutique, he noticed the figurines in the window. Most were cats, but he spied one in particular that called to him. Nik entered the shop and gently lifted a yellow and white ceramic hare. It wasn't a cute bunny, but it held his interest, nonetheless.

"She is the symbol of fertility and renewal," a female voice said from behind.

Nik turned toward the voice. The shopkeeper was an older woman dressed in the traditional style of clothing. He had seen a wide variety of styles as he was walking down the street. The older women preferred the customary clothing, while the younger women dressed more modernly like the women in the States.

"Fertility, huh? I'll take it." Nikolas had every intention of mating with Sophia and producing a houseful of little shifters. A fertility trinket couldn't hurt. After he paid for his purchase, he made his way back to his hotel. Even though he was tempted to stop once again at the Nile Grand, Nik forced himself to continue on. Once in his room, he took the hare figurine out of the bag and placed it on the desk in front of him.

Instead of calling Julian immediately, he hacked into the computer systems of both the large hotel and the smaller inn. Room ten seventeen was registered to a Clara Fort, but he couldn't rule out the possibility of an alias. He dug a little deeper to find her credit card and passport information. While he was waiting for that information to populate, he began another search at the bed and breakfast. There was no one registered by the name Sophia or Clara. He ran through the list of names and made note of them all. Once he did that, he set up a program to search credit card and passport information there as well.

His computer dinged indicating the first search was complete. He opened the window and studied the photo associated with the passport. The woman in the picture was an American, but she was not Sophia. Instead of Sophia's light brown hair and vibrant blue eyes, this woman had both dark hair and eyes. If this was a disguise, it was a damn good one. While Nik waited on the information from the bed and breakfast, he called his brother.

"Nikolas, how are you?" Julian asked instead of saying hello.

"Same as I was earlier. No closer to finding Sophia. At least I don't think I am."

"What does that mean? Did something happen to make you believe otherwise?"

Nik explained the honeysuckle, fully expecting his brother to give him shit about following a floral lead instead of a tangible one.

"Don't dismiss the possibilities just yet. You don't truly know your mate or what she is capable of. If, like Tessa, she has been influenced by one of the greatest minds the world has ever known, we have no idea what she has in her bag of tricks."

"That is true." Nik's computer sounded, letting him know the other search was complete. "I have some information to go over, so I'm going to let you go. I'll talk to you later." They said goodbye, and Nik focused on the guests at the bed and breakfast. There were no young, single women registered. The only single woman was an older lady named Beatrice Nightingale. She, too, was an American, but she was old enough to be Sophia's grandmother.

Nik wasn't ready to give up, though. He searched the airline logs for Clara Fort. If that didn't pan out, he would expand his search to neighboring countries. For now though, he was going to take advantage of the small gym in the hotel and hit the treadmill. His shifter was ready to exert some energy, and he couldn't take to the skies. It was going to be hard to keep the beast at bay until he found his mate.

BEATRICE was once again enjoying the company of the Waterfords. Everyone except Yvonne. She was being her usual catty self, and Sophia was doing her best to ignore the woman. Garret and Millicent were filling her in on their trip to the pyramids when Sophia became light headed. She took a sip of water and fanned herself as best she could with her cloth napkin, but the feeling wouldn't go away. The few times she'd felt that way before were when Nik was close by. *No frickin' way.*

"Beatrice, are you okay?" Millicent asked.

"Yes, please excuse me. I need a bit of fresh air." Sophia pushed back from the table and hurried to the door of the inn. When she reached the sidewalk, she looked both ways. Nik wasn't short, but he wasn't overly tall. Not like some of his cousins. Still, she didn't see his sandy brown hair anywhere. "Get a grip, Brooks," she chided herself. When she returned to the dining room, Yvonne and Fred were the only ones there. "The youngsters retiring early, huh?" she asked Yvonne with a grin.

The older lady made a rude noise and continued to sip her coffee. Fred gave Sophia an apologetic look, but she just smiled at him. If he wanted to live with her crappy attitude, that was on him. She knew relationships were hard work, and couples wouldn't always see eye to eye, but to marry a person knowing they were a miserable human being? That was insane.

Sophia was lucky, though. The fates had found the perfect life partner for her. Even if they hadn't spent any time together, she had followed Nikolas Stone around without him knowing it. She watched every news program his family was featured in, and she read every article in which he was mentioned. The only time she didn't follow was when he went on a date. The last time he'd taken another woman out, Sophia had nearly lost her mind and interrupted the evening just to prove a point. Had she strolled into the restaurant where Nik and the blonde were dining, he would have figured out then and there who his mate was. At that point, she was still under JoJo's influence. It didn't take her long to put a plan together to help Nikolas figure out that Gargoyles were mating with humans and had been for a long time. Had he not come into the library on his own, she was going to anonymously tip him off. It turned out she didn't have to.

The King of the States, Rafael, met his mate in the

human police chief, and that was the impetus needed to start the ball rolling. Now, Tessa and Gregor were together, and Isabelle and Dante had figured out their connection as well. Sophia and Nik would eventually get together. While the three women were actually half-bloods, there was still the human factor. She thought about her aunt and prayed Xenia would be able to convince Keene they were meant to be together.

Returning her attention to the older couple at the table, Sophia couldn't help herself. She knew poking the bear was wrong, but she turned to Yvonne and said, "I really can't blame the kids. I remember my honeymoon. Why, my husband and I didn't come out of our hotel room for days! That man knew how to keep the fires burning, if you know what I mean." She wiggled her eyebrows, and Yvonne sucked in her coffee at the same time she gasped. When she fell into a coughing fit, Fred swatted her on the back a few good times and grinned at Sophia.

"Bless your heart," Sophia consoled in her best southern drawl. She hated the fact that Millicent was missing the show. If she got the chance, she'd tell her about it later. Sophia was quite fond of the other girl. She and Garrett would be fun to hang around if Sophia were able to be herself. But she was not. Sophia wasn't there to socialize. She needed to go to her room and reschedule the ferry ride to Giza for the next day. Once Yvonne calmed down, Sophia excused herself and wished them a good night. Back in her room, she removed the prosthetics and turned on the water in the bathtub. It had been one hell of a day, and she had a feeling the next few weren't going to be any better.

CHAPTER SEVEN

IT took Ezekiel longer than expected to get to Egypt. Cordelia begged him to stay a couple more days, which he did. Eventually, though, he made her see the seriousness of the situation and promised to check on her once Sam and Monica were found. He didn't have a clue, literally, where to start looking for Sophia other than she had flown to Cairo. He wasn't an expert in computers, but hacking the airlines was pretty basic stuff. He called Elizabeth once he landed to see if she had heard from the girl. He may look only a few years older than his niece, but he was old enough to be her father. Zeke hadn't spent a lot of time with her while she was growing up, but once she started her watcher training, he was around her quite a bit. He knew she had studied Tessa intently, as her older cousin was an expert when it came to the cloak and dagger stuff. If Sophia didn't want to be found, she wouldn't be. Why she hadn't asked Jonas for help was one of the first questions he was going to ask her when he finally found her.

He settled into his hotel room and relaxed in the large Jacuzzi in his *en suite* bathroom. He had left his sister in a somewhat decent frame of mind in New Mexico. Zeke found talking someone around after they transitioned to be more challenging than convincing them they would eventually become what he was. He had another sister, Xenia, who lived in Africa. Last he heard, she was in South Africa. Even though Tessa was her watcher, the woman could be anywhere by now. Zeke doubted Sophia would risk her aunt's well-being by visiting her, but he would not rule out the possibility. All he knew for sure was Sophia had received a note stating Sam and Monica had been taken, and Sophia was to fly to Egypt.

Why would someone kidnap Sam? He was one of the kindest, most decent males Zeke knew, even if he was his brother. Zeke couldn't say the same thing for himself. He went off the rails for a while when he transitioned. Sam had been the one to talk him back around and even convince him to become a watcher. Jonas had come up with the concept of them helping their siblings transition, but he knew it would take more than one of them, considering they were scattered around the world. Ezekiel had nothing better to do considering he didn't have a mate to worry about. That was another reason Sam wanted Zeke's help; Sam wanted to be able to spend more time at home with Monica.

The only ones outside of the family who knew Jonas's true identity were the other Gargoyles of his former clan. If they were targeting Sam to get to Jonas, why wait two hundred years? It was possible his father had pissed someone off and Zeke didn't know about it. Hopefully not, and hopefully this would be an isolated situation. For now, though, he didn't want to think any more on it. He would do that in the morning. Zeke hit the music icon on his phone, turned on some Sully Erna, and leaned his head back against the tub, willing himself to relax.

SOPHIA woke early so she could make her way to the larger hotel. Hopefully, those who were watching her room would still be asleep when she slipped in. She was not going to take a chance and leave the bed and breakfast without a disguise. If, by some chance, those following her were awake, she could escape more easily as Clara than she could as herself. But if someone from the inn saw her, it would be best to leave as Beatrice, so she donned the grandmotherly disguise. When she made her way downstairs, she caught a whiff of a delicious scent. It was the same one she'd smelled the night before when she thought Nikolas had been there. Sophia inhaled deeply, allowing the aroma to invade her senses. She relished the reminder of her mate, even if he was thousands of miles away.

She stepped outside onto the quiet sidewalk where a taxi was waiting on her. It was a short distance to her hotel, but even she wasn't crazy enough to walk alone at this time of the morning. Sophia paid the man and entered the hotel through a side door. She felt she had a better chance at not being spotted if she took a few extra precautions. She got out of the elevator on the ninth floor and took the stairs to the tenth. Reaching out with her senses, she didn't detect anyone in the hallway. Carefully, she opened the door and walked softly toward her room. When she reached her door, she caught that familiar scent once again.

Sophia slid the keycard into the slot. The green indicator sounded like a bomb going off in the quiet corridor. She entered her room and closed the door as softly as she could, leaning her back against it once she was safe. She kicked off her shoes and went about removing the prosthetic, voice transmitter, and contacts. She had a few hours before her reservation for the ferry, so she flopped down on the bed and tried to go back to sleep. Instead of focusing on the task ahead of her, Sophia allowed her mind to drift back to the first day Nikolas came into the library. She hadn't looked her best. Her hair was gathered in a mess on top of her head, and she'd had on a pair of silly glasses. Having already transitioned, she no longer needed them. She wore them to throw her family off to the fact she had phased for the first time. Her looks hadn't mattered. Nikolas felt the effects of the mate bond almost immediately. When Sophia touched his arm, she thought he was going to pass out on her. She felt sorry for the gorgeous man.

Nik returned to the library, only he didn't come to the information desk. He went to the computer bank to search for Jonas's books himself. By now, he had probably figured out they were mates, but that day, he seemed to be fishing, and she couldn't resist torturing him. When he asked her if she preferred vampires in her reading choices, she quickly dismissed that crazy thought. The look on his face when she said she preferred shifters was priceless. The closeness of his body had her core pulsing. Sophia had never had sex, but at that moment, she had been ready to grab him by his beautiful wings and drag him into the basement where she could lock the door and have her way with him. She might have if he hadn't been so intrigued with the journal she had stashed just for that occasion.

She leaned around his back to look at the journal.

What she had truthfully been doing was pressing into his arm so she could feel the heat coming from his body. After that, she helped him check out most of the books Jonas had written. When Nikolas grinned at her, she felt her panties flood. Needless to say, she had gone home and put fresh batteries in her favorite toy. And now she was horny. *Great.* She hadn't packed any toys, because she didn't want anyone seeing them through the scanner at the airport. Instead, she rolled onto her back, unbuttoned her jeans and pushed them down her legs. She slid her hand down her panties and into the wetness of her folds. With her handsome as hell Gargoyle on her mind, Sophia scratched the itch Nikolas Stone caused.

A few hours later, with her belly full of room service breakfast and a pot of coffee, Sophia headed to the ferry. She was more nervous than she'd been since she arrived. What if those following her stopped her from getting to the zoo? What if they took her after she sat across from the leopard? Would she then be taken to her parents? Or was this truly a puzzle of sorts to actually find her parents? She stepped out of her taxi and opened her senses. She had to be more observant now than ever before. She made her way to the dock where she would take the hour-long boat ride. This seemed like overkill considering the short taxi ride two days before, but Sophia was going to comply with their instructions. Well, somewhat.

The ferry wasn't the largest on the water, and that was the reason Sophia chose this particular one. A smaller ferry meant fewer people. It also meant there were no cars allowed. Paranoid or cautious, either way she wanted less of a chance of being kidnapped herself. The pier was fairly busy, and Sophia tried to blend in with the pedestrians walking toward the gangway. She made her way to the ticket office and showed her digital receipt. After receiving her ticket, she walked to the designated loading area. Sophia was glad to see several families waiting in line as well. She would attempt to stick close to the larger groups instead of standing alone.

The weather forecast predicted sunshine and mild temperatures. It was currently sixty-six degrees, which called for Sophia to wear a jacket and cover her head while she was on the ferry. The wind coming off the water would be cool. It would also allow her to be harder to identify unless she had already been spotted. In that case, no amount of head covering would work in her favor. So far, she hadn't felt eyes on her, but they could be on the dock using binoculars. Or, she might have completely blown it by not showing up as herself the day before.

The boat moved away from the dock, and they were underway. According to the schedule, she had almost an hour until she arrived on the other side of the Nile. The ferry was a tourist boat, so the captain would take his time getting them from point A to point B. Sophia followed a family and stood against the rail as their tour guide began his spiel. She was intent on the words coming over the loud speaker as she gazed out at the land passing by. After half an hour, Sophia had begun to relax, until the hair on her neck stood up, and Sophia froze. She had let her shifter senses subside, but now they were kickboxing her from the inside. She might not have been aware of the stranger walking up behind her, but her Goyle half was. She concentrated on keeping her fangs where they currently were: safely sheathed away from unknowing eyes.

When the presence continued to linger where it was, she slowly turned her back to the rail so she could take in those around her. The family remained to her left, but two large men were now standing to Sophia's right. Instead of looking them in the eye, she kept them in her peripheral vision. After about ten minutes, the men walked away, allowing Sophia to get a good look at them. Both were well built, and they looked like locals. She didn't sense that either one of them were shifters. That didn't mean they weren't dangerous. Not wanting to appear conspicuous, she stayed where she was until the boat docked in Giza.

As she was debarking, Sophia kept her eyes open for her admirers. When she reached the end of the gangway, she noticed them walking ahead of her. One of them was talking on a cell phone. Sophia hadn't been instructed how to get to the zoo from the pier, so she opted for the cheapest, most occupied form of transportation. She hopped on the bus with several others. As they were pulling away from the curb, the two men were standing there watching. Next time she talked to Tessa, she was going to ask how her cousin did this job without taking nerve pills, because Sophia's were shot all to hell at that point.

Sophia followed several families off the bus, making their way to the ticket booth at the zoo. She was nervous, but she had gone over the scenario in her mind until she was certain she could pull off acting surprised. Once inside the zoo, Sophia opened the map and studied it as if she had no idea where the leopard pen would be situated. Once she gave herself sufficient time to be convincing, she walked along the same path on which she'd previously followed the blonde. When she reached the enclosure, there were people standing at the fence admiring the big cat. Sophia sat on the bench and looked around, not seeing the two men from the ferry. That didn't mean they weren't there, or that whoever they'd called wasn't now watching her.

Since the instructions only told Sophia to go to the bench, she didn't reach her hand underneath for the disk. That would have been a clear giveaway she had seen the woman put it there. Instead, she remained seated for over half an hour. When nothing happened, she decided to walk around the park and see if she could identify anyone else who might be tailing her. She stopped every so often to glance at her map, but after an hour, Sophia made her way back to the bench and had a seat. Still having no idea what to do, she sat there for another half hour. Just as she stood to leave, a park employee walked past her and shoved something into her stomach. Sophia had no choice but to grab onto the item.

It was a folded piece of paper. Sophia debated on whether to read the note there or wait until she got back to the hotel. On the chance she was directed elsewhere, she decided to go ahead and see what it said.

TRAVEL TO THE PLACE OF BEAUTY AND FIND THE LAST PHARAOH'S TOMB

Sophia had no idea where that was, so she needed to get back to her computer. She folded the note and slid it into the pocket of her jeans. With one last look around, she headed back to Cairo. This time by taxi.

CHAPTER EIGHT

NIKOLAS was ready to take out an advertisement on the side of a building that flashed "Sophia, where are you?" After coming up with nothing on either woman's credit card, Nik expanded his search. He was going to need a supercomputer if he kept up the extensive algorithms Julian had put in place. As it was now, his laptop was ready to blow, just like its owner. Nik's gut instinct told him the honeysuckle scent wasn't a coincidence. Even though he had nothing to go on other than his instincts, he was going to follow up on the hotel room occupied by the young woman. Taking a huge chance, Nik hacked into the reservation system and added his name to her room.

In over five hundred years, Nik had never felt so helpless. It had been centuries since he had more to worry about than where he would live next. When Rafael first took over the States as King, the immediate family spread out to keep the peace throughout the Clan. When Eduardo was slain, it was the perfect time for an uprising. Nikolas moved to Florida, one of the only times he and Julian were apart. Once things settled down and Rafael proved to be a competent ruler, Nik moved to North Carolina where Julian was. They had lived in the same city ever since. When you lived your life hiding in plain sight, it was easier to have a best friend who understood who and what you were.

Jules was his wingman when they went out. Not that Nik had trouble finding women. Quite the opposite. His trouble had been saying no. Nikolas

Stone loved women, and he rarely turned one down. His brother had saved his ass more than once when Nikolas said yes to more than one woman in the same night. Nik had never been opposed to having two or three women in his bed at the same time, but there were some women who didn't like to share. When that happened, Julian offered his services to one of the ladies so Nikolas didn't go home alone.

It was a rare occurrence when Julian went out alone, though. It always amazed Nik how his brother could go years at a time without a woman. Nik could barely go weeks. It wasn't only the sex, either. He loved the softness of a female's body. The way they smelled like flowers after a rain shower. How they were hardwired to care for others. He'd always envisioned his mate as a shorter, plumper female he could curl up around and enjoy the extra pounds on her hips as he thrust into her body. What was the old saying? *More cushion for the pushin'*? Somehow the fates envisioned someone entirely different. Sophia was average height and slender. Still, his bunny was beautiful. He had no problem with who the fates had chosen for him.

An alert sounded on his computer. When he saw what the search had unearthed, he was ecstatic. The two credit cards were issued by the same company. That wasn't what made him happy. The fact that they both had the same post office box number as their address was. That couldn't be a fluke. Nik was almost certain he'd found his mate. Why else would two women in different hotels have credit cards issued to the same address? There was a possibility they could be relatives, but if that were the case, they more than likely would be staying in the same hotel if they were on vacation.

Nik looked up the number for the Nile Grand Hotel and placed a called. When the operator answered, he asked for room ten seventeen. The phone rang several times with no answer. If he were Sophia, he wouldn't answer either, not unless he was expecting a call. She probably wasn't, at least not on the hotel phone. He called the operator once more and asked to leave a message for Miss Fort. Once he told *Clara* he wished to speak with her, he decided to head on over to the hotel.

If he was lucky enough that this was indeed Sophia, he was going to make the mating bond official within minutes. With her permission, of course. Nik wanted to jog the couple of blocks to the Nile Grand, but he made himself walk. He didn't need any unwanted attention, especially if someone was watching Sophia. He entered the lobby and walked up to the front desk. When the clerk got a good look at him, her demeanor changed from bored to interested.

"Good morning, sir. May I help you?" she gushed.

Nikolas didn't hesitate to flash his beautiful smile. It rarely failed to get him what he wanted. "I sure hope so. I left my key in the room. I'm so embarrassed."

"Oh, don't worry. It happens all the time, Mister…?"

"Stone. Nikolas Stone, room ten seventeen." Nik leaned his arms on the counter, smiling even larger.

The clerk had to enter the information several times. Her attention was more on Nik than it was the computer. She opened a drawer, retrieved a blank key card, and swiped it into the machine to register it to the proper room. She handed it over and asked, "Is there anything else I can do for you, Mister Stone? Anything at all?"

Nik winked and said, "You've been a doll. Thank you so much." He pocketed the card and headed for the stairs. That had been way too easy. Maybe it was an omen. When he reached the tenth floor, he walked with purpose until he reached Clara's door. When he didn't hear any noise coming from inside, he let himself in. Nik was immediately assaulted with honeysuckle. This had to be Sophia's room. He took a look around, noting the room looked unused with the exception of the laptop on the desk.

Wanting to be certain, Nik opened the top dresser drawer. He pulled out a pair of lace panties and held them to his face. Even though they were clean, the faint hint of Sophia was evident where she had touched them. Instead of putting them back, he shoved the sliver of material into his pocket. He moved to the bathroom. Toiletries were neatly lined up on the vanity. A large cosmetic box was on the shelf underneath the sink. Nik squatted down and tried to open the box, but it was locked. Why would her cosmetics be locked up?

Next, he opened the closet. There were a lot of clothes on hangers. He slid each item across the bar, noticing some were for a younger woman, while there were a couple of frumpy looking dresses a grandmother might wear. A grandmother named Beatrice, perhaps? "What are you up to, my bunny?"

Nik muttered. The safe was closed and locked. If he had time and his computer, he could get into the small box fairly quickly. Whatever she had locked up would have to remain that way for now. The last item Nik looked at was the computer. He opened the lid to the laptop and powered it on. When it booted up, he wasn't surprised to see the password bar appear. If Clara's computer was anything like Nik's, it would have a complex password that would require one of Julian's programs to break. Nik powered the system down and closed the lid.

The message light on the phone was blinking red. His message was still there, meaning she hadn't been in the room since he called. While debating on whether to sit and wait, a voice from the room next door made up his mind for him.

"We still haven't found the old woman, but the Brooks girl is at the zoo. Drago paid a worker to give her the note. We have eyes on her now."

Brooks girl? They were talking about Sophia. Was Beatrice the old woman they couldn't find? Fuck! Nikolas had to get to the zoo. He took his cell phone out of his pocket and did an internet search for the Cairo Zoo. He returned his attention to the voice next door.

"Yes, Princess. I will make sure she doesn't get away again."

Nikolas had planned on leaving a note for his mate, but he needed to get to the zoo before something happened to her. Why the fuck did he not get her phone number? Nik sneaked out of the hotel room and ran down ten flights of stairs. He exited the side of the hotel and jogged to the front of the building, hailing a taxi. When he got in, Nik told the driver, "I need to get to the zoo as fast as you can."

The Cairo Zoo was located in Giza. It was a fairly quick trip by car, but it was still enough time to give Sophia a chance to slip away. Nik's shifter was clawing to be released. It knew their mate was in danger, so Nik did his best to calm down on the short ride. When the taxi pulled up to the entrance, Nik had the appropriate pounds ready to give the man. He rushed to the booth and bought a ticket, stepping out of the way of other guests. The zoo was situated on eighty acres. That was eighty too many to guess where Sophia would be, so he inhaled deeply. Amid the numerous animal, plant, and people scents, there was a faint trace of something sweet.

Nikolas literally followed his nose along the walkway leading to the large animals. As he passed each cage, the animal residing there made it clear his presence was offensive, and most retreated to the back of their enclosure. When he walked through the area in front of the leopard, the scent of his mate was much more prominent. Nik stopped and looked around, hoping to get a glimpse of his beautiful woman. He continued on through the park, but his nose and his feet brought him back to the leopard. Something had happened there. The man on the phone said a worker had given her a note. If only he could figure out who the worker was. Nikolas looked around, noting the security cameras. He needed to get a look at the feed. He could barge in there now or come back later when the park was closed. Godsdamnit!

Nik made one more pass through the large park before heading back toward Cairo. Instead of going to his hotel, he stopped at the bed and breakfast. He was going to ask for Beatrice in hopes that Sophia was there. When he walked into the small inn, the familiar scent was barely detectable. She probably wasn't there, but he was going to ask anyway. When he reached the desk, there was an older woman standing behind it. He smiled and said, "Hello. I'm here to see Beatrice, but she isn't answering her phone."

"You must be her son-in-law," a voice said from his right. Two couples, one older and one younger, were walking toward him. The younger woman smiled and held out her hand.

Oh shit. If he was wrong about the woman, these people would probably call the cops on him. "Yes, I am. We were supposed to meet for breakfast this morning, but she didn't show." Nik hoped it was a plausible lie.

The older man spoke up. "I saw her leave early this morning around four."

"What were you doing up at four, and why were you watching Beatrice?" The older woman crossed her arms over her chest and huffed at him. If they were married, Nik felt sorry for the man.

"You were snoring, and I couldn't sleep. Besides, I wasn't *watching* Beatrice. I was down in the common area reading a book, and I just happened to see her leave."

"I don't snore!" The woman began a one-sided argument with the man who simply stood and took the bashing from his wife.

The younger couple appeared mortified, but Nik grinned. "I will return to my hotel and wait on her. She has a mind of her own, that Beatrice."

The young woman said, "She's a spitfire, that's for sure. I'm Millicent, and this is my husband, Garrett. Those are his parents, Yvonne and Fred." Nik shook hands with Garrett.

"It's a pleasure to meet you both. If you see Beatrice before I do, please tell her I was looking for her." Since he had no idea if Sophia was truly portraying the older Beatrice, Nik didn't give them his name. If she was, she would know he was in town. If she wasn't, at least the older woman wouldn't have a name to give the police when she informed them she had a stalker.

He exited the inn to the sound of Yvonne still going on about Fred's early morning activities. If she were his wife, he'd lock her in the Basement with the Unholy for a few days. What Nik wouldn't give to be home in New Atlanta, flying at night, fighting Unholy, and going home afterwards to Sophia. Since she knew all about Gargoyles, he wouldn't have to hide the blood from her. As a matter of fact, she could help him shower it off. Fuck, now his dick was getting hard just thinking about her. Nik ducked onto a side street with no traffic so he could adjust the hard-on in his jeans.

CHAPTER NINE

SOPHIA was being followed. This time there was no doubt as to who it was. The two men from the ferry had been waiting outside the zoo when she made her way to a taxi. Now, they were in the cab behind her. They knew she was staying at the Nile Grand, but they didn't know about the bed and breakfast. Hopefully.

She wasn't as nervous leaving as she had been entering. They had given her another clue. If they intended to abduct her, they could have done so before now. The people following her had to know she would need to get ready to travel to the intended destination once she figured out where it was. When she arrived at her hotel, she was alone. The two men continued on past instead of getting out with her. Sophia breathed a sigh of relief and made her way to her room. When she reached her door, she felt light-headed. She stuck the keycard in the slot and didn't try to be quiet. When the door was closed, she leaned her hand against the wall for support. *There's no fricking way…*

Sophia closed her eyes and inhaled deeply. If she didn't know better, she'd think Nik had been in her room. There was no other explanation for the scent or the way she was feeling. Her senses weren't as keen as a full-blood's, but she would never forget the way her mate smelled, and her room smelled exactly the same. She shook the fogginess out of her head. If someone had been in her room, she needed to make sure all her stuff was still there and intact. If it had been Nikolas, hopefully he would have left her a note. Her laptop was where she left it on the desk. She opened the closet. The clothes were pushed apart haphazardly instead of neatly as she'd left them.

She punched in the code to the safe, and the contents had been untouched. Her toiletries were still arranged as they had been; however, her case had been moved. She inspected the contents, noting everything was still there. Lastly, she checked the clothes in her drawers. Those also appeared untouched.

Maybe she was scenting someone from housekeeping. Other than the clothes in the closet being moved around, her things were as they should be, so she let the odd feeling slide. Sophia opened her laptop and booted it up. While she waited, she pulled the note from her pocket and re-read it.

TRAVEL TO THE PLACE OF BEAUTY AND FIND THE LAST PHARAOH'S TOMB

Sophia hadn't studied a lot of ancient history that didn't pertain to the Gargoyles. She seemed to recall Cleopatra being the last Pharaoh, but she would double check to be sure. The Gargoyles in Nik's family were of Italian descent on his father's side. Jonas's origins were Italian and French. Sophia had only paid attention to the history of those Gargoyles of interest to her and her family. If a computer search didn't help her, she would call Xenia. Her aunt was a history professor after all.

Her search for the Place of Beauty resulted in several hits, but Ta-Set-Neferu came up most often. It was the Valley of the Queens where the wives of the Pharaohs were buried. Both it and the Valley of the

Kings, where the Pharaohs were buried, were located in Luxor. When she looked up the last Pharaoh, she read that it was Cleopatra. According to everything she was reading, Xenia had been correct that nobody knew where the Queen was buried. Then why did her clue have her going to Ta-Set-Neferu? Unless someone had recently made an archaeological discovery that wasn't in the search engines, the clue was somehow incorrect. Anything that was newsworthy was on the internet within minutes of it happening, so the clue had to be wrong. Her search showed a glyph for the tomb, and she wanted to know if it was also pictured on the Cleopatra Disk. If it was, she would look there, even if it didn't make sense. If it wasn't, she would know she was being given the runaround.

Just in case, Sophia dialed Xenia's number. When her aunt didn't answer, Sophia left a message, "Hello, Xenia. I needed to ask you a question about the Valley of the Queens. Please call me when you get this." She leaned back in the desk chair and decided to order room service. When she reached for the receiver, she noticed the blinking red light on the phone. Someone had left her a message. Right as she picked up the receiver, her cell phone rang.

"Hello, Xenia."

"Hello, little dove. Sorry I missed your call. You said you had a question about Ta-Set-Neferu."

Sophia turned back to her computer and the hieroglyphs. "Yes, I received another clue as to where my parents are. It said go to the place of beauty and find the last Pharaoh's tomb. When I looked up both, it didn't make sense. Not unless Cleopatra's crypt has been found in the last five minutes. I wanted you to look at the disk and see if the hieroglyphs for the Valley of the Queens happen to be on there somewhere. I know it's a long shot, but if somehow she happened to be buried there—"

"Describe the glyphs to me," Xenia instructed, cutting her off. Sophia could hear her aunt unlocking a safe.

"From left to right there's a bird, a funky building, a box, then three of the same symbol that look like fish with crosses coming out of their heads. Hang on, I'll take a snapshot of it and send it to you." Sophia snapped a picture of the glyph and texted it to her aunt.

"I got it. I will have to get a magnifying glass out and study the disk. I doubt this particular sequence will be stamped on there, but I'll give it a look. I'll let you know when I find something."

"Thank you. Have you talked to Keene yet?" Sophia hoped Xenia and her mate worked things out.

"He's coming over later. I'm going to tell him the truth. Let's hope he doesn't run screaming."

"Call me if you need back-up. He would probably take it easier if he knew there were more of us."

"I appreciate the offer, and if he doesn't believe me, I'll take you up on it. Now, let me study this disk. I'll call or text you soon."

"Thank you and good luck." Sophia thumbed her phone off. A loud thump against the wall made her jump. It happened again, and she jumped again. When it happened a third time, Sophia figured out whoever was in the room next door was bouncing a ball off the wall. She drew her fist back to bang on the wall when she heard a loud voice say, "I told you, she's in her room. I followed her from the zoo."

"Oh, gods," Sophia whispered to herself. She knew they were keeping close tabs on her, but not that close. *Shit!* What if they had bugged her room and were listening to her conversations? If they were, they would know not only had she found the disk, but she'd passed it along to someone else. And she'd said Xenia's name out loud. "Oh, this isn't good, you stupid girl." Sophia forgot about ordering room service and began scouring her room for bugs. After an hour and a thorough search, she felt good about not finding anything. She still hadn't heard back from Xenia, so she decided to head over to the inn. She could enjoy a meal and possibly poke the bear known as Yvonne at the same time.

The door to the room next to hers had opened and closed several times. Sophia gathered her Beatrice disguise as well as her laptop. She placed everything in a large bag and listened for movement and voices next door. When she felt the coast was clear, Sophia left her room, taking great pains to close the door silently. She padded down the hallway to the stairwell and exited out the side door. When she reached the side street, she hailed a taxi. Once inside, she looked behind her. Sophia didn't see anyone following, but she still had the driver take her farther than she needed to go.

She made her way into the lobby of another large hotel and found the guest restroom on the bottom floor. She went into the handicapped stall and donned her Beatrice disguise. Luckily, no one came in while she was changing. She didn't want to have to hang out in the ladies' room any longer than she had to. Once the coast was clear, Sophia left the restroom and strolled through the lobby. The delicious scent that reminded her so much of Nikolas wafted over the air. When she got back home and got her hands on him, he was in big trouble.

Sophia arrived at the inn and took her bag to her room. She knew it was too early for supper, but she was hungry. She entered the dining room right as the Waterfords were coming in the front door.

"Beatrice. Did your son-in-law find you?" Millicent asked.

"My son-in-law?" What the holy hell was she talking about?

"Yeah, he stopped by earlier. Said you were supposed to meet him for breakfast, but he couldn't get you to answer your phone."

"Was he tall with light brown hair and beautiful blue eyes?"

"That was him," Millicent said, fanning herself.

Yvonne huffed. "Garrett is standing right there, Millicent."

Garrett laughed and put his arm around his wife. "Yes I am, but even I can admit how handsome he was." He winked at Beatrice. Everyone laughed except for Yvonne.

Sophia grinned at Millicent. "Yes, he's quite a looker. My daughter sure caught a good one. And yes, thank you. I did meet up with him later."

"And what, might I ask, were you doing out alone at four in the morning?" Yvonne asked, her eyes squinting accusingly.

"Mom, that's enough. Beatrice, please excuse us. It's been a rather trying day. We'll let you get to wherever you were going." Garrett pulled his mother along by the wrist.

Sophia just couldn't let it go. "Yvonne, for your information, I met a man, and I realized I left my bra at his place. I went back to get it." Yvonne's mouth gaped open then snapped shut.

As Fred walked past, he patted Sophia on the shoulder and whispered, "Good for you, dear."

Sophia went into the dining room, sat down at the table, and placed her head in her hands. There was no way Nikolas could be in Egypt, could he? She had been catching his addicting scent, but she chalked it up to coincidence. Now...

"Are you okay?" one of the caretakers asked her. The woman had been nothing but professional and accommodating.

"Yes, just thinking. If you don't mind, I'd like to go ahead and order. Please have it sent to my room when it's ready."

"Of course. Anything you need."

Sophia headed to her room so she could pace the floor in private. Someone who matched Nik's description was looking for her. It could be one of the men who had been following her, but how would he have known about Beatrice? Unless they went over the security feed from the zoo and tracked her that way, they shouldn't know. Even Nikolas shouldn't be able to figure out who Beatrice was. While she was waiting on her food, she remembered the message light blinking on her hotel phone. She called the Nile Grand and asked to retrieve her message. After giving her credit card number to verify her identity, the operator patched her through.

"Hello, Clara. I would love to talk to you. If you can, meet me in the hotel bar at three p.m. I'll be waiting."

Sophia listened to the message three more times. How was it possible Nik was there? Oh, gods, what if they had kidnapped him and it was a trick? Shit! She listened again. He didn't sound stressed. He sounded great. His voice was magical. Besides, he was a Gargoyle. He would be hard to abduct and harder to hold onto. No, Nik was there and wanted to see her! He had figured out she was Clara. She knew he was smart, but it was still impressive. She would have to ask him how he knew so she could be more careful next time.

Gah! She couldn't believe he'd followed her to Egypt. He *had* been in her room. Holy shit! He said he would meet her at three. It was twenty minutes until four now. "Oh, gods. No!" Not bothering to wait on her food or change out of her disguise, Sophia took off for the hotel.

Chapter Ten

NIK looked at his watch for the twentieth time. Either Sophia didn't get his message or something had happened. He wouldn't consider that she didn't want to see him, not after the note she left for him at the library. He ordered one more drink and looked around. While he was waiting on the bartender to pour his fourth vodka tonic, he recognized the man who had almost run him down on the tenth floor. He was talking excitedly on his cell phone. Nik threw some money down on the bar and took off after him.

Nik used his shifter hearing to listen in on the conversation. The man was talking about Sophia and a note. He turned down a side street, so Nik followed. As soon as he turned the corner, he felt uneasy. Normally, Nikolas associated the queasiness with being around his mate. If he turned back to look for her, he would lose the man. If he continued following, he might lose a chance at catching up with Sophia, if it was even her. His gut told him it was, but the man on the phone knew where her parents were. Nik would find his bunny later. When he did, he prayed he'd have good news for her.

Nik continued after the stranger. Instead of the unease lessening, it increased. When the man stopped at the corner, waiting for the traffic light to turn green so he could cross the street, Nik lingered back so he wouldn't be seen. The scent of honeysuckle assaulted Nik's senses. He bent over, putting his hands on his knees to calm himself. "Nikolas?" an older woman's voice asked.

Nik unfolded himself. Before he could confirm his identity, the woman flung herself at him and kissed him. His first thought was he was being molested by an old woman. His second thought, the one that made no sense at all, was that he was enjoying the hell out of it. She licked at the seam of his lips, her tongue begging for entrance. Before he allowed some strange grandma to French him, he pulled her off him. "Hold up. Do I know you?"

"Of course you know me, Nikolas Stone. I'm your frickin' mate." When she scrunched up her nose, he knew without a doubt she was Sophia.

Grinning, he said, "But you're... *old*," as if she didn't know what she looked like.

"Just call me Beatrice, sonny. Now kiss me," she husked as she pushed him against the side of the building.

"Well, alrighty then." Nik closed his eyes and pictured his bunny. He opened for her, their tongues mating the way their bodies were aching to. Sophia's hands grabbed his hair, pulling him in closer, if that were possible. He wished they were somewhere other than the sidewalk. She rotated her hips, the friction jumpstarting his dick. When she moaned in his mouth, his half-erect cock inflated all the way. Godsdamn, what he wouldn't give to strip her bare right there. They finally came up for air, and he remembered the man he'd been following. "Shit."

"What's wrong?" she asked as she held onto his arms for support.

"Other than we're not naked? I was waiting for you in the bar when one of your neighbors got a phone call. I overheard him talking about you and a note, so I followed him." Nik looked around and saw the back of the stranger's head a block away. "That's him, the one wearing the red sweatshirt," he said, pointing at the tall man.

"I think you should still follow him. See what you can find out. I'll go back to my room so I can get out of my disguise. I'll wait for you there."

"Okay, but be careful. I finally caught up with you. I can't lose you again." Nik leaned in and kissed her hard on the mouth. "I'll see you soon." He tapped her on the nose then took off running across the busy intersection. Leaving her there was the hardest thing he'd ever done, but knowing she would be in her room waiting for him made it easier. He would tail the stranger and find out what he could about the note and who was following Sophia. When he met her back in her room, he was going to spank her ass for worrying him. Then he was going to spend the rest of the day making her his.

The traffic light changed to red, but Nikolas ran across the street anyway. He had already lost valuable time. His heart was soaring, and his cock was aching. Even in her disguise, Sophia was the most beautiful sight Nik had seen in a long time. He couldn't believe he'd found her in a country so large. Actually, they found each other, but either way, he knew she was safe. He intended to keep her that way.

The red sweatshirt bobbed in and out of pedestrians, obviously in a hurry. Nik had no trouble keeping up with him. He closed the gap when the man stopped at the next corner. When he turned to look behind him, Nik ducked into the alcove of a shop. He waited a few seconds before peering around the bricks to see the man was on the move again, this time at a much faster pace. *Shit.* Nik was afraid he'd been made. Before he could close the gap, an SUV pulled to the curb and the stranger jumped in. *Fuck!* Nik ran out into the street and barely had time to take in the license plate number. If he wasn't a shifter, he would have missed it.

He begged the gods for a taxi, but none were on the busy street. Dammit, he'd been so close. At least now he could go back and spend time with Sophia. He would run the license plate while they got acquainted. Even though he'd let the stranger get away, his heart was pounding at the prospect of getting close and personal with his mate. Really close and personal.

SOPHIA couldn't believe Nikolas was in Egypt. He was there to help her find her parents. She should have asked him to help her in the beginning. If she had, she would probably be a lot closer to finding them. The note didn't say anything about coming alone or not telling anyone. She'd never even thought to call the authorities. There was too much at stake to involve the human police. She didn't know the King's mate, Kaya Kane, well enough to trust her. And besides, what could she do? She was a local chief in New Atlanta, not some high-ranking official in one of the government alphabets. Even if Chief Kane had been in the CIA or

FBI, Sophia wouldn't have gone to her.

Nikolas, she should have trusted. Sophia should have known he would accept the mate bond and be by her side. Now he was, or would be in just a little while. Sophia couldn't wait to get back to her hotel and strip out of her disguise. She wanted Nik to see the real her. Soon, she would be mated to Nikolas Stone, of that she had no doubt. Yes, she was there to find her parents, but the pull was too strong not to answer the call. Once they completed the bond, they would work together to find her parents.

"I've seen it all now," a familiar voice crowed behind her. Sophia turned to find Yvonne standing behind her, scowling.

"I honestly doubt that, but what are you going on about?" she asked the older woman.

"You attacking your son-in-law. That was despicable." Yvonne was looking down her nose, disdain evident on her face.

"Are you following me, Yvonne? Does Fred know you're off your leash?" Sophia was tired of this nosy bitch.

The older woman huffed. "Yes, I followed you. I wanted to tell you I don't appreciate you meddling in my family. I was right; you are nothing but trouble."

"Garrett's an only child, isn't he?"

"How did you know that?"

Sophia pulled up to her true height and got in the woman's face. "Fred must have good sperm, because as big a bitch as you are, there's no way he would screw you more than once. Now, I don't have time to stand here and trade barbs with you. Stop following me and worry about your own damn business." Sophia didn't give her time to respond. She left Yvonne wide-eyed and furious.

As soon as she was far enough away, Sophia burst out laughing. She could only imagine how it looked, Beatrice kissing Nik. She wished she'd seen the look on Yvonne's face as she watched them going at it. That would be one to tell the grandchildren. She was lost in thoughts of a naked Gargoyle when she reached her hotel. Waltzing in the front door, she went straight to the elevator instead of taking the stairs. The doors were almost closed when a male hand slid between, stopping the motion. Sophia sucked in her breath when the blonde woman and her partner entered the car with her. Instead of pushing the button for the tenth floor, the man pushed five.

Sophia averted her eyes, praying to the gods they didn't recognize her. When the doors opened, only the woman got off the elevator. *Shit.* She couldn't get off on the tenth floor and go to her room, or they would know where she was staying. She pressed the button for nine, hoping the man wouldn't follow her. When the doors opened again, Sophia stepped into the hallway and turned left toward the stairs. When she felt a presence behind her, she had a split second to decide - phase and hope like hell the man wasn't a Gargoyle, or scream for help. She opted for the latter. When she reached the end of the hall, she pulled the fire alarm and screamed at the top of her lungs. Her follower was so stunned she was able to shove him down on his ass and take off running. Instead of running up to her room, she went down. Sophia allowed herself to get lost in the throngs of hotel guests using the stairs to get to safety.

When she reached the bottom floor, she ran out the side door and flagged down a taxi. *Dammit!* She needed to get back to her room and wait on Nikolas. Now she would have to go back to the inn to wait. Hopefully he would figure out where she was. Why hadn't she bothered to get his phone number? She didn't even know what hotel he was staying in. If she could get to her computer, she could figure it out. When she got to the bed and breakfast, she prayed she could get to her room without anyone seeing her. The last thing she needed was another confrontation with Yvonne.

Her followers either knew she was both Sophia and Beatrice, or they only knew Beatrice had the disk and they wanted it back. Either way, she was screwed. The only option she could see was to become Clara and change hotels. At this point, she had little faith in getting back into the Nile Grand and retrieving her things. Earlier, Nik said he was chasing her neighbor. It was probably the same man she'd heard talking on the phone. If he was working with the blonde and her accomplice, then she wouldn't risk going back for her stuff. At least she had an extra computer and clothing at the inn.

As soon as she got to her room, she opened her laptop to search where Nik might be staying. While she was waiting on it to boot up, Sophia stripped out of her disguise. This afternoon was not going the way she thought it would after running into Nikolas. She was pulling a T-shirt over her head when she heard a commotion outside. Sophia looked out her window to see the blonde and her partner arguing with a couple of men on the sidewalk. *Shit!* They'd found her. She closed her laptop, and shoved it into her backpack along with everything else she could fit. Next, she grabbed her Clara disguise, her toiletries, and as many clothes as she could fit in her large bag.

Sophia couldn't go out the front door, and she wouldn't chance going through the kitchen. She kept out of sight while she waited to see if they were coming inside the inn. After a few minutes and some heated discussion, the couple headed toward the entrance while the two men split up. If she was lucky, the inn owners would turn the couple away and she could stay in her room. If her luck was continuing as it had been, Yvonne would be the first to tell them where she was. Sophia wasn't going to put any faith in hiding out in her room.

The front window with the balcony looked out over the street. That was out. The side window faced the garden area. Garden it was. Sophia opened the window and tossed her bag to the ground amidst the bushes. She strapped her backpack on and climbed over the window ledge. Two stories up was higher than she'd ever jumped, but she was a shifter. She called her Goyle half forward and dropped the twenty-something feet to the ground. She landed on her feet then fell back onto her butt. Not very graceful, but she'd take it. She stood and wiped the dirt off her jeans, grabbed her bag, and took off behind the building.

Sophia needed to figure out where Nikolas was registered. Since she hadn't been able to search on her laptop, the next best thing was to call all the hotels and pray to the gods he wasn't using an alias. Sophia ducked into the first coffee shop she came to. Instead of sitting at a booth, she headed for the restroom. Once she was secluded in a stall, she pulled up the area hotels on her phone and began calling each one. When she tried the Sitela West, she hit the motherlode. He didn't answer, but at least she knew at which hotel he was staying. Sophia left a message on his room phone, leaving her phone number for him. That way if they kept missing each other, at least he could call her.

Her safest bet was to hop a train to Alexandria and hide out with Xenia for a while, but she didn't want to chance being followed and putting her aunt in danger. Xenia had enough on her plate without Sophia adding to it. She would have to take her chances on her own. She pulled up the search engine on her phone and typed in public library. It wasn't too far away, but she wouldn't take a chance on walking. She made her way back to the front of the café and stepped out onto the sidewalk to flag down a taxi.

As she was getting into the automobile, a man yelled, "There she is. Get her!"

Sophia didn't look behind her. She climbed into the taxi and yelled, "Go, go!" Only when they had pulled out into traffic did she dare turn to see who was following her. She recognized the big man from the airport. He and his partner were yelling and rushing to find their own taxi. Sophia felt safe for the moment. "To the library, please," she told the driver.

CHAPTER ELEVEN

KALLISTO was furious at Sergei for allowing the old woman to get the jump on him. As soon as she heard the fire alarm, she'd taken off down the stairs, her gut telling her it wasn't a fire. She saw the old woman just as she got into a taxi. Luckily, there was another right behind it. Sergei jumped in the cab right before she could close the door. Drago and one of his men, Crane, met them at the bed and breakfast where Kallisto was certain the taxi had stopped.

Crane explained, "I don't know who the man was or why he was following me. If he hadn't stopped to talk to some old woman, he'd probably have caught me."

"Old woman? Did she look like this?" Kallisto held up the photograph they had of the woman from the zoo. Sergei had been able to hack into the security feed and freeze frame on her face. The picture was a little grainy, but it was clear enough to show it was the same woman they were now chasing.

"Yeah, that's her. Why would a young guy be kissing an old woman?" Crane asked, cringing.

"Might be his mother," Drago offered.

"If you ever catch me kissing my ma with tongue, just fucking shoot me," Crane protested.

"How do you know there was tongue involved?" Drago asked.

Kallisto growled. "Would you two shut up? I'm pretty sure she ducked into this inn. Sergei and I will check it out. You two split up. Crane cover the area outside. She might be old, but she's tough and fast.

Drago, you go to the hotel in case she circles back. If either of you spot her, don't let her out of your sight. We have to get the disk back," Kallisto instructed.

"What about the Brooks woman?" Drago asked.

"She should be looking for clues to her parents' whereabouts, not that the note will do any good. Our first priority is retrieving the disk. Now go. Call me if you see either one of them."

When the two men walked off, Sergei asked, "Don't you think it's a big coincidence the old woman was going to the tenth floor?"

"Yes, I do. After we leave here, I plan on getting into her room and see what we can find. For now, I want to see if the old woman went in here." Kallisto walked up the steps to the inn and went inside. It was a quaint little place, if you liked that sort of thing. She lived in a huge villa fit for a princess. Considering who her father was, she expected nothing less.

Several people were in the foyer arguing. She interrupted them. "Excuse me. Did any of you see this woman come through here?" she asked, showing them the picture on her phone.

"That's Beatrice," the older woman of the group exclaimed.

"Why do you want to know?" the younger woman stepped in front of the older one and asked.

"We only want to talk to her. There was an accident, and she might have been a witness," Kallisto lied.

The younger woman placed her hands on her hips, but the older one stepped around her. "Yes, I will show you to her room."

"Now, wait just a minute, Yvonne. You can't go disrupting someone's privacy. I won't stand for it." The older man grabbed the woman's arm. She jerked her arm away and started to give him a piece of her mind, but a caretaker from the inn stopped her.

"Excuse me, Mrs. Waterford. I must insist you leave this matter to me. We take our guests' privacy seriously, and I'm sure if you were in the same position as Mrs. Nightingale, you would feel the same way. Now, Miss...?"

"Miss Verga. I do apologize for the commotion. I was only hoping Mrs. Nightingale could tell us what she saw. It is unnecessary to disturb her at this time." Kallisto grabbed Sergei's hand and pulled him outside. "We know she's there. Now we'll wait until she leaves. She can't hole up in there forever. Let's take a look around, make sure there's not a back way she can escape."

NIKOLAS arrived at the Nile Grand to find the building had been evacuated. He pulled out his cellphone and dialed Sophia's room, doubting she would still be in the building. He got no answer, so he looked around the crowd for her. Firefighters were allowing guests to return to their rooms, so she might be on her way upstairs. Nik hovered around one of the emergency vehicles, close enough to overhear two men talking. A fire alarm had been pulled on the ninth floor, but no fire or smoke had been found. They chalked it up to a kid playing a prank. Hotel surveillance would give them more information. Even though it was the ninth floor, Nik needed to see that video feed for himself. First, he needed to find his mate.

He took the stairs up to the tenth floor and used the key card to let himself into Sophia's room. He fully expected her to be right up, even though he hadn't seen her downstairs. While he was waiting, he called Julian to check on things back home. He didn't tell his brother about running into Sophia. He would wait and give him the good news once they were mated. After thirty minutes had passed, he began to get worried. She should have been back by now. Another thirty minutes later, and Nik wrote a note for her, telling her he was going to his hotel to run the license plate of the SUV. He remembered to write down his cell phone number for her.

The one time he wanted to run into someone in the hall, the strangers who were following Sophia were nowhere to be found. Nik made his way to his own hotel room where he plugged in the license plate number. Next, he opened one of the tiny bottles of whisky in the mini-bar. He swallowed the liquor in one gulp and opened another. These little samples were just enough to piss someone off. He checked the computer, and as he suspected, the SUV was a rental. It was assigned to someone named K. Verga. The initial K didn't give him much to go on, and if they were smart, it was an alias.

He noticed the red light flashing on the room phone just as his cell phone pinged with an incoming text. He grabbed his phone and frowned. The number was unknown, but he opened the text anyway.

In trouble, please help.

Fuck! Nik texted back: *On my way*

Sophia had to be at the hotel, or she wouldn't have known his number. She must be using a burner phone, or else she had her name blocked for security. All this back and forth was getting on his nerves. As soon as he got his hands on her, he was going to chain her to him. A lesser man would already have an ulcer. Since Nik wasn't really a man, he would be fine. Eventually.

Guests were still milling around the lobby of the hotel, but the emergency crews had left the premises. Nik kept his shifter senses open, especially his hearing. He blocked out all sounds except for voices and then he listened for anything that would alert him to Sophia's followers.

He stopped when he was outside the door to her room. He didn't hear any movement inside, but he did feel a presence there. Oh, gods, what if she was hurt? Nik slid the key card in the slot and shoved open the door when it unlocked. Instead of Sophia, Nik was facing someone from housekeeping. The tall woman jumped when he burst through the door.

"Where is she?" Nik asked, grabbing the woman by the arms.

"I'm sorry, sir. I'm just cleaning the room," she begged. Nik let go and took a look around. The woman tried to run past him, but he grabbed her wrist. There were no cleaning supplies in the room. If there was a cart in the hall, Nik didn't remember seeing it.

"What exactly were you cleaning?" Nik demanded. Instead of answering, the woman pulled something out of her pocket and sprayed it in his face. "Fuck!" His eyes were burning and tearing up. He couldn't see. The sound of the heavy door handle turning let him know the woman was getting away. "Godsdamnit!" Nik stumbled to the bathroom, running into the bed along the way. He flushed his eyes with water until he could see again.

Back in the sleeping area, Nik looked around the room and saw his note to Sophia was gone. *Fuck!* Instead of doing the smart thing and finding a way to get in the room next door quietly, Nik knocked. When he didn't hear voices inside, he used his Goyle strength to open the door. The dickheads following Sophia could explain to the hotel manager how it got busted.

Nik calmed his shifter and took in the room. It didn't look as though anyone had been in there. If they had checked out, he would be surprised. Unless they had Sophia. No. Nik wouldn't allow himself to believe she had been captured. He opened each drawer on the dresser and found they were all empty. There were no toiletries in the bathroom. The garbage can, however, contained a crumpled-up piece of paper. He pulled it out and unfolded it. Nik was holding the note he'd written Sophia.

After another cursory glance around the room, Nik shoved the paper in his pocket and left. The woman who'd been in Sophia's room was probably the one to text him and lure him away from his hotel, but for what? *To identify you, you idiot.* Now the ones following Sophia knew he was there with her. Not only that, but they had probably seen him with Beatrice, too. If they were worth their salt, they would already know where

Beatrice was staying. This was getting worse by the minute. Nik left the room and ran down the stairs.

He called the bed and breakfast again, asking if Beatrice was there. The woman who answered the phone was not polite. "I've already told you, my guests' privacy is all that matters. Do not make me call the police." The woman hung up, and Nik looked at his phone. What the hell? Obviously, someone else had been to the inn looking for Beatrice. If they knew she and Sophia were the same person, Sophia was screwed. He wished he had one of Sophia's disguises. Her followers knew what he looked like, and they knew he was there to help her.

He walked the long way to the inn, keeping his eyes and ears open for any sign of someone following him. He memorized the layout of the building, the garden on the west side, and the balconies on the second floor. As he turned the corner, the back door opened, and a man in a chef's hat deposited a black plastic bag in a trash receptacle. When he went back inside, he didn't pause to lock the door. Nik could use that to his advantage later. Just as he was headed to the front door, a loud argument sounded from an open second floor window.

"I'm telling you, Fred. Stay away from Beatrice. That woman is trouble, and I forbid you to talk to her again."

"You forbid me? Yvonne, I've put up with your crap for thirty years. I'm done. This was supposed to be a nice trip for the kids, and you've ruined it. Beatrice was right; you need to cut the cord where Garrett's concerned. He's old enough to take a trip with his wife without you butting in. They haven't had any alone time since we arrived. As far as we're concerned, I think once we get home, we need to take a break."

"See what I'm talking about? You never would have talked to me this way before you met that hussy! I hope that nice couple finds her."

"Beatrice is not a hussy. And that couple didn't seem so nice to me. They looked like trouble."

Nik didn't listen to any more of their argument. As soon as Yvonne mentioned a couple, he knew Sophia's cover was blown. Why else would they be looking for her? He would come back when it was dark and look around for Beatrice's room.

Nik made his way back to his hotel room and remembered the flashing red light. When he picked up the receiver, the light was no longer flashing. He pressed the button anyway, but there were no messages. His stomach growled, so he decided to call for room service while thinking about what to do next. He was pleased to see a steak on the menu since he wasn't fond of foreign food. While he was waiting, he decided to meditate. Too much had happened for one day, and Nik wanted to clear his mind. He kicked off his boots and sat down on the floor, crossing his legs. He closed his eyes and slowed his breathing. Gargoyles could sit unmoving for hours at a time. Nik sat for hours in the lab with Julian, or in his home office with the archives. Rarely was he completely still, though. He had a lust for life that hadn't waned in five hundred years. Now that he'd found his mate, that lust was only going to get stronger. He had someone to share his days with, have babies with. He concentrated on

Sophia's face and let her beauty wash over him.

In his mind, she was wearing her long, colorful skirt. Her toenails were as bright as the fabric covering her legs. Her hair was blowing in the wind. She was laughing. Even though he'd never seen her on the beach, that's where his thoughts took her - to white sands with blue waters rolling in behind her. Sophia twirled around, her skirt billowing around her ankles. She began running. Not toward Nik, but away from him. When she glanced over her shoulder, she was not smiling. She was afraid. A hand reached out for her shoulder as a pounding noise grew louder.

Room service knocking on the door brought Nikolas out of his meditation. Gargoyles didn't sweat, but there was a light sheen of perspiration on his face. Okay, that was weird. Nik had no psychic powers. Dante was the gifted one in the family. There was no reason for his fantasy to turn dark the way it had.

Nik rose from the floor and looked through the peephole. His nerves were on edge when he opened the door. The last hotel employee he encountered incapacitated him. He stood back with the door open as the man brought the tray in, set it on the table, and asked, "Can I get you anything else, Mister Stone?"

"No, thank you." Nik pulled some money out of his pocket and tipped the man. Once he was alone, he removed the lid from his supper. The idea of a thick, juicy steak had lost its appeal, but he needed to eat something anyway. It didn't take long to demolish the meat and potato. As an afterthought, he picked up the dinner roll and stuck it in his mouth. When he went to place it back on the plate, he noticed a piece of paper.

His intuition told him he wasn't going to like what it said. He was right. Printed in block letters were the words:

WE HAVE THE GIRL

Nikolas fell to his knees and roared.

CHAPTER TWELVE

ZEKE spent most of the day on the computer. He had no leads to go on, nothing indicating where his niece might be. Once she landed in Cairo, she could have gone anywhere. She wasn't using her own credit card, so he had no clue where to look for her or how to find her. He called Elizabeth, making sure she hadn't heard from Sophia or Sam. She hadn't, but that wasn't the worst of what she told him. Elizabeth filled him in on what happened with Tessa and how she'd been injured in a car chase. Elizabeth was waiting until Xavier returned from Italy so they could go see their daughter. Zeke had never met Xavier, but he'd heard his cousin was a force to be reckoned with, especially where Elizabeth was concerned.

Zeke looked up his sister Xenia's address, pleased to find she was no longer living in South Africa but Alexandria. Since he was no closer to finding Sophia than he had been when he got there, Ezekiel decided to pay his sister a visit. He was going to tell her who and what she was. If nothing else good came from his trip, at least he would have the peace of mind in doing this for her. He decided against calling first, so he boarded a train and settled in for the three-hour ride.

His mind drifted to Tessa and what she had endured at the hands of her father. Not Xavier, but the man who thought he was her father. Gordon Flanagan was a monster. He had been searching for Tessa since Elizabeth disappeared with the girl when she was a baby. Now, it seemed the search was over. The helicopter Gordon had been flying in had been shot down, and he was presumed dead. Tessa was in a coma thanks to him and one of his goons. Zeke knew Tessa. She was a fighter. He also knew his father was masquerading as Chief of Staff of the hospital where Tessa was being treated. Jonas would take good care of his prodigy. She might not be his daughter, but she was Jonas's pride and joy. Zeke wasn't jealous of the girl. He was just as proud of her as Jonas was. What Jonas didn't realize, though, was Sophia was as smart and cunning as Tessa.

The train rolled into the station, and Zeke stood and stretched his legs. He was anxious to meet another sibling but apprehensive to do it unannounced. Still, he made his way to the street and flagged down a taxi. Even though he had traveled many places, it never ceased to amaze Zeke how a lot of houses and neighborhoods looked the same all over the world. The street Xenia lived on could have easily been in the States. When they reached her house, he paid the taxi driver and stood on the sidewalk in front of the smaller home. He took a deep breath before walking to the door and knocking.

The similarity between the woman who opened the door and his mother let him know he had the right house. "Hello, Xenia. My name is Ezekiel. I'm—"

"My brother, I know. Come on in. Can I offer you something to drink?" Xenia surprised him.

Zeke stood in the door, unmoving. "How do you know who I am? And how do you know I'm really Ezekiel?"

Xenia stopped when he wasn't behind her. "Because Sophia told me about you, and you look just like Jonas. She showed me pictures."

That got him moving. He entered her house and closed the door. "I'll have whatever you're having, please. When did you speak with Sophia?"

"This morning. She called to ask about the Valley of the Queens." Xenia handed him a tumbler filled with amber liquid and no ice. He took a sip and coughed. "I see you like your Scotch neat."

"Yes. It's the good stuff, so I don't see the need in watering it down with ice. Won't you have a seat?" she asked as she sat on the sofa.

Zeke took the armchair across from her. "If you don't mind my asking, how did you meet Sophia? I've been sent by the family to locate her, and it's surprising she came to visit you when she's supposed to be looking for her parents. Did she tell you that?"

"Yes, she told me everything. I'm surprised you didn't call her cell phone. I'm pretty sure she would answer, especially if you're here to help her."

Zeke felt like a fool. Of course, he should have called her phone. "You're absolutely right. Don't I feel like an idiot? I just assumed since nobody knew her whereabouts, they had already attempted to reach her on her phone. Can you please tell me what you know?"

Xenia recounted the events of the previous day, from Sophia walking in to find a phased Xenia, to the disk, to her phone call that morning. "She told me I have a lot of siblings. I never thought I'd meet one so soon. How old are you, if I'm not being too forward?"

"I'm fifty-seven. I am the middle child, but Sophia probably already told you that."

"She gave me a list of names with ages and their

whereabouts. It's a lot to take in. First the phasing, then the news that I'm adopted with so many brothers and sisters. But it is what it is. I've had almost twenty-four hours to come to terms with it all. Everything except for my mate. I'm meeting Keene tonight to tell him the truth. What about you? How did your mate take the news?" Xenia asked, sipping her Scotch.

This was the one thing Ezekiel hated discussing with his siblings. They had a right to know, but it still stung having to relay such a hurtful, personal detail. "I don't know who my mate is. I transitioned in my late twenties. I dated a lot of women at the same time. I guess you could say I was a womanizer. Still, I never felt the mate pull with any of them. Back then, I didn't know what caused our kind to transition initially. Now that I do, I look back on that period of time, and I cannot for the life of me figure out who it could have been."

"I'm sorry. I don't know what's worse, knowing who it is and having them reject you, or not knowing at all."

"Definitely not knowing at all. Xenia, I've never seen a mate reject a shifter. The pull is too strong. It might seem shitty on the part of the fates, but the mates I have been around are nothing but loving, loyal, and accepting. I have a feeling Keene will be the same way once the initial shock has worn off. You aren't alone in this. I'm here. I might have come searching for Sophia, but we are family. I will not abandon you if you need me."

"Seems like the fates knew what they were doing when they gave me family, too. I just met you and

Sophia, but it feels like I've known you my whole life. That's crazy, but it's true. Thank you for offering. I will be fine, though. Sophia talked me through the history of our family, if somewhat briefly. I have been working on getting my phasing under control, and I feel confident I will be a pro at flashing fangs very soon. Sophia is the one you need to worry about. We need to help her find her parents. These people who are after her have her on a wild goose chase. That may be what they intended, to send her on fool's errands just to keep her from finding Sam. I have a feeling whoever it is has some really deep pockets and strong connections. If the authorities had caught her with the Cleopatra Disk, she would have been detained indefinitely."

"What can you tell me about the clues they've given her?"

"The disk was her first clue. Sophia happened to see the blonde woman and her male companion while out walking, so she followed the woman. The blonde hid a disk under a bench at the zoo. Sophia retrieved it and brought it here. She needed help deciphering what it was. Since the disk has been missing since the time of Cleopatra's death, it didn't show up in the databases Sophia looked in. When she went back to pretend to follow their instructions, she was handed a note. This is where I believe they are trying to confuse her. The note told her to go to the place of beauty and find the last pharaoh's tomb. The place of beauty translates to the Valley of the Queens. That's where the pharaoh's wives are buried. The last pharaoh was Cleopatra; her place of burial is unknown."

"Is it possible someone might have discovered

where the Queen's tomb is?" Zeke had studied Egyptian history and knew it was a long shot.

"I'm pretty sure it would have been all over the news. No, I have a feeling whoever has Sam and Monica is toying with Sophia."

Zeke stood and pulled out his cellphone. "Excuse me for a moment. I want to see if I can reach her." He dialed his niece's number, but it went to voice mail. He left her a message, telling her he was in Egypt and to call him as soon as she got the message. While he was on the phone, there was a knock at the door.

Xenia downed the rest of her drink before going to answer it. When she opened the door, a handsome man who Zeke assumed was Keene came in. He stopped short when he saw Zeke. "Is there something you want to tell me?" he asked Xenia.

She grabbed Keene's hand and said, "I'd like to introduce you to my brother, Ezekiel. Zeke, this is Keene Tyson."

Zeke reached his hand out to shake the other man's. "It's a pleasure to meet you."

Keene nodded but told Xenia, "I didn't know you had a brother."

She grinned. "I didn't either until yesterday. It seems I have several. That's why I asked you over here, so I could explain what I found out about my birth parents."

Keene nodded again before raising an eyebrow at Zeke. He took that as his cue to leave. "Xenia, before I go, did Sophia happen to say where she's staying? I have searched the hotels in Cairo, but her name isn't listed at any of them."

"She mentioned the Nile Grand, but she's probably using an alias considering she's been in disguise the whole time. If I talk to her again, I'll be sure to have her call you."

"Thank you. Here's my number," he said, handing her a card. "Call if you need anything." Zeke turned to go but was stopped when his sister pulled him in for a hug. He returned her embrace, inclined his head to Keene, and left them alone to discuss their future. Hopefully, they'd have one.

NIKOLAS was going crazy. He had paced the floor of his room, waiting until it was late. As soon as he stepped out into the night air and felt the pull of the moon, his Gargoyle clawed at him from the inside, begging to be turned loose. Nik would love nothing more than to take to the skies, spreading his wings and soaring. He tamped down his beast but kept it close enough to the surface to be aware of his surroundings. He was pissed at himself for letting the blonde get the jump on him with whatever she'd sprayed in his eyes.

When Nik arrived at the inn, he checked the back door. He turned the knob slowly and pushed the unlocked door open enough to listen for movement inside. When he heard none, he entered the hallway behind the kitchen. The place was small enough that he found the stairs easily. He made his way to the second floor and followed his nose to the door where honeysuckle was present. Nik tried the knob and surprisingly, it was unlocked. He opened the door and let himself into Sophia's room.

This room was not neat and tidy like the one at the hotel had been. Drawers were open as was the window. Even though the days were pleasant, the night air could get chilly. The thin curtain was flowing from the breeze. Nik looked out the window to find it overlooked the garden. At first glance, everything looked normal. Nik continued to study the area below the window. A bush had branches broken off, and the dirt next to it had been disturbed. His mate had jumped. *Dammit.* That wasn't good. If she had to escape out the window, someone had been looking for her downstairs.

A large bag was on the floor by the bathroom. Nik picked it up and looked through the contents. A gray wig along with the Beatrice prosthetic were mixed with some clothes. Either Sophia's alter ego had been compromised, or she was in too much of a hurry to grab it. Otherwise, she wouldn't have left it behind. Various items of clothing were in the closet, most of those belonging to an older woman. A couple of shirts hung on hangers that he could see someone like Tessa wearing. Nik tried to imagine Sophia dressed as a female version of Indiana Jones. Even though their situation was dire, Nik grinned when he envisioned his mate wielding a whip. Maybe she would whip him. *Get your head out of the bed, Nikky boy. Your mate is in trouble, and you're thinking of sex games.* As he pushed through the hangers, a wave of lightheadedness washed over him, and he allowed the feeling to flow through his body. He should have never separated from her once he found her. He wouldn't make that mistake again.

Instead of going back through the inn, Nik decided to go out the window as Sophia had. He climbed through the open frame then dropped to the ground. He landed, knees bent, hands on the dirt. His right hand was resting atop a piece of paper. He picked it up and read what had been written. Sophia must have dropped it when she jumped. Finally, a break. Nik was holding the clue to where Sophia's parents were being held.

Chapter Thirteen

SOPHIA thought New Atlanta's library was large. It was nothing compared to the one she was hiding out in. The building boasted seven stories that held millions of books. It was almost closing time, and Sophia hoped the security guards bypassed the bathrooms on their final walkthroughs. She prayed their security system didn't have infrared lights or motion detectors. She hadn't had the chance to check it all out before she ducked into the small room.

She sat quietly as the minutes ticked by, one slow second at a time. When she was certain the building was closed down, only then did she step out of the cramped stall she had been waiting in. Sophia pulled her laptop from her backpack and plugged it in. She couldn't believe there was an outlet in the women's restroom, but she was thankful for it. Her first order of business was to hack into the library's system and check out the security situation. Unfortunately, it was coded in Egyptian. She could either stay put until morning when the library reopened, or she could take a chance on getting caught. If she was caught, she could say she was in the restroom when the building closed. It would be the truth, and she should be able to talk her way out of getting into too much trouble.

Sophia had never been one to sit idly by, so she decided she'd take her chances. She stowed her laptop in her backpack and slung it across her shoulders. She grabbed her larger bag and headed toward the floor where she could research books on Cleopatra. The note she'd been given indicated she should go to the last

Pharaoh's resting place. Her followers also intended she have the Cleopatra Disk. Both those clues had her believing her parents were being held somewhere that had to do with the Queen.

Several hours passed, and Sophia could barely hold her eyes open. She knew if she lay down for a nap, she would definitely be found by someone when the library reopened. She remained standing so she wouldn't be tempted to close her eyes. When none of the previous books gave her any indication where Cleopatra could be, she decided to read up on Marc Antony. When that offered no help, Sophia realized it was time to stop speculating and to follow the clue she had been given.

Since the first part of the note instructed her to go to the Valley of the Queens, that is where she would start. It might be a lost cause, but it was better than twiddling her thumbs while her followers got closer. She once again pulled her laptop out of her backpack and decided on the best way to start her journey.

If she had been smart, Sophia would have figured all this out and taken the train overnight. She would have been able to sleep so that when she arrived, she would be ready to go. As it were, she was still going to sleep during the trip, but it was going to screw up her schedule. She booked her trip, and before making her way to the train station, Sophia donned her Clara disguise. She prayed the men who had followed her the night before had given up on her location and would be nowhere near the library when she left.

Sophia packed all her things and waited until the building opened for business. She gave the staff twenty minutes to get in place before emerging from the restroom. During the night, she had made note of where all the exits were. The one on the bottom floor on the west side of the building opened to a one-way street. That was the exit she used and strode directly to the taxi she had arranged for a few minutes prior.

Since a train to Luxor was only available leaving from Giza, it took longer than Sophia expected to arrive at the station and get boarded. She had read there could be delays, but she preferred the longer commute so she could rest. An hour later, Sophia was on the train, sitting safely in her private sleeping compartment. She had passed through an extensive security checkpoint, much more so than any airport she'd been in. She locked the door and pulled the shade on both the door and the window. She didn't wait for the train to move before she stretched out on the small bunk and allowed herself to rest.

A knocking woke Sophia. She rubbed her eyes and sat up. When the knocking continued, Sophia realized it was coming from her door. She rose from the bed and took the few steps necessary to cross the small compartment. When she opened the door, a guard was standing there. "Can I help you?" she asked.

"We've arrived, Miss. You are the only passenger on the train."

"I'm sorry. I fell asleep. Let me get my things." Sophia couldn't believe she'd slept the whole time. She really needed to pee, but the man standing at her door didn't look like he wanted to wait on her to take care of personal business. She grabbed her still packed bags and followed him down the hallway. Every few steps he glanced over his shoulder. After about the twentieth time, it started freaking her out.

When they reached the exit, the man stood in front of the door and eyed Sophia up and down. One side of his lip snarled as he asked, "What's a beautiful woman doing traveling alone?" He pulled a strand of her hair between his fingertips, raising it to his nose. He closed his eyes as he inhaled. "Ah, honeysuckle." If it had been Nikolas, she'd have been flattered. Instead, she was scared. She was crazy for traveling alone in a foreign land where she had no backup. Why had she not waited until Nik was with her?

Instead of showing fear, Sophia drew on her shifter strength and stood up straight. Her claws were ready to break through if she needed to use them. "I'm not alone. The rest of my family chose to ride separately so I could get some rest. They are probably wondering where I am, so if you'll excuse me," she said as she stepped toward the door. He didn't move out of the way, so when she walked past him, their bodies touched. Sophia could sense the evil inside the man.

Right before she descended the steps to the platform, the guard said, "I'd watch your back if I were you."

Sophia didn't give him the opportunity to say anything further. She hurried down the platform toward the exit. She found the taxi stand and waited among the other travelers for her turn. When she was seated, she told the driver to take her to the Luxor Embassy Hotel. It was a nice hotel that catered to tourists. Once *Clara* was checked in, Sophia ordered room service. She had missed breakfast and lunch on the train while she was asleep.

The first thing she was going to do when she got back to the States was to binge on junk food. The food in Egypt was not what she was accustomed to, but it gave her nourishment if nothing else. While she was eating, she decided to schedule a tour of the Valley of the Queens with a guided group. This going off alone was nerve-wracking.

Sophia was going to have a hard time sleeping since she'd slept all day on the train. It was nearing nine, and she was wide awake. She ate her supper, unpacked her things, and decided to take a bath. She rarely took the time to luxuriate in the tub, but she had plenty of time to relax and think. As the water filled the oversized Jacuzzi, she allowed her thoughts to stray to her mate. Nik still hadn't called. Eventually, he'd see the red blinking light on his hotel room phone.

She piled her long hair on top of her head and lowered herself into the water. She turned the jets on and let the massaging bubbles do their job. She tried not to think of her parents and what they were going through. She did think about why someone would take them. It was time Sophia called JoJo and asked him if he had any clues. She also needed to give him the number to the burner phone she was using. She decided to wait until after the tour tomorrow to see if she came up with any clues on her own as to their whereabouts.

Sophia closed her eyes and let the hum of the tub soothe her spirit. Too many faces ran through her mind, the latest and most disturbing was the man from the train. If she had been fully human, she doubted she'd have felt the evil intentions coming from him. Too often, bad people ended up in roles where they were supposed to protect people. She was thankful she had gotten away from him unscathed. If her mate had been there, the man wouldn't have even dared to look at her.

Picking up her phone for the hundredth time, there was still no word from Nik. She trusted he was safe; he was a Gargoyle after all. Now that she knew he was in Egypt, she had no doubt he would accept the mate bond. When she first found out about the fates and how they chose mates for the Gargoyles, she balked at the idea of not being able to pick who you spent eternity with. Once shifters were mated, it was a decision that lasted a lifetime. Who were the fates to think they knew best? But after seeing mates together with her own eyes, Sophia became a believer. Fated mates might sound like something out of a fairy tale, but she couldn't wait to start a life with Nikolas. Having watched him all this time had been hard.

Other than Jonas, Gargoyles of other Clans had never mated with humans that she was aware of. Now, the King was mated to the chief of police, and the cat was out of the bag, so to speak. Sophia had been the one to put the cat in the bag in the form of JoJo's journal. She had gotten tired of waiting on Nikolas or one of his Clan to figure it all out. When Tessa asked her how the journal got into the library, Sophia skated around the truth. Eventually, she would tell her cousin what she'd done, but for now, it was her secret.

When the water lost its heat, Sophia drained the tub and dried off. She opened her computer and researched the Valley of the Queens. She booked a tour so she would be among other people. It didn't mean she wouldn't wander off on her own to explore some of the more secluded areas. If her parents were anywhere in the ancient tunnels, she'd find them.

After a few hours of research, she put her laptop aside, set the alarm on her clock, and closed her eyes. Hopefully, she would get some rest before it was time to get up.

NIKOLAS hated airplanes, but it was the quickest way to Luxor. If he had traveled by train, he'd have probably jumped at some point during the ten-hour trip. The first available flight had been at five a.m. Even though he had to wait until the following morning to travel, flying would get him to Luxor before the overnight train arrived. Before he left, he had gone to the manager of the hotel and paid a large sum of money to switch rooms as well as have his privacy protected. Whoever had Sophia knew which room he was in. If they knew that, they could possible break in and take his equipment. That just wouldn't do.

Before time to leave for the airport, he researched as much as he could about the Valley of the Queens. While he wasn't one hundred percent certain that's where the clue intended Sophia to go, it was the most logical. The second part of the clue was confusing. Everything Nik read about the last pharaoh stated Cleopatra's burial spot had never been found.

Still, visiting the first part of the clue was better than sitting idly by and worrying about his mate. Nik mentally kicked himself in the ass for not grabbing Sophia when he had the chance. Even if she was dressed as an old woman, his shifter knew who she was, and his body had reacted immediately. If Sophia truly was in the hands of her followers, he had no idea how to proceed in finding her. The second best thing he could do was locate her parents. If by some small chance she wasn't really being held captive, she would more than likely be following the clue. Either way, he could not sit idly by hoping he ran into her or her captors again.

The airport had been crowded, and his flight was delayed. Instead of arriving at six as scheduled, it was now almost eight a.m. He couldn't check into a hotel that early, and there were no tours of the tombs scheduled for a couple hours. Even though it wasn't technically allowed, Nik decided to take a look around the ancient burial caverns by himself. Before the apocalypse, tourists could purchase a ticket and visit certain areas of the site unguided. Immediately after the apocalypse, the tombs were taken over by rebels. Now, the rebels had moved on to less populated areas of the country. The once-thriving tourist area was just now rebuilding itself.

Nik found his way to the ferry and traveled across the river. Once he arrived, he made his way to an open-air market where he purchased a scarf and sunglasses. Even though he was a Gargoyle and the elements wouldn't affect him, he wanted to blend in as much as possible. Instead of finding a taxi, he briefly considered renting a camel. If he were to travel by animal, he would have more freedom in where he went. As soon as he neared the roped off area, he realized his idea was ludicrous. The first camel he approached spit at him. The animal sensed the beast within Nik and wanted no part of being around him. Even though Nikolas tried soothing the four-legged beast, it wasn't working.

The man working the rental area came forward, grabbing hold of the camel's harness. He spoke to Nik while trying to calm the animal. "He is a feisty one. We will find one more suitable to your needs. Fifty pounds, and we'll get you saddled up."

As badly as Nik wanted to travel by camel, he knew it would be a headache. "I have changed my mind, but thank you."

"Forty pounds. We get you a girl. She will not be feisty. Yes?"

The man was insistent; Nik gave him that. "Let me see this non-feisty girl you speak of. Then we'll talk money." He highly doubted even the most docile animal the man had would put up with a Gargoyle on its back.

"Yes, yes. Wait here." The man disappeared only to return a few minutes later with a smaller animal.

Nik held his hand out to the female, and she sniffed his hand. When she didn't spit on him, he felt this one might be okay. When he took a step closer, she remained calm. Okay, he could do this. "Thirty pounds," he told the handler.

"Forty," the man countered.

"Twenty-five," Nik said. He wouldn't be bullied

when a taxi would be so much easier.

"Thirty," the man relented.

"Deal." Nik pulled the correct currency out of his pocket and handed it over to the man. He watched as the camel was adorned with a blanket, saddle, and a harness. Nik was glad to see stirrups were attached. He stuck his left foot in the slot and hoisted himself up onto the animal's back. Before he was settled, the creature took off across the sand. All Nik could do was hold on.

CHAPTER FOURTEEN

NIK used the strength in his thighs to stay seated on the runaway animal. The din of laughter and yells of people in the market floated over the air as he tried to grab onto the reins. When he finally managed to snag them, he wrapped his hands around the leather straps and pulled back. The camel didn't come close to slowing down. At that point, Nik had no other choice than to ride it out. He was still too close to civilization to phase and fly off the animal's back.

He tried talking to the camel, soothing her with soft words. He yelled. He smacked her on the rump. Nik wouldn't hurt the animal, but damn if he wasn't irritated. It was his fault for thinking she would be okay with a beast riding her back. The bouncing was doing a number on his nuts. He braced his feet against the stirrups, giving his balls a rest. When the camel finally slowed to a walk, Nik sat back and studied the scenery. He couldn't see his original destination since it was down in a valley, but he knew the direction he needed to be going in. If he and his ride went too much farther, he was going to miss his opportunity to visit the tombs before the tours started.

Nik pulled the reins to the east, hoping she would follow his directions. "Please go that way. I need to visit the tombs, and I really don't want to walk that far. Besides, I don't want to have to pay for a lost camel."

She completely ignored him and continued walking the direction she wanted. "Fuck my life. I'm talking to a camel," Nik said to the sand. As if she agreed, she jerked her head forward and grunted, or made whatever sound a camel makes. She continued sassing him for at least thirty seconds. When she stopped, he chastised her. "Seriously? You have no reason to complain. I'm not the one who took off across the fucking sand with no thought to my passenger's well-being. That was all you, Bessie."

Obviously, the animal didn't like the name he chose for her. She took off at a trot again, sending Nik farther away from where he needed to be. He shouted to the heavens, "Really? A little help here?" When he received no answer from the gods, he had a choice to make - either ride it out or jump. He could remove himself without harm, but what would he do about the camel? Would she return to her owner or continue on her journey? Fuck it; Nik decided to bail. She was better equipped to be alone in the desert than he was. He took a look around to make sure nobody had decided on a last-minute rescue effort. When he saw no one, he removed his shirt before calling forth his wings. Nik phased and lifted himself off the animal's back.

He landed on the sand and retracted his wings. Nik shook his head as the camel stopped running and turned around. She let out another loud groan. "Don't yell at me, you mangy beast," Nik shouted as he turned back toward the tombs and began walking.

TOURS started every two hours. Sophia figured she could ditch the first tour over halfway in, do a little reconnaissance on her own, and join the next tour. She removed the scarf from her head and stuffed it in her bag. She placed herself in the middle of the families as they descended into the corridors. Even though there were almost a hundred tombs in this location, the tours were only allowed to see a handful. During the night, she had studied as many maps as possible of the popular tombs as well as those that were blocked off. Nefertari's was the most popular, and she wasn't going to miss seeing it.

Sophia was in awe of the beautiful colors and pictures on the walls of the tomb. She would love the opportunity to come back when she could study them at length. It never ceased to amaze her how so many different theories regarding the gods and afterlife were still in existence. As she stood and gazed upon one of the images of the ancient queen, Sophia smiled as she hoped to herself that Nefertari had been mummified appropriately and her spirit had passed the test to be transformed into another body. Gargoyles knew what immortal life was like. The half-bloods encountered an extended life once mated. Maybe reincarnation was just a different version of immortality.

When she realized she was alone, Sophia decided it was an excellent opportunity to look around. She followed a corridor away from the voices of the tour group. She allowed herself to go as far as her eyesight could take her. She reached out with her shifter senses, listening for any indication of life farther into the tombs. She stood still and calmed her breathing so she was in tune with her surroundings. Scratching came from a few feet in front of her. It wasn't like something being raked over a stone wall. It was closer to something being dragged. A thud reverberated through the corridor to her left. The air behind her grew warmer. The hair on her neck stood as if she'd passed her hand over an electrical current.

"I warned you to watch your back," a familiar voice spoke in her ear. Sophia turned to run, but a large hand grabbed her shoulder, pulling her backwards. The guard from the train clamped his hand over her mouth and pushed her against the cold, hard wall of the tomb. "I'm going to enjoy this," he seethed into her ear as one of his hands found its way under the hem of her shirt. She struggled to get free, but he tightened his grip. Sophia allowed herself to become dead weight. She slid to the floor, landing harshly on her hip. The man cursed and grasped a handful of her hair, attempting to drag her across the floor. Refusing to be a victim, Sophia called forth her claws and swiped at the man's arm. He let go of her hair long enough for her to find her feet.

"You bitch," he growled. The glint of a knife came toward her face. She jerked her head backwards. The blade grazed her jaw instead of cutting a path across her neck as she was certain he intended.

"You really don't want to do this," she warned him.

"Oh, I assure you, I definitely want to do this. You smell too sweet and are way too beautiful for your own good. I intend to have a taste of you." He stepped forward but instead of his hand finding purchase, he found his wrist cut and bleeding. "What the fuck?" he howled. The man lunged for Sophia, and without thinking, she slashed across his throat. The knife he was holding plunged into her side, and they went down to the floor together. She cried out as the pain registered, but she had bigger problems to worry about. Like the two-hundred-pound guard lying on top of her bleeding out. Gurgling sounds came from his throat as he tried to staunch the blood flow with his hands.

Sophia used her half-blood strength to roll the man off her. She crab walked backwards until she hit a wall. She placed one hand over her mouth and the other over the cut in her side. Between the blood leaching from man she was sure was dead and her own wound, the rich coppery smell was nauseating. Her fingers were wet and doing no good against the cut. She felt around on the floor until she found her bag she had lost in the scuffle. Sophia removed the scarf and placed it against her skin. She needed to get up and get help, but her head felt woozy. She would rest a few minutes and regain her strength.

When Sophia opened her eyes, bright lights made her head hurt worse than before she'd closed them. She was being lifted off the ground and placed on a stretcher. Why was she being carried, and why did her body ache so badly? She couldn't see the man at her head, so she focused on the one at her feet. He was dressed similar to the guard she had encountered on the train. The guard. He had attacked her in the tunnel. Oh gods, she had killed him. She had killed a man, and now she was being hauled off. She tried to find her voice to tell them it was an accident, but the words wouldn't come.

When they reached the mouth of the tomb, police

vehicles and a couple ambulances were waiting. She couldn't understand what was being said. Too many people were talking at one time. An angry man strode to her and got in her face. He began yelling questions at her, but before she could answer, her world turned black.

Sophia woke with an excruciating pain in her side. Her back was aching, but considering the hard floor she was lying on, it was no wonder. She opened her eyes to the faces of approximately twenty women, most of whom were eyeing her like she was their next meal. She probably would have been if she had been in the same cell as they were. It didn't take a genius to figure out Sophia had been unceremoniously dumped into an Egyptian prison for murder. Did they not care that it was self-defense? They hadn't even asked her what happened.

The gash on her side had been stitched, but the blood had not been cleaned off. Her shirt was torn where the knife entered. She pushed herself up to sitting, but that was as far as she tried to go. Instead of looking at the other women, Sophia kept her eyes straight ahead, willing a guard to come tell her what was going on. The women talked about her, some talked to her, taunting the *white girl*. She wanted to yell at them and tell them she killed a man, warning them not to mess with her, but she had to play it smart. She would not admit to anything except self-defense.

Sophia had no idea how much time had passed. She did know she was hurting, hungry, and thirsty. When a guard came to her cell and unlocked the door, she was hopeful. "Let's go," he snarled.

"Where are you taking me? Do I get my phone call now?" she asked.

"This is not America. You do not get a phone call when you murder someone."

"I did not murder anyone. Please, can I have some water?" Sophia was going to pass out again if she didn't get something on her stomach. She was taken to another area of the prison. She knew it wasn't a mere jail because of the size of the place. Several levels of square boxes contained not so nice-looking men and women. They weren't segregated. Instead, they were scattered throughout, with the men making lewd comments to the women next to them. They continued on through a door into a hallway with very few cells. Sophia saw no prisoners. The guard opened the bars and pushed her into the cell, this one of the permanent kind. "Please, I need to talk to the American Consulate."

The guard slammed the bars shut behind her. The cell contained a cot, a sink, and a crude toilet. That was it. It appeared she was in isolation. For that she was grateful. She sat down on the bed and leaned against the wall. A few minutes passed and a different guard brought her a tray of food, or something that was supposed to pass for food. The guard opened a slot in the metal bar, pushed the tray through, waiting on her to take it. She rose from her cot and took the tray. "Please, I need to speak to the American Embassy." Her pleading fell on deaf ears. The guard walked away without a word.

Other than the piece of bread, Sophia couldn't identify what was on the tray. It resembled day-old oatmeal, but she doubted it would taste that good. Still, she was starving. She had no idea how long she had been unconscious. Probably not long, but long enough to be stitched up, if crudely, and hauled to her prison. She picked up the spoon and dipped it into the mush. Before she put it in her mouth, she sniffed the oatmeal-looking gray goop. Thankfully, it had no odor. She took a small bite and found it tasted as bland as it smelled. She continued to scoop it up, alternating it with the stale bread until she had eaten it all. She hadn't been given anything to drink, so she walked over to the sink and turned on the faucet. She let the water run into her cupped hands, and she slurped it as best she could.

She had to be careful with the Clara disguise. Even though it was practically indestructible, she didn't have a mirror to make sure it was properly in place. If she removed it now, there would be more questions she would have to answer if she ever had the chance to speak to someone. Sophia did wet her hands and wash her arms, using her blood-spattered shirt to dry them. Her boots were missing, and her socks were as nasty as the rest of her clothing.

She sat back down on the bed and leaned against the wall. She refused to cry. Eventually, they would have to let her see the Consulate, and then she would get out of there. At least she hoped so.

CHAPTER FIFTEEN

THE time dragged on as did the pain in Sophia's side. Two more trays of slop were brought to her cell along with new clothes. When the guard brought the clothes, Sophia begged him to let her at least see the prison's physician. If she could speak to him or her, hopefully she could convince them she was being held unreasonably. She was an American citizen, and as such, she had a right to speak to the Consulate. At least she thought she did. As with the others, this guard ignored her.

After she ate, she removed her blood-splattered shirt and jeans and washed off as best she could, considering she had no soap. Sophia then put on the drab, cotton pants and top. At least they were comfortable, if not a little on the large side. She really wished she had a toothbrush and deodorant. She had a feeling by the time she got out of there, she was going to be ripe.

The lights went off, and Sophia was left in the dark. She lay down on the cot and closed her eyes, bringing forth an image of Nik. She had spent the day going over the events at the tomb and her story, should she ever get to tell it. Now, she needed beauty in her thoughts, and there was none more beautiful to her than Nikolas Giancarlo Stone. At some point over the years, Nik had changed his surname from Di Pietro to Stone. It suited him, though. She didn't care if his name was Barney as long as he was her mate.

She willed herself to get some sleep, praying tomorrow would be a new day with better results. It felt as if she had just closed her eyes when a voice woke her. "Get up."

Sophia opened her eyes to see the guard who brought her the clothing standing at the open cell door. Surely it wasn't morning already. She sat up and blinked, trying to focus in the still dimly lit cell. The only light was coming from down the hallway. She stood and followed the man out the way they had come in. He led her to a small room, large enough only to accommodate a table and four chairs - one on her side, three on the opposing. She knew then she wouldn't get the courtesy of legal counsel.

She thanked the gods when he didn't shackle her hands. Sophia sat on them in case she had the urge to claw someone's eyes out. The guard who led her in stood across the room, leaning against the wall. Two more men came in, sitting at the table across from her. Great - good cop, bad cop, worse cop. She doubted any of them were going to be nice to her, not after the treatment she'd received so far.

"What is your name?" good cop asked.

"Clara Fort." She had to stick with the disguise since they probably found her bag in the tombs somewhere.

"Miss Fort, why did you murder the guard?" bad cop asked.

"I didn't murder anyone. He attacked me and stabbed me with his knife." That was the truth.

"His throat was cut. How do you explain that?" That came from worse cop. By the look in his eyes, she had pegged him correctly. There was something oddly familiar about him.

"I can't. He stabbed me, and I screamed. I heard a scuffle. I didn't cut his throat. I was in too much pain."

"You're saying it was someone else?"

"It had to be, because it wasn't me. I'd really like to speak to someone from the American Embassy."

"You will speak to us. You have committed a crime on our land. We will handle this our way," bad cop declared.

"My only crime is getting separated from my group. I did not kill that man. He attacked me." Sophia wanted to add *he got what he deserved,* but she did not. "Please, at least let me speak with a doctor."

Worse cop slammed his hand on the table causing Sophia to jump. "You will speak with no one until you tell us the truth, Miss Fort!" he yelled.

Sophia's Gargoyle half was attempting to dig its way out. *Stop it. You're the reason we're in this mess in the first place.*

I'm the reason we're still alive, her shifter half responded. That was a first. Sophia decided it was best to keep her mouth shut from that point on. She looked straight ahead, not allowing them to intimidate her. If her beast happened to get loose, she had a chance at one, possibly two of the men. But three? Those weren't very good odds. If a Gargoyle male was shot, the bullets bounced off their impenetrable skin. Females weren't so lucky.

"You killed my brother, and for that you are going to pay." Worse cop stood so quickly his chair toppled over backwards. His brother? That's why he looked so familiar. The rage coming off the man was palpable.

Good cop stood and stepped in front of worse cop.

"Perhaps a little time in solitary will do the trick, hmm?"

Solitary? Wasn't that where she'd already been? Well, shit.

AS Nik trod through the hills and sand of the desert, he debated whether or not to continue on to the Valley of the Queens. By the time he reached the ancient landmark, tours would be in full swing. Worst case scenario, he would be arrested for camel evasion. Best case? He could bum a ride back to the marketplace. Not that he was tired from walking. He was a Gargoyle, and as such, his stamina was off the charts. He just hated the sand swirling around his face with no water to wash it off.

His internal compass led him to the Valley with no trouble. When he rose over the last hill before the descent that would take him to the landmark, he stopped. Police cars were parked haphazardly at the opening, blue lights flashing. An ambulance was being loaded with a body, and it drove off soon after. Curiosity got the better of Nik, so he continued on. As he neared the chaos, another body was brought out of the tombs, this one in a black bag. He walked over to one of the tours and insinuated himself among the people standing around. From what he could gather, a guard was dead, and the woman who allegedly killed him had been stabbed.

Nik reached out with his senses, searching for any

sign of Sophia. There was the slightest hint of honeysuckle floating on the air, but not enough for him to make a definite determination. The tombs were now cordoned off since they were a crime scene. Nik wouldn't be able to search the interior any time soon. When the group he was lingering with loaded up on a bus to return to the marketplace, he climbed aboard with them. Luckily, nobody stopped him.

What a fucked-up morning. One thing was for certain – Nik would never try to ride a camel again. He should go back to the vendor and let him know the beast was somewhere in the desert, but he didn't want to have to pay for the animal. Besides, it was a camel. Surely it would be okay until someone retrieved it.

With nothing but the clothes on his back and money in his pocket, Nik went in search of a cheap hotel where he could take a shower and grab some food. Without his computer, he was at a loss on where to go from there. His best bet was to return to Cairo and continue his search with the aid of his equipment. If Sophia really had been captured, he wanted to be in his hotel on the small chance she somehow escaped and returned to him. He also wanted to figure out who was after her, if possible.

By the time he returned to Cairo and his new hotel room, Nikolas was ready to call Julian and ask for his help. He knew his brother was needed elsewhere, but truth was he missed him. Spending five hundred years with someone almost daily formed the type of bond rarely seen in siblings. If Julian were in Egypt, Nik would have someone to bounce ideas off of. At the least, he'd have someone to yell at. Julian would take the verbal abuse, because that's what brothers did when one was hurting. Then he would tell him to buck the fuck up and calm the fuck down. Yeah, Nik missed Jules.

Instead of calling home, Nikolas decided to go for a swim. In the Nile. Since he couldn't fly, swimming was the next best thing. It was late, and he figured he could find somewhere to slip into the water without being seen. If a camel didn't want to be near him, Nik figured any type of creature swimming in the river would also offer him a wide berth. He knew he should be on the computer searching for something, but his beast was clawing at him. Being so near to his mate only to lose her had the beast roaring, ready to tear something or someone apart. Since that wasn't an option, Nik decided to wear himself out.

Doors slamming, people laughing, kids running up and down the hallway were the last thing Nik needed. He couldn't focus with all the extraneous noise. His shifter hearing was too keen, and he couldn't block it all out. He was already on edge. The little sleep Nik got once he returned from swimming was filled with nightmares of his mate being captured by unknown assailants

His first order of business when he rose was to find a house to rent. At the rate he was going, it would be cheaper to lease a villa than to continue paying to stay in a hotel. And that way he would have his privacy. He would be able to phase if he wanted to, letting the beast loose momentarily. Sixx was the keeper of the Clan's properties, but Nik was almost certain they didn't have any in Egypt. He wasn't going to wait on him to wake up and find out. He opened his laptop and did a search. By the time his breakfast was delivered, he had found a secluded villa that was furnished with everything he would need except food. He had no problem going to a grocery store and cooking for himself.

As soon as he knew Julian would be up, Nik called him to check in.

"Nikolas, how are you?" Julian yawned into the phone when he answered.

"Going crazy. I have a feeling I'm going to be here a while. I called a realtor and am going to lease a villa for the duration. I've already been found by the bastards who have Sophia."

"They have her? Are you sure?" Jules sounded wide awake now.

"I don't have proof other than a note they slipped me with my meal. I changed hotel rooms after that, but they probably still have eyes on me. At least with the villa, it's gated and no one can get in without tripping the alarm. I had a vision that someone was after Sophia, but before I could see the outcome, it dissipated. It's been a crazy few days. How are things at home?"

"Interesting, to say the least. Tessa came out of her coma yesterday while Xavier and Elizabeth were at Gregor's."

"Why were they there?"

"It turns out Xavier is Tessa's real father. We also found out that Alistair is probably behind the threats to the Clan. He not only hates Rafael, but he's also the one who had Jonas ostracized."

"So, what is the elusive Elizabeth Flanagan like?" Nik would love to have met the woman.

"She's the spitting image of Tessa, or should I say, Tessa is the spitting image of Elizabeth. We believe that's how Gordon found Tessa. The only difference is their attitudes. Tessa's a spitfire, whereas Elizabeth is calm and gracious."

"I'm sorry I missed that. I thought Rafael and Xavier were at war, so to speak."

Julian laughed. "They were before yesterday, but once Xavier found out what was going on, he pledged his Clan's loyalty to ours. I think Tessa being Gregor's mate had something to do with it. That and Xavier and Aunt Athena know Alistair better than most."

Nik whistled. "I'm glad they're on our side. We need all the inside information we can get. Do you think Alistair is behind this shit with Sophia?"

"At this point, anything is possible. Guard your back, Brother. If he is behind this, he will have his Gargoyles out and about. Speaking of Goyles, I have located a small clan in South Africa, but I've yet to find out who they are loyal to, if anyone. I'll keep working on that. Is there anything else I can do from here?"

"Yes. I want you to monitor all activity in and out of Cairo for either Clara Fort or Beatrice Nightingale. Beatrice is a longshot since Sophia left her disguise behind, but Clara is still an option."

"Your girl's using an alias? Smart."

"Yes, and she has disguises to go along with them. I'd love to have one right about now. It would be easier to get around without being identified."

"I'm on it. What else?"

"That's it. Give Gregor and Tessa my best."

"Will do. As soon as things settle down here, I'm coming to help you."

"Honestly, I look forward to it. I miss you, Brother."

"And I miss you. Be well, Nik."

"Later." Nik hung up before he couldn't speak. It took a lot for him to get emotional, but Jules was a good reason. He began packing the items he'd only unpacked the day before and prepared to meet the realtor at the villa. Instead of taking a taxi, Nik called for a car service. He instructed them to park in the underground garage of the hotel so he would have better clarity of his surroundings. Thirty minutes later, he was securely in the limo with nobody following him.

CHAPTER SIXTEEN

KALLISTO sat unmoving as the breaking news report on the television made her want to throw up. An anonymous patron had donated several ancient artifacts to the Cairo Museum of Egyptian Antiquities. Among them was the Cleopatra Disk, an item so rare it was thought to be one of a kind. The news anchor stated the items were dropped off at the museum minutes after opening that morning. "Sources say the patron, a woman in her mid- to late forties, walked in, demanded to see the curator, and handed over the box. She didn't wait around to give her name. The cameras weren't able to get a good picture of her face. The curator told us this was the single largest donation to the museum in its history."

When the telephone rang, Kallisto picked up the remote and turned the TV off. She took a deep breath before answering. "Hello?"

"Hello, Princess. I have another job for you."

"But this one isn't complete. We have no idea where the girl is."

"No, but we know where her parents are. Now, I need you to gather a team and fly to the States. I have received information on another of Montagnon's mongrels. It appears his youngest daughter has a son she has kept hidden from the world. I need you to kidnap the boy, dispose of his adoptive parents, and convince his mother to come with you to Greece. All the information you need is being sent to your phone."

"And what of the other man? We've been keeping tabs on him, but he doesn't seem interested in Sophia.

He spends most of his time in Alexandria. Nikolas Stone has rented a house here. He won't give up until he finds the woman."

"The other man is of no consequence. He's just another of Jonas's offspring. As for Mr. Stone, the longer he stays in Egypt, the better. One more thorn in my side out of the way. Now, forget about them and head to your next assignment."

"We'll leave immediately." Kallisto was ready to hang up, thinking she'd dodged a bullet.

"I know about the disk, my darling. We'll discuss that when you return home."

"Yes, sir." Kallisto thumbed off the phone and let out a breath. The fact that he didn't yell at her did not bode well. She would much rather take her berating from thousands of miles away than face to face. She turned to Sergei who had heard only her side of the conversation.

"We have another job. It involves kidnapping a child. Choose two of your best men and have them meet us at the plane. Instruct the others to continue looking for the Brooks woman."

"Did he mention the disk? That donation had to make world news."

"Yes, but he said we'd discuss it later."

"Oh, shit."

"Yeah, shit. Now, let's get to our next mission and hope we don't fuck it up." Kallisto left her companion to make his phone calls. She began packing their things for the trip to America.

EZEKIEL sipped his coffee while Xenia cooked breakfast. He had been in Egypt for almost two weeks and was no closer to finding his niece or his brother. Xenia hadn't been able to get hold of Sophia either, and they were both worried about the girl. Zeke had followed her alias from Cairo to Luxor where the trail dead-ended. She had checked into a hotel there, but whenever he called, he got no answer. He spoke to the manager, telling him he was worried about his niece. The man took Zeke's name and number and said he'd call if she showed up. He hadn't.

"What made you turn in the disk anonymously? You could have given your father a great deal of credibility, even if it was posthumously."

Xenia turned the bacon before answering. "If I gave the curator my father's name, it would be easy for anyone to find out my name and address. My life has been disrupted enough in the past two weeks. I don't need random people calling and stopping by for interviews. They would want to know where he discovered the disk. That is a question that needs to remain hidden."

"True. Hopefully that will keep the people who are after Sophia from looking for Beatrice any further."

"Yes, but their focus was split between Sophia and the old woman. Now, they can focus solely on Sophia. Maybe I should have waited." Xenia bit her bottom lip. When she did, blood ran down her chin. "Oh, shit."

"You need to keep your emotions in check, my

dear." Zeke stood and wet a paper towel. He dabbed the blood until it stopped leaking from her lip.

"I know, but I forget about the fangs. They tend to pop out at the most inopportune moments."

"Is that why Keene walks around with his hands over his crotch?" Zeke joked.

"Very funny. And no, it's because of the claws, not the fangs," she said with a wink.

"Ouch." Zeke had spoken with Keene more than once since Xenia told her mate the truth. He still hadn't agreed to complete the bond, but he was spending time with her. Xenia had refused to tell Keene that there was one mate for Gargoyles, and if he walked away from her, she would never find true happiness. While she was getting control of her new shifter half, she had taken a sabbatical from her teaching position stating medical reasons.

Xenia had opened her home to Zeke. Staying in a hotel indefinitely seemed crazy when she had plenty of room. He helped her with her phasing, and she schooled him in Egyptian history. The only time he made himself scarce was when Keene came to visit. They needed to be alone if they were to work out their future.

While he was sipping his coffee, Zeke's phone rang. "Hello?"

"Mr. Seymour? This is the manager of the Luxor Embassy. I told you I would call if your niece showed up. I'm sorry to say she hasn't. Since she only paid for one night, we cannot hold Miss Fort's room any longer. We will need you to either retrieve her belongings or pay for the room until she shows up. Of course, I'll need proof you and Miss Fort are related."

"Of course, I understand. Let me pay now, and I will be there soon to pick up her things. Thank you for calling." Zeke gave the manager his credit card number before hanging up. He sighed. "That was the hotel in Luxor. I have to go get Sophia's things."

"Do you want me to go with you?" Xenia asked.

"I would like that. First, I have to have proof that she and I are related. I'm not sure how I'm going to do that since she's using an alias."

"Do you know how Sophia gets her fake IDs?"

"She probably makes them. It's not that hard."

"Can you do it? I'm thinking if I go in as Clara, I can tell them I was mugged and lost my key. They'll give me a new one."

"Xenia, I don't mean to be rude, but the manager knows I'm looking for my niece. You don't exactly look young enough."

Xenia huffed. "Well, I never." She threw a dishtowel at him, laughing. "You won't be with me, silly. I'll get into the room, then I'll call you and you can come up."

"I guess it could work, if only I had the necessary supplies. I wish I knew someone who was into forgery."

"Hmm. I might know someone. He owes me a favor, too. Let me make a phone call." Xenia handed Zeke the spatula and disappeared down the hall. A few minutes later, she returned, smiling. "We're good to go. After breakfast, we'll go see a colleague of mine. We should have what we need by this afternoon."

"I don't want you to get in trouble," Zeke offered.

"I won't, and neither will he. Besides, this beats sitting at home painting my claws."

After they finished eating, Zeke went ahead and made plane reservations. Xenia assured him they would have what they needed and be able to make a later flight. She hadn't been wrong. Her colleague was an art curator who authenticated paintings. While that had nothing to do with forging passports, he was an expert in handwriting. He also had the equipment to produce an alternative ID. Xenia gave him the note Sophia had written, and the man was able to recreate Clara's signature based off the lettering on the note. He made a copy of Zeke's driver's license, replacing the information with Clara's and the picture with one of Xenia. Within an hour, Xenia had a license claiming she was Clara Fort.

While they were making their way to the airport, Zeke said, "I was thinking about visiting the Valley of the Kings while I'm there. Would you like to be my tour guide?" Zeke wasn't leaving Egypt until he knew Sophia and her parents were safe, but he could enjoy the sights while he waited.

"I would love that," she beamed.

Zeke and Xenia arrived in Luxor that evening. Zeke went ahead and checked into a room at the hotel across the street so they had somewhere to put their things. With Xenia claiming to be someone who'd been mugged, she couldn't stroll in the Luxor Embassy pulling a suitcase behind her. Zeke impatiently paced the floor, looking at his phone periodically. When she had been gone thirty minutes, he debated whether or not to go check on her. He was headed to the door when his phone rang.

"Xenia?"

"No, Clara. And I'm in the room. Fourteen twenty-nine."

"I'll be right there." Zeke grabbed the room key and made his way across the street. He avoided looking at the desk clerk and continued to the elevators. Once he reached the fourteenth floor, he turned left and strode down the hall with purpose. He wasn't one for telling lies, but desperate times called for desperate measures. He knocked once, and Xenia opened the door.

Together, they went through Sophia's things to see if there was any clue as to where she could be. All of her things were put away neatly with the exception of her laptop. It sat unused on the desk in the corner of the room. After trying to access her computer, Zeke said, "I've tried to get in there and take a look, but she's a whiz when it comes to that kind of thing. I doubt too many people in the world could hack her system."

Xenia voiced what Zeke already knew in his heart: something had happened to Sophia. She packed their niece's clothing and toiletries while he stored her computer in its case, then double-checked to be sure they hadn't overlooked anything. Xenia left the key card on the desk, and they took Sophia's things, slipping out through the back entrance. They made their way to the hotel across the street. Zeke would call the manager in the morning with the good news his niece had safely returned to him.

Even though he was only a half-blood, Zeke

needed to get out of the small hotel room and breathe in some of the night air. His shifter hated being locked inside. It was one of the reasons he lived near the ocean. Since it wasn't too late, they decided to visit the Luxor temple complex. It housed five temples, one being the Karnack. It was a vast, open-air complex. Before the apocalypse, it was one of the most visited religious sites in the world. It was still popular since it was lit up at night, offering a completely different experience.

As they strolled through the complex, Xenia gave him a history lesson. The locals tried to infringe on their privacy, offering to provide the history, but Zeke made it clear they didn't want to pay for someone to guide them. Ezekiel found himself entranced with his guide. Her knowledge was vast, and he could tell by the way she described everything that she loved history. He wished he'd had a history professor who loved the subject as much as she did. It would have made taking the class that much more enjoyable.

Once they had visited everything there was to see, they headed to a restaurant that had international dishes as well as local flavors. Zeke opted for Spaghetti Bolognaise, while Xenia chose fish and chips. Being a world traveler, he was used to eating foreign food, but sometimes he wanted a taste of home. If he was honest with himself, he was looking forward to the day he could retire from being a watcher. He didn't mind the traveling so much, but he wanted to go to a nice, sunny island instead of the hole in the wall places his siblings had been shipped off to.

He and Xenia talked of her life growing up in

South Africa and her parents. Zeke told her everything she wanted to know about Jonas and Caroline that Sophia hadn't already shared. He talked about Tessa's life and her being cloned. The last phone call he'd made to Elizabeth had been full of exciting, if not horrific, information. He was happy to know Tessa was going to be okay. He hadn't been around her often, but when he had, she had kept him highly entertained.

He explained the Unholy and Tessa's father's part in that. Zeke sadly told her about their brother, Conrad, going undercover as Magnus Flanagan and how he lost his life. It was his opinion that the siblings be told everything, not just the bits and pieces Jonas wanted them to know.

Even though they had met only recently, the two were falling into an easy comradery. As they talked and laughed, they finished off three bottles of wine. Having shifter metabolism allowed them to drink more than humans, and neither one was feeling the effects of drinking that much. They walked the short distance to the hotel and turned in for the night.

In the morning, they set out for the Valley of the Kings. Zeke was more excited about this excursion than any since he would be seeing the burial chamber of King Tut. He had studied the young pharaoh in his college years and found the stories fascinating. Having Xenia as a guide would only enhance his visit.

Zeke was not disappointed. The chamber was decorated with colorful images and text designed to aid in the pharaoh's trip into the afterlife. Xenia kept quiet during most of the tour unless the guide left out something important or made a false statement. She had no problem correcting the young man. Once their tour was finished, she said, "I'd like to visit the Valley of the Queens. It's much less impressive, but part of Sophia's clue mentioned it. I want to see if there is anything I pick up on. It's only about twenty minutes away."

"Let's go." Zeke was all for visiting another ancient landmark. It would probably be a long time before he could return, and he was having a good time despite the reason he was in Egypt.

Once inside the Valley of the Queens, the tour guide instructed them that part of the corridor was closed off due to the recent murder of a guard in one of the cordoned off areas. "I heard about that on the news. Do you think it's safe to be in here?" Zeke asked Xenia.

She whispered so only he could hear, "Between the two of us, I think we can protect ourselves."

He knew she was referring to their shifter halves, and she was correct. The news report had stated a guard had been killed by a female tourist, but no names were given. As they descended farther into the tombs, Xenia stopped. "Do you smell that?"

The rich coppery tang of blood was present off to the left. "Yes. That must be where the murder took place."

"Yes, but there's something else, something… familiar." Xenia inhaled deeply.

"Please stay with your group," the tour guide chastised them for getting separated.

Zeke and Xenia continued on with the rest of the tour. It wasn't until they were outside that Xenia said,

"I think Sophia's been here. She has that distinct honeysuckle scent that few women can pull off."

"I smelled it too, but it was so faint. She could have been here a week ago." Zeke had a bad feeling about his niece. "Xenia, is there any way to find out who the woman was involved in the murder? I know I'm grasping at straws, but what if it was Sophia? The timing is about right since she disappeared."

"You think she killed the guard?" Xenia asked, frowning.

"Anything is possible," Zeke said, praying it wasn't true and his niece wasn't being held in an Egyptian prison.

CHAPTER SEVENTEEN

KEYS jingled in the lock. Time for lunch. Or was it supper? Sophia's days were running together. At first, she was able to keep count of how long she'd been locked away in the dark, dank hole. Now, she was losing all concept of morning versus night. When your home was a five-by-five concrete box with no bed and only a bucket to relieve yourself in, things became foggy. Her meals were the same as they had been since she arrived. Her pleas were the same, too. Every time a guard brought her tray, Sophia begged to speak to a consulate. Every time, she was ignored.

Her body was weakening, as was her resolve. If she didn't find a way to get out of this hell, she would surely die there. She knew the only thing keeping her alive was her shifter half. More than once, the voice in her head had told her to buck up and figure a way out. Sophia was smart. If only she had as much faith as her Gargoyle half did.

She didn't bother to move when the door opened. She knew the routine - a new tray replaced the old one. The guards had only emptied her bucket once, so she was used to the smell of stale piss. It was mixed with the odor of a woman who hadn't bathed in weeks. One who was due to start her period any day now. That ought to be fun. She didn't bother looking at the guard. The first few days when they sneered at her, she was ready to do to them what she'd done to the man in the tombs. Her shifter was urging her to fight her way out. When she convinced the beast she would not kill someone without physical provocation, it quieted inside her head.

This was one of the few things Sophia focused on – her inner Gargoyle talking to her. She had never heard of that happening. Maybe it did and no one spoke of it. If she ever got out of there, she would ask someone.

"When you get out of here. I told you, Nikolas will not stop until he finds you."

"You keep saying that as if you know it for fact," Sophia said to her inner voice.

"Who are you talking to?" the guard asked. "The dark's broken you, has it? Maybe now you'll speak the truth." He slammed her door shut, the darkness once again her only companion.

Sophia pulled the tray closer to her and picked up the bowl. She carefully spooned the slop into her mouth until it was all gone. She saved the stale bread for later in the day, but she did take a few sips of the bottled water.

"No, not your only companion. I am here, and I will never abandon you."

"Then help me figure a way out of here," Sophia pleaded.

NIKOLAS split most of his time between trying to crack into Sophia's computer and meditation. He had gone to both the hotel and the bed and breakfast and retrieved Sophia's things. It was easy at the hotel since he had put his name on the reservation. The inn was another matter entirely. When he went to the front desk to sign Beatrice out, the Waterfords were still staying there. As soon as Nik walked in the door, he was accosted verbally by Yvonne.

"You are one sick, perverted human being. How can you look your wife in the eye when you're gallivanting and carousing with her mother? You should be ashamed of yourself!"

Nik had no idea what the woman was going on about until she added, "Kissing like that on a public sidewalk. That's just… wrong."

Holy shit. She had seen him and Sophia. "I assure you, ma'am, I was not kissing Beatrice."

"Don't try to deny it! She admitted as much. And then those people came asking about her. She's nothing but trouble. All I can say is good riddance." Yvonne huffed off. It was a good thing, too. Nik didn't believe in hurting females, but that woman was asking for it.

"Can I help you?" the woman tending the desk asked.

"I'm here to get Beatrice's things and pay for any extra she owes."

"That won't be possible, sir. Your name isn't on the registry. You can pay her bill, but I'm afraid her things will have to remain where they are."

"Did you clean out her room already?" Nik hoped not. He had a plan.

"No, we kept hoping she would return for her things herself. But since it's been almost two weeks, we have no other choice."

"I will pay for an extra day if you will leave her things where they are. I will make sure she gets them tomorrow." Nik placed a credit card on the desk, praying his request was granted.

"Very well, but only one more day. We need her room." The woman swiped his card and printed out a receipt.

"Thank you. You've been kind." Nik folded the receipt and slid it into his back pocket. He was able to exit the small inn with no further run-ins with Yvonne. Looking back on it, seeing Nik kissing Beatrice must have been a great shock to the other woman's system. Hell, it had shocked him. He returned to the bed and breakfast under the cover of night, thankful the window wasn't locked. He packed all Sophia's things in a huge bag and took them to the villa.

That was over a week ago. There was no sign of the people following Sophia, not since the day he caught the blonde woman across the street taking his picture. He had tried to follow her, but an SUV had been waiting on her. If there was anyone left, they were doing a great job of hiding. He knew in his heart something bad had happened to his mate. Whether the blonde and her goons had really captured Sophia, or something else had happened to her, he felt her despair when he meditated.

After seeing Sophia in a vision being chased by someone, Nik had spent hours trying to find her with his subconscious. Now, all he saw was darkness. He could feel her presence, but he couldn't see her. Couldn't see anything. Wherever she was, he prayed she was holding on. If something happened to her before he got to her…

His phone rang. He didn't have to look at the caller I.D. to know it was Julian. "Brother, please tell me you have something."

"I have something. I'm sending a new program to your computer. You will need to upload it to a thumb drive and install it on Sophia's laptop. It will work regardless of whether or not you have her password. Once it finishes running, you'll be able to access all her files."

"I hope there's something in there that helps me find her. Otherwise, I'm invading her privacy for nothing."

"Nikolas, I can't begin to imagine what you're going through, but do not give up hope. We will find Sophia and bring her home."

"When are you and Gregor getting here?" Nikolas hated to sound so fucking needy, but he needed his family around him.

"About that. We have another problem. Are you sitting down?"

Nik sank down on the sofa. "I am now. What the fuck is going on, Jules?"

"I told you Dante and Isabelle have been spending time together. What none of us knew was Isabelle has a kid, a son named Connor by her late husband. He has been kidnapped, and Isabelle is now on her way to Greece at the behest of the kidnappers. The kid's foster father is dead, the foster mother in a coma. Long story short, Tessa was going to disguise herself as Isabelle and go in her place with the kidnappers, but Isabelle got away before that could happen. Gregor and Tessa are on their way with Dante to Greece. I am so sorry we have to postpone our trip to Egypt. I promise you I don't think Sophia's life is any less important than

Isabelle's or her son's. It's just, well, he's a kid."

"I totally understand. Jules, what the fuck is happening? First Kaya, then Tessa. Now Sophia and Isabelle? If Alistair is behind all this trouble with our females, it's only getting started. Imagine all the Clan going through this when they find their mates."

"Yeah, I'd rather not. I have to tell you, though. Tessa's disguise threw everyone for a loop. She was the spitting image of Isabelle. Jonas's creations are like nothing I've ever seen before."

"I've witnessed it firsthand, remember? Had Sophia not kissed me, I'd have never known she was really the old woman on the sidewalk."

"I remember. Listen, there's something else. It seems one of Sophia's uncles is there in Egypt looking for her, too. Tessa was going to go, but her mother intervened and called in a replacement. He's another watcher, and his name is Ezekiel Seymour. I'm texting you his phone number. Other than that, I have no information as to where he's staying. Hopefully, together you can find her faster. I promise, Brother, as soon as we find Connor and get Isabelle safe, Gregor or I will be there with you. Preferably both of us. Until then, I'll help you as much as I can from here."

"I understand. I appreciate all you're doing. I'm going to get off here and run the program. While it's doing its thing, I'll give this Ezekiel a call. Thanks for everything, Jules."

"I wish I was doing more. I'll talk to you soon." The phone disconnected. Nik could swear Julian choked up before he hung up.

Nikolas found a thumb drive in his computer bag

and pushed it into the USB port on his laptop. He opened the file Julian created and began transferring it. While that was working, he placed a call to Sophia's uncle. Ezekiel didn't answer, so Nik left a detailed message stating who he was and how he could be reached. A few minutes later, his phone rang with the man returning his call.

"Hello, Ezekiel?"

"Yes, this is Zeke. I apologize for not answering your call, but with things as tentative as they are, one can never be too careful."

"No apology necessary. Please tell me you have some kind of lead on my mate."

"Is it possible we meet in person? There's a lot to tell you, and I believe some things are better kept off the airwaves, if you know what I mean."

Nik totally agreed. "That's an excellent idea. I'm renting a villa that's secluded. I think we'll be safe talking here. I'll text you the address."

"Sounds good. I'm coming from Alexandria, so it will take me a few hours to get there."

"No problem. If you'd like, bring an overnight bag. There's plenty of room, and I have a feeling we'll need more than a few hours to go over everything that's happened since we've both been here."

"Will do. I look forward to meeting you, Nikolas."

"Please, call me Nik. I'll see you soon." Nik hung up, and for the first time in a few weeks, he felt a tinge of hope.

While he waited on Sophia's uncle, Nik transferred the program from his computer to Sophia's. Once it was installed, he was able to access her files, just as

Julian predicted. He was not surprised it worked; his brother was a genius. What did surprise him was the number of folders on the desktop. They were arranged alphabetically, and there were hundreds of them.

Nik opened the one titled *Aliases* and scrolled through the numerous names listed. Clara and Beatrice were two of the many alter egos Sophia had created. Within each subfolder was the photo, the credentials needed for a driver's license and passport, along with the address used for credit cards. With these folders open, Nik plugged the various names into his own computer program and prayed one of the names would show up.

He closed that folder and opened the one with his name as the title. He was eager to see how much information his mate had on him and how long she had known they were mates. He opened a folder with pictures in it and froze. Some of these had to be several years old. One was at a charity fundraiser for the hospital. Nik and Julian were shaking hands with the Mayor after presenting them with a huge donation. He clicked through the hundreds of photos, some taken as recently as a month ago, right before Sophia left for Egypt.

When the buzzer at the gate interrupted the silence, Nik realized he had spent hours going through the information Sophia had on him alone. He cleared his mind and spoke into the microphone. "Yes?"

"Nik, it's Zeke." The man was holding his photo ID up to the camera.

"Great, come on in," Nik said as he pressed the button that opened the gate. He wished he had more time alone to go through the other files. Sophia's computer was filled with information on not only the half-bloods but the Stone Society as well. He wasn't sure how he felt about his privacy being invaded for so long. He couldn't dwell on it now, though. Now, he had to meet with her uncle and find his female.

CHAPTER EIGHTEEN

NIKOLAS opened the door and welcomed Ezekiel inside. "Zeke, it's a pleasure to meet you. I only wish it was under different circumstances."

"Likewise," Zeke replied. For some reason, Nik had been expecting an older man. If he was Sophia's uncle, he should look like an uncle, not a good-looking, thirty-something blond. He and Dane could almost pass for twins. The only difference was Dane's eyes were the color of a deep sea, whereas Zeke's were closer to sapphire.

"I'll show you to your room before we settle in." Nikolas led Zeke down the hall to one of the larger bedrooms. It was on the other end of the house from the master suite, but it was nice and offered plenty of privacy.

Once back in the living area, Nik asked, "Would you care for a drink?"

"I'll have whatever you're having, thanks."

Nik refilled his Scotch and poured one for his guest. He handed the glass to Ezekiel and asked, "So, do you have any idea where our girl could be?"

Zeke took a sip of the liquor and nodded. "We think she's in jail."

Nik inhaled and swallowed his Scotch the wrong way. He coughed and beat himself on the chest until he could speak again. "Jail? Why would she be in jail?"

"May I sit?" Zeke didn't wait on Nik to agree. He went ahead and took one of the overstuffed armchairs and leaned back. "Let me start at the beginning." Zeke explained everything that had happened since he arrived in Egypt, including Sophia meeting up with Xenia. He recounted the feeling both he and Xenia got when they visited the Valley of the Queens. "It was faint, but I swear it was her scent. I know it's a long shot, but the timing fits. She showed up in Luxor the day before the murder. She hasn't been seen since."

"Dammit! If she is the killer, I saw her being put into an ambulance. Dammit to the deepest pits of hell. She's hurt." Nikolas began pacing the floor.

"You were there?"

Nik stopped moving and leaned against the arm of the sofa. "Not exactly. I was trying to get there and had trouble with my transportation." There's no way in hell Nik would admit to being bested by a stinky camel.

"Nik, if she was injured, they would have taken her to the hospital. Xenia and I have tried to find out who they arrested. Even Xenia being a citizen of Egypt isn't bearing any weight. We've been locked out at every turn."

Nik pushed off the sofa and went to his laptop. He sat down and started typing away on the keys. "If she's been arrested, I'll find out. Did you contact the Embassy?"

"And say what? I think my niece murdered someone. Can you please tell me if she's in jail?"

"No, you could say she is missing, and you believe she's been wrongfully imprisoned. If Sophia did kill that guard, she had to have a good reason. I can't see her murdering someone in cold blood, but then again, what do I know? Other than she's my mate and has known it for years."

"That was a shock to me as well. I didn't know

until Xenia told me."

"It seems our little bunny is full of surprises," Nik murmured.

"Bunny?"

"You know that thing she does with her nose? It's cute, like a bunny." Nik grinned. He was pissed at his mate, but he still found her mannerisms endearing. "Look, here it is." Nik motioned for Zeke to come see what he was pointing at.

"Is that Sophia's computer?" Zeke asked when he saw the other laptop.

"Yes. I was hoping it would give me a clue as to where she is."

"How did you get access? I'm pretty smart, but I couldn't crack her password. I retrieved her things from the Luxor Embassy Hotel when she didn't return. Another laptop was there."

"My brother Julian is a genius. I'd put him right up there with your father. Now, these are the patients taken to the hospital on the day of the murder. There is no one fitting Sophia's description. I'll bet you money they took her straight to the prison, and she was seen in the infirmary there. If something has happened to her because they were negligent, I'll kill them all myself," Nik fumed.

"Slow down. We need to figure out a way to see if she's actually in the prison. Can you hack their records as well?"

"Yes, I can." Nik typed away, and within two minutes, he was looking at the people detained in the Luxor jail.

When Zeke looked over Nik's shoulder, he

corrected Nik. "No, that's a small holding facility. The prison is in Cairo."

"You mean to tell me they transported an injured woman from Luxor to Cairo with no medical attention first? I doubt the ambulances here are adequate for more than a fucking hangnail." Nik had to calm his Gargoyle. The beast was roaring inside his head, begging to be turned loose. "Calm the fuck down!" he chastised.

"Excuse me?" Zeke backed up.

"Not you. Sorry, but my beast is ripping my insides to shreds right about now. I'm calm."

"Yeah, I can't imagine what it's like being a full-blood. Having half a monster inside is bad enough," Zeke said as he returned to where he'd originally been standing.

As Nik tapped away on the keys, he looked up at his guest and asked, "You think we're monsters?"

"Don't you?" Zeke shrugged. "I've seen the damage done when the shifter half is out of control."

"So have I, but we call them Unholy. Gargoyles are nothing like the creatures we hunt." Nikolas returned his attention to the computer. "There were twenty-two women detained the day of and the day after the murder. Most were picked up for prostitution or petty crimes. There is no record of Sophia, Clara, or anyone matching her description or crime being locked up."

"Dammit. Now what?"

Nik shoved his chair away from the table and retrieved his Scotch. After downing it and pouring another glassful, he said, "Now, we call the Embassy."

"And tell them who is missing? When Xenia and I

gathered Sophia's things from the Luxor hotel, she had checked in as Clara, not Sophia. Her disguise was nowhere to be found."

"Then we tell them Clara. I have her Beatrice disguise. If she's been held for this long, is her disguise even holding up?"

"Those are extremely durable. My father knows what he's doing."

"Clara it is then." Nikolas found the number for the American Embassy and gave them a call. After explaining their situation, the consulate he spoke with requested they come to the Embassy in person. The two of them loaded up in Nik's rental vehicle and headed downtown.

THE lock turned, and the cell door opened. Sophia was flat on her back with her knees bent and twisted away from her. She was lying partially on top of the empty tray. The guard would have to either move her or pull it from beneath her. "Move your ass, bitch," he snarled. When she didn't move, he kicked at her with his boot. She had been ready for the kick and didn't flinch when it was delivered. The man bent down and shook her. "Wake up." Sophia had calmed her breathing to the point it was barely detectable.

"Fuck," the guard cursed before speaking into his radio. "The American isn't breathing. Hurry up." He stepped out of the cell into the hallway. She didn't blame him. The stench coming from both her and the bucket was enough to cause the strongest stomach to hurl. Within a few minutes, another guard was outside her cell.

"Help me get her onto the gurney," the first guard told the newcomer.

"Gah! She reeks," the second guard spat when he got a whiff of her.

"Yeah, you would too if you were stuck in the hole. Now, shut up and grab her feet."

Sophia kept her body lax as the two men not so gently hoisted her onto the stretcher. It was easy to keep her eyes closed since she was used to the dark. The two men carried her in silence until they got to what she prayed was the infirmary and not another cell. They didn't transfer her body to a table. Instead, they placed the stretcher down and left her.

When she didn't hear voices for a few minutes, Sophia took a chance and barely cracked her eyes. She didn't open them all the way, just wide enough to take in the room where she was. While she was waiting, voices from the hallway grew louder. Crying drowned out the men speaking. The door to the infirmary opened again, and a hysterical woman was brought into the room with Sophia. It was all she could do to keep her eyes closed. She was curious as to why the woman was there.

"Strap her down," a male voice instructed.

"No, no please. I'll behave. Just get me something for the pain," she begged.

"Shut up. It's your own fault you're in here," another voice chimed in.

Sophia had wanted to get out of her cell, but now

her plan at playing dead was getting the best of her.

"What is that smell?" one of the guards asked.

"It's her. She's been in the hole for a while."

"Someone needs to hose the bitch down. Fuck."

Sophia wished someone would hose her down. Even if they stripped the hide off her skin, it would be better than the way she smelled. The woman next to her continued to get louder. "No, don't stick me, please," she begged again. A few seconds later, the room was quiet. The shuffling of the men's feet sounded as they left the room. They had obviously drugged the woman, because she wasn't moving. Sophia opened her eyes barely a slit and looked over at where the woman was strapped to her table. From what Sophia could see, the woman was light skinned. Her voice had sounded American, but just because she didn't have an accent didn't mean anything.

As she lie there on the table, Sophia began formulating a plan. If only she knew how long she had before someone returned to the room. Even if she was able to switch places with the other woman, her plan wouldn't work until she had the chance at bathing. No, her only hope at this point was the other woman waking up and Sophia pleading with her to tell someone she was there. If this woman wasn't in solitary, she was probably being held for some minor infraction. Not murder. Gods, how did self-defense become a guilty verdict with no trial? Because she wasn't in the States.

The doorknob turned, and Sophia calmed her breathing once again. If this was the doctor, she needed him to believe she was close to death. The smell of cologne tickled her nose, and she prayed to all that was holy she wouldn't sneeze. The scent grew stronger as the man closed the distance. He placed his fingers on her wrist to check her pulse. The smell dissipated as he stepped away from her. He must have sat down because a chair squeaked. Papers were shuffled right before he said, "Sir, the American is very weak. I can start an IV. Sir, if she doesn't wake up, we'll never get the truth out of her. Will do. And Sir? She really needs a bath. Yes, Sir." The receiver was replaced on the base, and the chair squeaked once again.

Drawers were opened and closed. Wheels rolled across the floor. Sophia's arm was lifted, and a tourniquet placed around her bicep. Having fluids pumped through her body would allow her to remain where she was for a while as well as help her gain a little of her strength back. The man tapped at the veins, and soon she felt a slight sting. The needle was removed from the catheter, and tape was placed over the tube to hold it in place. When the tourniquet was released, Sophia had to stop herself from rubbing the area. The liquid nourishment was a welcome respite from the mush she'd been eating for however long she'd been there. She relaxed even further into herself and waited to see what happened with the woman.

She didn't have to wait long. The doctor obviously gave her something to counteract the effects of the earlier drug, because the woman gasped. When she became aware of her surroundings, she began begging again. "Please, I need something for pain. I can't take it anymore."

"I suggest you be quiet. You should have thought

about pain before you slapped one of the guards. Our men do not take it lightly being struck by a woman. I will stitch your face, and you will keep your mouth shut. If you utter one word, I will leave the wound open, and you will have a nasty scar for the rest of your life. What will it be?" the doctor asked hatefully.

"I'll be quiet," the woman whispered.

More drawers opened and closed. Water turned on and ran for a few seconds before being turned back off. "I'm going to clean the area before I stitch it." More rustling and rolling of wheels followed. Sophia prayed for the woman, asking the gods to give her strength to get through the next few minutes without speaking.

A hissing noise floated across the air. Hopefully, the man had sprayed something on her skin to deaden the area. Without looking, Sophia knew when the doctor touched the needle to skin. The woman whimpered, but didn't cry out. Instead, she inhaled and didn't let out her breath until the man was finished. The wheels rolled across the floor, and the water turned on once again. "I'll send someone to take you back to your cell," was all the doctor said. He offered her no pain medicine, no kind words, nothing.

Once the door closed, Sophia blinked several times, making sure the colored contacts were in place. "Hey," she whispered to the other woman.

The woman sniffled but couldn't wipe her face since she was still strapped down. "I thought you were dead," she said through her tears.

"I almost was. Listen, they've been keeping me in solitary. It's a small black hole with no light. They won't let me talk to an American Consulate. My name is Clara Fort. Please, when you get out of here, tell someone they're keeping me captive. I'm begging you. You're my only hope of getting out of here."

"What are you in for?"

"Murder, only I didn't do what they said I did. I was attacked by a guard at the Valley of the Queens. He died, but I didn't murder him. Please, you've got to help me."

The woman nodded. "I will. If *I* ever get out of here. They don't take too kindly to women."

The doorknob turned, and Sophia closed her eyes. Her only hope of survival was unstrapped and taken back to a cell.

CHAPTER NINETEEN

NIKOLAS and Ezekiel spent several hours at the Embassy. By the time they left, Nik was ready to let his beast loose. He explained more than once how they weren't positive Sophia had been arrested, but the timeline fit. If she wasn't sitting in prison wounded, they needed to know so they could look elsewhere. The consulate explained the Egyptian laws, and if Sophia had been arrested for murder, she was looking at a long stay. The laws were different there than in the States. Nik understood that. He wanted to know, one way or the other, if she was in jail. If she was, he would continue looking for her parents. If she wasn't, he'd need to search for her.

Before they left, the consulate assured them he would do everything he could to find out if she had been arrested. Now, they were to sit tight and wait. Nikolas was tired of waiting. Tired of not knowing where his mate was or whether or not she was okay.

Even though it was early morning, Nikolas decided to lie down for a while. He knew he wouldn't be able to sleep, but he wanted to meditate. He told Zeke to make himself at home, and he retreated to his suite. Once he was comfortable in the middle of the king-sized bed, he relaxed his body and his mind. He closed himself off from everything around him and focused on one thing - Sophia. When he found her, she was no longer in the dark. The air around her was bright, yet stale. His spirit called out to hers, but there was no answering tug. As Nik continued to focus on that tether he'd found before, his beast tried to add his energy.

That had never happened before. Normally, when Nik was deep in his subconscious, the beast shied away and let him do what he needed. This time, his shifter was front and center. He didn't want to lose the tenuous connection he had with his mate, so instead of dropping it and arguing with the Goyle inside, he allowed it to join him. His spirit felt heavy, like it would burst forth from his chest, but once the Goyle found where it wanted to be, the spirit settled down and was better focused on Sophia.

I was wondering when you'd find me. Sophia's in trouble, and I don't know how long I can keep her strong. You have to come get her.

Nik was startled at the voice. Who the fuck could possibly be in his head? He was just about to ask when he felt words flowing from his mind. ***We are trying. Do you know where you are?***

Prison infirmary for now. Won't be for long.

Keep her safe until we can get there. We're coming.

The beast retreated, and the connection was lost. What in the holy fucking hell just happened? Did his shifter take over his mind? *Did you take over my mind?* Nik had always spoken to his inner Gargoyle, but it had never spoken back. It still didn't. Besides, who was his beast speaking to? Nik was pretty fucking sure if he told anyone what just happened, they'd think he was crazy. He replayed the short conversation between his shifter and whoever he'd spoken to. The voice said they were in the prison infirmary. Zeke's suspicion had been right, but how did they prove it? Tell the authorities the voice in his head told him so? They'd lock Nik up in a psych ward somewhere.

After thinking about it, the only logical explanation was that his shifter was talking to Sophia's. If they had already completed the bond, that might make sense. Might. They had shared one kiss. Never mind that the kiss had gotten Nik's cock hard as stone, it was still a limited amount of physical contact. In all his years of documenting the Gargoyles, Nikolas had never heard of inner shifters being able to contact one another. If his and Sophia's were able to do it, it was likely others could as well. They were probably like Nik, though - afraid someone would think they'd lost their minds.

His phone rang in the living area, so he rose and headed to that part of the villa to answer it. Surprised to see Rafael's name on the I.D., he answered, "Is Julian all right?"

"Hello to you too, Nikolas. As far as I know, he's fine. How are you?" The tone of Rafe's voice was tense.

"Crazy. I'm going out of my fucking head trying to get to my mate."

"That's why I'm calling. Julian replayed what happened with Xavier, yes?"

"He told me; dear old Uncle Alistair is gunning for you."

"Yes, well, it seems I'm not the only one he's targeting. Nik, I received a package in the mail. It contains photographs of you, Sophia, her parents, and Ezekiel. The postmark was New Atlanta, but that doesn't mean he isn't behind having you followed."

"That doesn't surprise me. Whoever was targeting Sophia found out about me. It seems they knew about Zeke, too. Hold up. How do you know who the people are in the other photos? You've never seen them."

"I had a sit down with Jonas earlier. He's ready to help any way he can."

"Rafe, I need those pictures, especially the ones of Sophia's parents. The clues she was given are vague and make no sense."

"Clues? So you've found Sophia?"

"Not exactly. I saw her once, but she disappeared again. Elizabeth put Zeke and me in touch with one another. Sophia had visited one of her aunts who lives here and shared the clues with her. Zeke hooked up with his sister. I mean, they didn't hook up because that would be wrong, but they met up. We're working together to figure this out. Have you shown the pictures to Jules yet?"

"No. I wanted to give you a heads up first. I'll take them over there right now."

"I appreciate it. The sooner we can take a look at them, the sooner we can see if they give us any insight as to where her parents are."

"I have to warn you; the pictures are pretty dark. I don't want you to get your hopes up."

"I understand. But I also have a super genius for a brother. I have no doubt he'll be able to brighten the photos enough to see the backgrounds."

"I hope you're right. I'll head over to the lab now. Take care of yourself. Be well, my brother."

"And to you, my King."

"What was that about, if you don't mind me asking?" Zeke had been sitting next to Nik while he was on the phone with Rafael.

"It would appear whoever is behind Sam's and

Monica's disappearance has been keeping tabs on us all. They took photographs and sent them to Rafael. He is taking them to the lab so Julian can scan them and send them to us. If we can get clear shots of Sam, we might be able to figure out where they are."

"That would be wonderful, since the clues were useless."

"I agree. It shouldn't take too long until we get a copy. Again, all we can do is wait. I'm going to make breakfast. Would you like something?"

Zeke stood and stretched. "Yes, if you don't mind. I'm going to take a quick shower while you cook."

"Sounds good." Nikolas pulled stuff out of the fridge to make omelets. His stomach was churning with anticipation, but he needed to keep his strength up. He started a pot of coffee and whipped up some eggs. While he was waiting on Zeke to shower, he considered telling the man about what happened during his meditation. They hadn't talked about Zeke's mate. They hadn't talked about Zeke at all, really. Nik had no idea how old the man was. His parents met approximately two hundred years ago, so he could be anywhere from thirty-something to way over one hundred.

When Zeke returned to the kitchen, his feet were bare and his hair still damp. Nik never paid much attention to men before, but his guest was good-looking.

"Why are you staring at me?" Zeke asked.

"I was wondering how old you are," Nik answered almost honestly. No need in making the male uncomfortable.

"I'm fifty-seven. How old are you?" he asked as he poured himself a cup of coffee.

"Five hundred and twenty-three. The reason I was wondering is you look like you're in your early thirties. You must have met your mate, right?" Nik asked, but almost wished he hadn't when he saw the frown that came across Zeke's face. "If that's a bad subject, forget I asked."

"It is a sore subject, but the way I see it, we are going to be one big happy Clan before long. Well, maybe not happy, but Clan, nonetheless. Tessa's the one who figured out what triggers the initial transitions in half-bloods. Actually, she read it in one of Jonas's journals, but to this day, my father swears he doesn't know what causes the initial change. Tessa feels he is trying to keep the family safe in his own misguided way. I disagree with his thought process. Once I found out what the trigger was, I made it a mission to help my siblings not go through what I did."

"And that was?" Nik asked as he put their plates on the table. The men sat down, and Zeke took a sip of his coffee.

"I transitioned right after my thirtieth birthday. Had I known the cause, I'd more than likely have my mate by my side. As it was, I had no idea. My mate could be anyone I was around at the time, but I would have known what signs to look for. So instead of spending the rest of my life with the one the fates chose for me, I'm now alone and will be the rest of my life. I know I could date, and don't get me wrong, I go out for an occasional one-night stand. I do have needs. But it's not fair to string someone along who falls in love with me when I cannot return that love one hundred percent. I vowed to tell my siblings who have yet to transition the truth.

"Take Xenia, for example. Had Sophia not arrived when she did, Xenia would probably have torn Keene apart from sheer frustration. She had no idea what was happening or why. I'm not saying that Sam and Monica getting kidnapped is a good thing, but at least one good thing came from it."

Nik put his fork down and wiped his mouth. "What happens if you run into your mate again after all this time? Would the pull still be there?"

Zeke swallowed the bite he was chewing. "I would assume so, but she would have continued aging. Not that I'm so shallow I wouldn't still want her, but how would she feel to see her intended looking so much younger? For human women, they continue aging until they have a baby."

"Let me ask you this then. What about two men? If a Gargoyle is gay and mates with another man, they'll never biologically have children. Will the human continue aging? That doesn't seem too fair to me."

"I've never known any gay shifters. That's a legitimate question."

Nik hated to think of Jasper spending the rest of his long life with no true mate by his side. "Hopefully the fates are keeping up with the times and have that figured out. For now, we need to figure out how to get Sophia out of that prison."

"If she's even there. I'm having my doubts," Zeke said.

"She's there. I know for sure."

"And how do you know this, exactly?"

Nik took a deep breath and answered, "Because I spoke to her."

Zeke laughed, but when Nik maintained a straight face, Zeke sobered. "You're serious?"

Nik nodded. "Actually, I think my shifter spoke to hers. I know this is going to sound crazy, but when I went to my room to rest, I meditated. In a previous session, I saw Sophia. She was running, and a hand reached out to grab her. The next few times, it was dark. Sophia was there; I could feel her presence. But she was being kept somewhere dark. Normally, my shifter stays in the back of my mind while I'm relaxing. This time, he shoved his way to the front, and I swear to all that's holy, it connected with Sophia. Or her shifter, to be more precise. The voice in my head said we needed to hurry. It wasn't sure how long it could keep Sophia strong. My spirit asked where they were, and hers replied the prison infirmary. Zeke, I know it sounds crazy. Have you ever heard tale of any of your siblings being able to talk to their mates that way?"

Zeke shook his head. "No, but I don't know if anyone meditates, either. I'm not dismissing what you say happened, though. If the gods make creatures that have wings and can fly, why wouldn't they give us the abilities to communicate with each other? At least some of us."

Nik hadn't thought about it that way. "Thank you. I was beginning to doubt my own sanity."

Zeke stood and took his plate to the dishwasher. "I doubt mine every day, my friend." He grabbed Nik's plate when he finished eating and cleaned up the kitchen. "Have you heard from Tessa? The last time I spoke to Elizabeth, Tessa was still healing from her wreck."

"She's actually in Greece, believe it or not. What I didn't tell you earlier is that we believe Rafael's uncle is behind all the trouble our mates are getting into. He's the one who ostracized your father all those years ago for mating with a human."

"Alistair. I've heard about him. Why would he start targeting mates now?"

"Rafael and the Counsel have been going round and round ever since his father died and he became King. He refuses his seat at the proverbial round table. On top of that, he is now mated to a human. Gregor is mated to Tessa, who is related to Jonas. Dante is mated to Isabelle, who is Jonas's daughter. Now, I'm fated to be with Sophia. As you said earlier, we will eventually become one interconnected Clan. How Alistair knows who is mated to whom is beyond me, but it is becoming clear he does."

"Why is Tessa in Greece? Don't tell me she's already on her honeymoon."

"Unfortunately, no. Isabelle's son was kidnapped."

"Isabelle? As in my sister Isabelle? She doesn't have a son."

"Yes, your sister, and yes, she does. She kept him a secret. He's been living with a couple up in Tennessee all these years. His name is Connor, and she didn't want his biological grandfather to find out about him. Someone found out and took him. Whoever it is convinced Isabelle to get on a plane with them. They said it was the only way to get the boy back. Now, Isabelle is being held on one island and Connor somewhere else. The fates might be bringing our families together, but there are others at play who are trying to keep us apart."

"Damn. It almost makes me glad I don't know who my mate is. At least this way I know she's probably a lot safer."

"Truth, but once I get Sophia back, I'll be damned if she ever gets hurt again. I'll stake my wings on that."

CHAPTER TWENTY

SOPHIA had to be dreaming. The fluid running through her veins must not be helping her gain her strength back. Not only was her shifter talking, but a voice had responded. She was worse off than she thought. Too much longer in the hole and she'd probably have died. Someone entered the room. Voices told her there were two men and a woman. They were talking about her. "You need to bathe her before we put her back."

"She is too weak to be put in the hole. Please, at least put her back in a cell."

"It is not your business what we do with this prisoner other than cleaning her up. Remember your place, woman."

"Yes, Captain."

Sophia's IV was removed. Her stretcher was lifted off the table and taken to a different room. The woman worked quickly to remove Sophia's clothing. Rough hands lifted her into a tub of hot water. If she was strong enough, she might have cared that she was naked in front of strangers. The sound of footsteps retreated from the room. Then she was alone with only the woman. She took a chance and opened her eyes. The woman was of African descent and had a kind, motherly face.

"I didn't do it," she whispered to the lady.

"Shh, it doesn't matter, child. I've heard them talking. They know you aren't strong enough to have killed Asaad, but they need to pin it on someone. You were there; case closed."

"But I didn't do it. My parents are missing. I've got to find them," Sophia vowed. "Nobody knows where I am. I can't die in here."

"I will do my best to have you moved back into a cell. I cannot make you any promises, though."

Warm water flowed down Sophia's face. She had no idea if it was the bath water or tears. At that point, it didn't matter. Her life was over.

No, it isn't. Nik knows where you are, and he's coming for you. Hang on a little longer.

Sophia closed her eyes and let the woman bathe the stench off her body. A few minutes later, the water was being drained, and she was being dried off. The woman put clean clothes on her, not asking if she could help. Sophia did raise her hips when the pants were being slid up her legs. Her hair was still a ratted mess, and her mouth tasted like roadkill smelled. At least her body was clean. "Open up, child," the woman said as she pressed something to Sophia's mouth. "It's not a toothbrush, but if you chew on it, it will help." Sophia accepted the gift into her mouth. She didn't expect it to be enjoyable. Whatever the plant was had a minty taste mixed with something she couldn't identify.

"They will be back for you soon. I suggest you play a weakling as long as you can," the woman said with a small smile.

When she started to stand, Sophia grabbed her arm. "Thank you. My name is Clara Fort, just in case."

"I will remember you in my prayers, Clara Fort." With that, the woman left her alone. She realized she was still sitting in the tub when the men came to retrieve her. Once she was loaded on the stretcher, they bypassed the infirmary and took her to the original cell she'd been held in. She thanked the gods for small favors.

Sophia settled back into the dull routine of waiting on her tray to come. No longer was she so weak she thought she was dying, but she wasn't so strong she felt like dancing. If she ever got out of that square room she now called home, she was going to dance every day.

NIKOLAS and Zeke were waiting at the airport for Gregor and Tessa. Dante had Isabelle and Connor safely on their way home to the States. Nikolas had enjoyed Ezekiel's company, but he was anxious to see his cousin. Gregor was more like a brother since their fathers had been close and raised the boys together. Tessa's father had been kind enough to lend his private jet to them since Dante and Isabelle were on the Clan plane. When the jet landed, Zeke let out a low whistle. "Life is good being a Gargoyle."

Nik laughed. "You do realize that's your cousin's jet, don't you?"

"Tessa doesn't have a jet."

"No, but Xavier does. Don't tell me you didn't know that." Nik frowned at the other man whose mouth was wide open. "There they are," Nik said and got out of the car. He jogged over to the plane and met Gregor at the bottom of the steps. "Brother, it's so good to see you." Nik and Gregor wrapped each other in a tight embrace, slapping each other on the back. When they broke apart, Nik held onto Tessa's arms and grinned until Gregor growled.

"Tessa, good to see you again. I guess you know this guy," he said, thumbing at Zeke. "Zeke, this is my cousin, Gregor."

Zeke shook hands with Gregor and hugged Tessa. He also got a growl from her mate, but if he noticed, he ignored it.

"Let's grab your luggage so we can get back to the villa. We have a lot to tell you," Nik said as they waited on the crewman to unload the plane. Once the bags were in the back of the vehicle, they all piled in.

"Please tell me you've found Sophia," Tessa said from the backseat.

"She's in jail," Zeke told his cousin.

"Jail? Sweet little Sophia's in jail? For what?"

"Murder," Nik and Zeke responded in unison.

"Yeah, right. Really, where is she?"

Zeke turned in his seat. "So much has happened in the last few weeks, and we'll explain it all once we get to the villa. But for now, our biggest concern is getting Sophia out of prison. The Egyptians aren't known for speedy trials or fair treatment of inmates."

"You weren't kidding. And you know for sure she's there?" Tessa asked incredulously.

"I do," Nik said.

"How do you know, Brother?" Gregor asked.

Nik and Zeke looked at each other. Nik had no problem telling Gregor, but he didn't know Tessa very well. Zeke nodded, so Nik told them honestly, "Through our minds." He looked in the rearview mirror for Gregor's disbelief.

Instead of frowning, Gregor gave a small smile. "That's how Dante found Connor. Even though they'd never met, the boy drew pictures for Dante, giving him clues to where he was being held. It's no surprise you and Sophia can connect the same way."

"It's not exactly the same. I didn't speak to Sophia. My shifter spoke to hers."

Tessa butted in. "That's impossible. She isn't a half-blood yet. You must have been talking to her."

"Oh, she's a shifter all right and has been for a few years now," Nik said, shoving his hands in his pockets.

"I would know if she's been through the change." Tessa leaned back and crossed her arms over her chest.

Zeke confirmed what Nik told them. "It was a surprise to me, too, but Xenia saw proof for herself."

"Xenia? Your sister Xenia?"

"Apparently Sophia phased to talk Xenia off the ledge, to show her she isn't the only one with fangs and claws. As Nik said, there's a lot that has happened. Here we are. Let's go inside and get you and Gregor settled. Then we'll tell you everything."

"I can't believe she didn't tell me," Tessa muttered as the car rolled up to the front of the villa.

Nik and Zeke helped Gregor get their luggage inside. Once they had their bags unpacked, everyone met in the living room and took a seat. Nik had poured Scotch for Gregor, but he had no idea what Tessa drank. She didn't hesitate to let him know. "I'll take a beer if you have it. I have a feeling I'm going to need more than one though."

She wasn't lying. By the time Nik and Zeke told

her and Gregor everything that had transpired, she was on her eighth longneck. If they didn't have shifter metabolism, they would all be tipsy. The beautiful redhead was pacing the room. Gregor was giving Nik the details of their adventure in Greece. When he finished, he said to Tessa, "Red, come sit down. You're making everyone nervous."

Tessa sat down next to her mate but hopped back up again. "I can't believe she's kept this from me. Why wouldn't she tell me she's transitioned?"

Gregor stood and grabbed her, stopping her from pacing. "You didn't know Isabelle had a child, either."

"Is that what's really bothering you? Or is it the fact that Jonas trained her without telling you?" Zeke asked. "You should know by now that Jonas has plenty of secrets of his own. It seems keeping secrets runs in our family. Speaking of which, now that Cyrus is the only sibling left who has yet to transition, I'm going to see him as soon as we find Sam and Monica. I won't have another Cordelia on my hands."

"I agree you should tell Cyrus. Jonas's secrets cost him his relationship with Isabelle, and in turn, almost caused her to lose Connor. I think we're past all that. Now that Rafael knows about us, he will want to absorb us into his Clan. Since I'm Gregor's mate, I'm already part of the Stone Society. As for Sophia, I guess I can understand. I kept Gregor at bay for years, too."

Nik picked up a stack of photos and started passing them out. "Julian scanned the photos that were sent to Rafael and emailed them to me. I have printed them out so we can all study the markings. Since Xenia is a history professor, we are going to enlist her help as well." Before Nik sat down in front of his computer, he grabbed the remote and turned on the TV, lowering the volume. He kept the news channel on just on the off chance someone found Sam and Monica.

Tessa set up her own computer and began looking at the clues they had so far. While Nik and Gregor discussed getting Sophia out of prison, Zeke called Xenia.

"I wonder if Xavier has any connections here. It's a long shot, but as old as he is, he might know of a clan in Africa," Gregor said.

"Julian found a clan in South Africa, but he hasn't been able to find out if they're connected to Alistair in any way. I have yet to sense any other Goyles other than the ones who were following Sophia. I'm pretty sure at least one of the larger men was a shifter."

"That makes sense if Alistair is behind this. We had the pleasure of running into Theron in Greece." Gregor grinned as he glanced at his mate. "You should have seen the look on his face when Tessa stabbed him with a hypodermic needle. It was priceless."

"It was great. Only he thought I was Isabelle. I'm telling you, Jonas's disguises are brilliant," Tessa added.

Nik smiled when he remembered Beatrice. "I've seen them firsthand. I'm praying Sophia is wearing one now. When we get her out of that prison, she'll be able to ditch the Clara disguise, and the media will be none the wiser."

"I could always ask Jonas to recreate the disguise," Tessa said aloud, more as a thought to herself.

"What are you thinking, Red? I know that look,

and I'm not going to like it, am I?" Gregor frowned at his mate.

"Doubling as Isabelle worked. It could work with Clara, too."

"We had the element of surprise on our hands, not to mention you had a team of Gargoyles backing you up. I don't think we can all get thrown into prison at the same time. I know you want to help your cousin, but we'll figure something out." Gregor pulled her into his arms and kissed her forehead.

Nik was happy for his cousin. The Gargoyles had gone too long before finding their mates. Seeing the two of them together had Nik even more anxious to find a way of getting Sophia out of prison so they could begin their life together.

The intercom at the gate buzzed. "That should be Xenia," Zeke told them.

Nik hit the button and said, "Hello?"

"This is Xenia Carmichael. Ezekiel asked me to come over." Nik motioned Zeke over to look at the screen. When he nodded, Nik opened the gate.

A few minutes later, the doorbell rang. Since she was Zeke's sister, Nik asked him to see her in. A strange man's voice was added to Zeke's and Xenia's. When they came into the living area, Zeke introduced them. "This is Xenia and her mate, Keene. This is Nikolas, his cousin Gregor, and our cousin Tessa."

After the men had shaken hands, Xenia spoke to the group. "I hope it's okay that I brought Keene. I believe he might be able to help us with Sophia."

"Yeah, how?" Nik asked.

"My father does a lot of business in Cairo. He has

influential acquaintances who would hate to lose him in their circles."

"Who exactly is your father?" Zeke asked.

"Brock Tyson," Keene answered honestly.

"The arms dealer?"

"Before you get your knickers in a twist, I have nothing to do with him or his nefarious way of life. We aren't estranged, but he understands I don't agree with his lifestyle."

"Then what makes you think he'd help?" Tessa asked.

"Because I am my mother's favorite child. Actually, I'm her only child, but if I ask her to intervene on my behalf, she will see that it's done."

Xenia stepped closer to her mate and slid her hand around his bicep. He smiled down at her lovingly. She smiled back and said, "It took him a while, but Keene is on board with the whole shifter mating. We have made the bond official, so technically, he's family. We're here to help any way we can."

Nik clapped his hands together. "This is the best news I've heard in a long time. Thank you, Keene." Inside, his shifter pushed his way to the front of Nik's mind and told Sophia's beast, ***Keep Sophia strong a little longer. We are coming for you.***

CHAPTER TWENTY-ONE

ANGRY voices woke Sophia. According to the amount of light in the hall, it was daytime. She sat up on her cot and turned so she could lean against the wall. She bent her knees and pulled her feet up onto the bed. Sophia wrapped her arms around her legs and listened. The voices were getting louder and closer. Two guards approached her cell. Instead of bringing her tray, the cell door was unlocked and slid open. "Get up," one of the men seethed.

Sophia had no idea what was going on, but by the unhappy look on his face, it couldn't bode well for her. She placed her sock-covered feet on the dirty floor and stood. Her body was still weak, but the dizziness didn't have time to take hold. The guard grabbed her arm and began dragging her behind him. Instead of going out through the main area where the other prisoners were housed, she was led through a series of hallways that had no doors. She wanted to ask where they were taking her, but she had found it best to keep quiet. The guard stopped and said to the other man, "Now." Before she could ask *now what*, a black bag was placed over her head, shrouding her world in darkness once again.

Her mind associated the lack of light with the small hole she'd been placed in. Her body protested, and Sophia began lashing out at the guards. "Fuck, grab her arms. Miss Fort, I suggest you behave. If you want to get out of this prison, you'll stop fighting us."

Sophia stopped swinging. Surely, they were messing with her. Why put a sack over her head if they were releasing her? The guard grabbed her arm, and, once again, they were walking. She did her best not to stumble considering she couldn't see where she was going. The jangle of keys sounded, and a door was opened. The bright sunshine bore down on Sophia's arms. Had they not placed the black hood over her head, she would have been blinded.

"I'll take her from here," a deep voice said. A gentle hand held Sophia's, and she was led away from the building. Sharp gravel bit into her feet. "Don't be alarmed; I'm here to take you to your family. Not much farther now, Miss Brooks. Here we are. I'm going to place your hand on the car door. Can you get inside the vehicle, or do you need assistance?"

Sophia reached out with her other hand and touched the door frame. She reached inside and came in contact with a leather seat. Tentatively, she eased her way into the vehicle. The door was closed beside her. Why was she getting into a car with a stranger? He could be taking her to her death. Or, he could be telling the truth. The door on the other side opened then closed. "Who are you?" she asked when the car began moving.

"I'm Brock Tyson. I believe you know my son, Keene. You can take the hood off now. The windows are tinted, so the bright sunshine shouldn't hurt your eyes too bad."

Sophia pulled the cloth from her head. She blinked a few times, adjusting to the light, but he was right. She turned to see who had rescued her from prison. The man was older, but he did resemble her aunt's mate. "How did you get me out? Where are you taking me?

Where's Nik?"

The man reached over and grabbed her hand gently. "Shh, slow down. I am taking you to Keene. He will take you wherever it is you need to be. I don't know where your Nik is. Don't want to know." He patted her hand then placed it back in her lap. "Relax."

Easy for him to say. Sophia had no idea if he was telling the truth. She had no idea of a lot of things, like how long she had been away, or if she was about to meet her death.

He's telling the truth. You will be with Nikolas soon.

And there was another thing she had no idea about. Should she feel relieved that her shifter half was comforting her? Or was it a sign she'd lost her mind? Either way, she prayed it was also telling her the truth.

The car slowed and turned into an abandoned parking lot. Brock told her, "Stay here until I come get you." He got out of the car and walked over to where Keene was waiting, leaned against an SUV. She reached out with her shifter hearing to eavesdrop.

"Hello, Son."

"Father, you're looking well."

"Because your mother won't let me eat the good shit. She misses you."

"I had to promise to bring Xenia over for supper, so she'll see me soon ."

"Don't forget the promise you made to me."

"I won't. Just don't wait too long. I want to get it over with."

"I'll call you when I need you. Now, let's go get the girl."

"How is Sophia?" Keene asked as they headed toward the car.

His father shrugged. "About as well as a woman can be after what she's endured." He opened the door and held out his hand to her. "Let's get you out of here." Sophia placed her hand in his and stepped out of the car.

When they approached Keene, he said, "Hello, Sophia. We really need to stop meeting under such troublesome circumstances. Come on. I'll take you to Nikolas." They made their way to his SUV, and he opened the door for her. She climbed into the passenger seat and buckled up. Before he closed the door, Keene asked, "Are you all right?"

"As well as can be expected, I suppose." She wasn't okay, not by a long shot, but she wouldn't tell him that. When he was in the driver's seat, she asked, "How long 'til we get to Nik?"

"About thirty minutes. Are you cold, hot?"

"I'm fine," she responded and turned to look out the window. She really didn't feel like talking.

"Okay, let's get rolling then."

Nik was pacing the area between the living room and kitchen. His Goyle was uncharacteristically calm. Keene did as he said he would and contacted his mother. Once she told his father what was going on, the man was more than happy to assist his son. Even though he kept a lot of the details to himself, Keene explained Sophia was the cousin of his fiancé. All he had to promise his mother was he would bring Xenia for a visit. His father called him once he had made the arrangements. The warden would only release Sophia to Keene's father, no one else. Brock would pick up Sophia and then he would take her to Keene at a prearranged location. Keene was to come alone. Nik refused to stay at the villa, wanting to go with Brock, but Keene convinced him it was the only way his father would comply.

Nik should be ecstatic. Not only was he getting Sophia back, but Julian was on his way to Egypt as of that afternoon. Instead, he was nervous. Scared at what condition Sophia would be in. The others were doing a good job of giving him space while they looked at the photos of Sam and Monica. Tessa turned the volume up on the television. "Listen to this."

A breaking news story was flashing on the screen. "An inside source has confirmed that Clara Fort, the American woman being held for the murder of transit guard Asaad Halim, has been released. Miss Fort was found inside Ta-Set-Neferu alongside Halim's body. No word on why she is being released or if they have found the actual killer. We will update you when we know more."

"Clara Fort, really?" Tessa said as she shook her head.

Nik frowned at his cousin's mate. "What are you talking about?"

"Rearrange the letters. Clara Fort is Lara Croft. At least she chose someone fun."

"Yeah, well, I doubt she's had too much fun being

locked up in a foreign prison for weeks," Nik responded. He knew from his shifter that Sophia was weak. "I can't imagine what she's been through."

"Sorry, you're right. But she's a half-blood now. That means she's tough. And she has you to come back to. Who wouldn't fight for that?" Tessa smiled until Gregor growled. "Oh, stop it, Stone. You know you're the only big, bad Gargoyle for me." She slid her arms up his chest and pulled his head down for a scorching kiss.

Nik felt like a voyeur watching them, but it was really hot, even if Gregor was his cousin. The intercom at the gate buzzed, breaking up the visual party. "Oh gods, she's here." He hit the control that opened the gate and ran out the front door. The SUV pulled into the circular drive in front of the villa, and Nik slung open the door before the vehicle came to a complete stop. He started to pull his mate from the car, but noticed she had no shoes. "Where are your shoes, Baby?"

"They took 'em," she said, nonchalantly.

Nik started to scoop her up in his arms, but upon seeing a splotch of blood on Sophia's pants, he stopped. "You're hurt."

"No, I'm weak, but I'm not hurt," Sophia told him.

"But you're bleeding." His beast could smell the blood on his mate.

"Help me out of the car or get out of the way, Nikolas Stone."

"Sophia, your pants…" Nik backed up so she could get out of the car, but he grabbed onto her arms in case she needed his assistance.

"Oh, that." She sounded unconcerned about having blood on her clothing. "I do that every month."

"What? Oh. That." Nik pulled his shirt off and wrapped it around her waist, tying the sleeves together so the others wouldn't see the blood and think the same thing. "Sophia, gods, I'm so sorry. I should have never let you go back to the hotel without me. Please forgive me." She had yet to look at him, and it was breaking his heart.

"No, it's my fault. I shouldn't have wandered off alone in the tombs." Sophia started toward the villa then paused when she saw all the people on the wraparound porch. "Wow, a welcoming committee. You shouldn't have," she joked.

"You had a lot of people worried." Nik kissed her on the hair, but she pulled back.

"I'm really gross, and I need to get out of this disguise."

"You're not gross. Okay, maybe a little, but I don't care. I'm just so thrilled to have you in my arms again. As for the disguise, yes, I'm ready to see your beautiful face."

Tessa met them at the bottom of the steps. "Welcome back, Lara Croft. You sure did pick one hell of an adventure for your first one," she said before she hugged her cousin. "I'm glad you're okay."

"Thanks. I see you finally came to your senses about Gregor."

"He was persistent. Let's get you cleaned up and then we'll compare stories." Tessa put her arm around Sophia and guided her to Nik's room. Nik wasn't about to let his mate out of his sight. He would let

Tessa get Sophia to the bedroom, but Nik was going to be the one to take care of his mate.

When they reached the bedroom, Nik told Sophia, "I retrieved your stuff from both the Nile Grand and the inn, and Zeke got your things from the Luxor. Your toiletries are in the bathroom. Tessa, thank you, but I'll take it from here."

Surprisingly, she didn't protest. She probably remembered the way Gregor was when she was hurt. Tessa closed the bedroom door, leaving them alone. He walked Sophia into the bathroom and started the shower. She turned to look in the wall-to-wall mirror and removed the Clara mask from her face and the contacts from her eyes. He smiled at the real Sophia. When she pulled her toothbrush out of the holder, he squeezed some toothpaste on the bristles. While she was brushing, he began removing his clothes. She kept her eyes on him in the mirror. When he was naked, she spat out the foam and asked, "What are you doing?"

"Taking care of my mate," he said softly. "I'm not going to take advantage of you. I only want to take care of you." When she nodded, he removed his shirt from around her waist. After she rinsed the toothpaste from her mouth, he slid the prison uniform shirt over her head. Nik growled when he saw a scar marring her side. "I thought you said you weren't hurt," he hissed as he gingerly touched the skin around the puckered wound.

"It's almost healed, Gorgeous. Please, I need a shower."

Nik calmed his beast who was ready to find the man who did this, dig him up, and kill him again. He grabbed the waistband of the cotton pants and pushed those along with her ruined panties down her legs. He unclasped her bra and slid the straps down her arms. His head knew now was not the time to ogle his female, but she was the most beautiful sight he'd ever seen. "You're so beautiful." He placed his hands on either side of her face and kissed her softly on the lips. The taste of mint invaded his senses. If he thought he'd been lightheaded when he met her for the first time at the library, now he was truly feeling the effects of being in the presence of the one the fates had chosen for him.

Nik opened the shower door and helped her in. He stepped in behind Sophia and turned her so that her back was under the spray. She dipped her head under the water and let out a loud sigh. Nik grabbed the shampoo, pouring a large amount in his hands. When all her hair was wet, Nik lathered her long strands and massaged her scalp. He helped her rinse the suds away before he shampooed it a second time. When the water was running clear, he turned her so the spray wasn't hitting her head and wrung the excess out before adding conditioner. Sophia kept her eyes closed as Nik applied body wash to a washcloth. The scent of honeysuckle invaded his nostrils. "So that's it," he murmured.

"Hmm?" she asked without actually asking.

"You always smell like honeysuckle. It's your body wash." Nik loved the fact that his mate didn't smell like every other woman in the world. Hers was a unique scent, one he could get lost in. He took great care in washing her body. When he got close to her mound, she opened her eyes.

"Nik..."

"Shh. I've got you. Unless you don't trust me," he said and patiently waited for an answer.

CHAPTER TWENTY-TWO

AFTER being taken and held in prison, Nik wouldn't blame her if she said she didn't trust him. He held his breath until she looked him in the eyes and said, "I trust you. It's just, I'm, well, you know."

"I don't know how many men you've been with. I really don't want to know. But you are my mate. I'm still upset with you for keeping that from me for so long, but that doesn't mean you aren't mine. You are, just as I am yours. What that does mean to me is I will take care of you. I will care for you. I will put your needs and wants above mine, always. You are my female and as such, you are the most exquisite creature ever created. Every single thing about you calls to me on a level so deep I can't explain it. The fact that you bleed once a month has no bearing on how I feel. It's part of what makes you who you are. The part that's going to let you give me babies one day."

Nik rubbed her flat stomach with the back of his hand, then continued, "If you would feel better washing yourself, I'll understand. But know this - you can trust me. With your body, your heart, and your spirit."

Sophia reached a hand up and cupped his face. She closed her eyes and tears rolled down her cheeks.

"Hey, talk to me. Did I upset you?" Nik lifted her chin.

"No, you're just so sweet. I'm sorry I didn't tell you about being mates, but you have to know that JoJo can be pretty persuasive." Sophia sniffed, scrunching her cute nose.

"JoJo?"

"Jonas. He was adamant about nobody knowing Gargoyles can mate with humans. It's one reason he put most of his children up for adoption. He didn't want them to be targeted."

"I think he might have been right. Not about keeping it a secret, but the targeting part. We're pretty sure we know who took your parents. We just don't know where they are yet. Have you heard Jonas talk about the Goyle who had him ostracized when he mated with Caroline?"

"Yeah, Alistair. He's behind this?"

Nik kissed the tears off Sophia's cheeks and went back to bathing her as he talked. "Yes. He has a chip on both shoulders. Not only does he despise Jonas, but he has a hard-on for Rafael, too."

"That's right; Alistair is the King's uncle. Well, hell. How did you find out he took my parents?" she asked as she grabbed onto his shoulders.

"A lot has happened while you were being held. Let's finish getting you cleaned up, and then I'll fill you in." Nik helped Sophia rinse her body as well as the conditioner from her hair. She insisted on shaving, so he held her upright while she placed her leg against the wall. When both legs and her underarms were to her satisfaction, Nik turned the water off and opened the shower door. Sophia wrung the excess water from her hair before he handed her a towel. She flipped her head over and twisted the towel around it like a turban. When he held another towel open, she stepped into it, and Nik wrapped it around her body. Instead of letting her go, he pulled her to him and held her close.

They stood silently for several minutes until Nik's cock was no longer behaving. He kissed Sophia on her temple before grabbing his own towel. He turned his back to her, forgetting she could see his profile in the mirror. "Somebody's happy to see me," she breathed across his back as she ran her hand down his spine.

"Sophia..."

"Don't you want me, Nikolas? Your body says you do."

Nik secured the towel around his waist and faced his mate. "Oh, I do, but you've been through quite an ordeal. At least I assume you have. We have all the time in the world to be together. I want to get some food in you and just hold you. I need to feel you in my arms, to know you're really here and safe."

Sophia nodded and began opening drawers. She retrieved various items, placing them on the counter. Nik slathered on deodorant and left her to do what she needed to do. He was in the bedroom putting on clothes when she walked into the room naked. Nik groaned. "Are you trying to kill me, woman?"

"If we are going to live together, you're going to have to get used to this."

"You want to live with me?" Nik had hoped she would, but he didn't want to jump the gun.

"You put my things in your bedroom. I assumed you wanted me to sleep in here."

"Of course I do. But only when you're ready."

"Gorgeous, I've been ready for three years. Do you know how hard it was watching you with other women? I should win some kind of medal for not maiming your dates."

"You followed me?" Nik couldn't believe she had kept her distance knowing they were mates.

"For a while, but it got to be too much. I knew eventually you or one of your Clan would find the journal I planted." Sophia rummaged through the drawers until she found the clothes she wanted. She returned to the bathroom to dress.

Nik followed her. When she retrieved a tampon from her things, he turned to give her privacy. Once Sophia had her clothes on, she picked up the comb. He took it from her and told her to sit. She closed the lid on the toilet and did as she was told. He ran the comb through small strands until all the tangles were gone. While he worked, he asked, "How did you know it was me?"

"I wasn't sure at first. Once I transitioned, I started following you all, because I refused to believe my mate was human. I knew it wasn't Gregor, because he was Tessa's mate. There aren't that many of you who go out in public as much as you and Julian. Geoffrey keeps to the gym, and I don't work out. One day, you were giving a press conference about a new building your family had designed and erected. You passed by me afterwards, and it was all I could do not to tackle you right there on the sidewalk. I thought back to the times I'd seen you before that and remembered sitting close to you at Giovani's. You eat there a lot."

"If you know I eat there a lot, you must too," Nik said and nudged her with his knee. "I wish you would have tackled me. It would have made the last three years so much more enjoyable. Plus, it would have explained why I felt so off kilter at random moments."

"Like I said, JoJo can be pretty convincing, but I think his days of telling his adult children what to do are over." Sophia stood and faced him, placing her hands on his shoulders. "Do you forgive me?"

Her beautiful blue eyes were wet with unshed tears. Nik set the comb on the counter and snaked his arms around her waist. He touched his lips to her forehead and whispered, "I forgive you." Sophia ran her fingers through his hair and pulled his head down to hers. She pressed their lips together. Nik allowed her to take control. He wanted nothing more than to rip her clothes off and make their bond official, but she had been through a traumatic experience, and he would wait until she was ready.

A pounding on the bedroom door interrupted their moment. Tessa said, "Is everything okay in there? I don't hear wild monkey sex, so you need to get your asses out here."

"Red, leave them alone. They'll come out when they're ready," Gregor chastised his mate.

"We're coming," Sophia responded. She scrunched up her nose at Nik. "She's a little crazy."

"I heard that," Tessa yelled from the living area.

They both laughed. Nik wasn't ready to share Sophia with the rest of their families, but now that she was safe, they needed to locate her parents. He asked her, "Are you ready to go out there?"

Sophia twisted her damp hair and secured it on top of her head with a clip. "Now I am."

SOPHIA allowed Nik to lead her into the living area. His fingers were entwined with hers, and she never wanted to let go. He was her lifeline. He was her life, period. She was grateful he forgave her for keeping their being mates a secret. She wasn't sure she'd be as forgiving. All talking ceased as they entered the room. She felt like a specimen under a microscope. Everyone started asking questions at the same time, so she held up her hand. "I'm hungry. I've eaten slop for however long I've been gone. How long *have I* been gone? What's the date?" she asked Nik.

He let go of her hand and wrapped his arm around her shoulder. "Today is the twenty-fourth. You were gone for three weeks."

Sophia soaked in the information. She knew it could have been a lot worse. "Who do I have to thank for getting me out of there?"

"Keene," Xenia answered.

Keene frowned and added, "My father to be precise."

"I am in debt to your father then." She looked up into the face of her mate and told him honestly, "I knew you would try to find me, but I had given up hope. I thought I would die in that place."

"Egyptian laws suck. Their judicial system is nothing like it is in the States. But I would never have stopped until I had you back." Nik kissed her temple. He had to be a little disappointed that he wasn't the one to break her out of jail. As her mate, he would feel she was his responsibility. She had lived with a Gargoyle and a half-blood long enough to know how the males thought.

"I haven't eaten anything with substance or taste for three weeks. I could really go for something with a little flavor to it. I know you all have questions. So do I. If someone will feed me, I will tell you all about what I remember. Then you can fill me in on everything that's happened here."

Nik led her to the table and pulled out a chair. "What would you like to eat?"

"Pizza. Tacos. A cheeseburger and fries. Make those chili cheese fries. Bacon. Lots of bacon."

Nik smiled. "And which one do you want the most?"

"All of them." Everyone laughed, but she was serious. "Whatever you have is fine. I doubt I can eat a lot anyway considering I was given so little these last few days." She probably should have kept that tidbit to herself, because Nik's claws popped out and his breathing came faster. "Stop, Nik. Calm down. It's over. I brought it on myself. If I hadn't gone off alone, I wouldn't have gotten arrested."

Nik did retract his claws, but he didn't immediately calm down. He retreated into the kitchen and stuck his head in the refrigerator. While he was looking for something to feed her, Tessa asked, "So, who killed the guard?"

"I did." When everyone began speaking at the same time again, she held up her hand again. "It was self-defense." Nik growled louder and slammed the door. He moved so fast she gasped when he knelt in front of her. She placed her hands on his face. "Gorgeous, he didn't hurt me. I stopped him before he could. I'm not going to tell you everything that happened if you keep this up. Can you remain calm?"

"It depends on what you tell me. If you tell me someone hurt you, I'm going to kill them."

"I already took care of that. Now, are you going to feed me or what?"

Tessa offered, "Nikolas, I'll find her something to eat. Why don't you two sit on the sofa so you can be close? I have a feeling it's the only way we're going to get to hear her story."

"That's a great idea." Sophia stood from the chair and took Nik's hand. Instead of letting her sit beside him, he pulled her down onto his lap. She snuggled in and told them everything that happened to her from the time Beatrice kissed Nikolas on the sidewalk to being released from prison. Nik tensed up a few times during her recollection, but she squeezed his hand, and he kept quiet.

She took bites of food when someone asked her a question. Eating slowly was helping her digest the bacon and egg sandwich Tessa had fixed for her. It wasn't as spicy as she wanted, but her stomach probably would have resisted if it had been.

Sophia needed to know exactly how close to death she'd been, so she turned to Nik. "I have to tell you something. It's more a question, but I need to know… There were a couple of times I felt my shifter speaking to me. That's never happened before, so I'm thinking it might have been my imagination. When I was at my weakest, I thought I heard you talking to me in my mind. Was I dreaming that?"

Nik grinned. "It wasn't me."

"So, I was going crazy."

"No, I didn't say that. I said it wasn't me. Somehow our shifters were connected. If it hadn't been for yours talking to mine, I'd never have known for sure you were in prison. Xenia and Zeke had a feeling that's where you were, but we couldn't get anyone to give us any information. Even the American Embassy was helpless in finding out anything. In all my years, I've never heard of the shifter being separate from the body; I always assumed we were one and the same. I could hear what was being said, but it wasn't *me* talking. That doesn't mean we're the only ones; I just haven't heard of it before now.

"Dante found Isabelle's son through their minds. They aren't related by blood, and he and the boy had never met one another. Dante and Isabelle hadn't completed the bond either, but somehow Connor and Dante communicated with each other."

"What are you talking about? Isabelle doesn't have a son." Sophia knew she'd been out of the loop for a few weeks, but that was something she would have known before now.

"I told you a lot has happened while you were gone. I think it's our turn to fill you in. Yes, Isabelle has a son. Alexi was his biological father. Also, Alexi didn't die when he went overboard all those years ago. He hid out until after Isabelle returned to the States."

"Where is Alexi now?"

"At the bottom of the sea," Tessa answered. "It's an interesting story, but one that can be told over beer and pizza once we find Sam and Monica."

"Agreed. Have you learned anything new that will

help us find them?"

They filled her in on the photos that were sent to Rafael, and Nik set her on the sofa while he retrieved his stack. "We aren't sure when these were taken, but Julian has done an excellent job of cleaning them up and enlarging them. With the glyphs visible in the background, we're hoping they will lead us to the location."

Xenia stood. "Keene has to get back to work. I'm going to have him drop me at home so I will have access to my father's journals and manuscripts. If only he'd have documented his findings electronically, I could share them with you. I will not stop until I have searched every last shred of information."

Everyone stood and said their goodbyes. Sophia held out her hands to Keene. Nik, who had his front to her back, growled low, but she elbowed him in the stomach. She took Keene's hands and said, "I will never be able to thank you for the debt, whatever it may be." She squeezed his hands then released them. Her aunt's mate inclined his head to her before ushering Xenia out the door. When they were gone, Sophia asked, "What exactly does Brock Tyson do for a living that he was able to get me out of an Egyptian prison?"

"He's an arms dealer," Nik said.

"Oh, shit." Sophia had a bad feeling about the conversation she'd overheard between the elder Tyson and Keene. "I heard Keene and his father talking. He owes his father for his help, and I doubt it's something as simple as mowing the lawn."

"Keene acted freely. He knew what he was doing,"

Tessa said.

"Doesn't mean I have to like it. But it's done, so let's get busy."

Chapter Twenty-Three

NIK kept an eye on Sophia while everyone worked on their own computers researching the hieroglyphs in the photos. She drank lots of water, and when it came time for supper, she cleaned her plate. Her mood was positive, and her spirits were high considering what she'd been through. Nik was proud of his mate for the way she was handling what happened to her. He kept waiting for the reality to sink in and for her to come crashing down. So far, it hadn't happened.

When she couldn't stop yawning, he told the others he was putting her to bed. They said goodnight, and Nik carried his mate to their bedroom.

"I can walk, Nikolas Stone."

"And I can carry you, Sophia Brooks." He placed her on her feet when they passed over the threshold and closed the door. Nik pulled the covers back on the bed and removed his clothes. He left his boxer briefs on so Sophia wouldn't get the wrong idea. Not that making love to his mate would be wrong. He was ready. No, he was beyond ready to make her his in every way, but he wasn't going to push it. She would let him know when she was ready.

Sophia removed her clothes with the exception of her panties. They stood facing each other, neither one moving, both drinking in the other's body. She had lost weight while in prison, and she hadn't had any extra to lose. Still, she was the sexiest female he'd ever laid eyes on, and that had been a lot of females. He prayed her experience in the sex department was lacking. He couldn't stand thinking of her with other men. Yeah, that might be hypocritical, but he didn't care. He was over five hundred years old. Sophia wasn't even thirty. He wanted to be the one to teach her what a male wanted. Liked. Needed.

She closed the distance and traced over his pecs with her fingers. Nik wasn't as muscled as most of the other Gargoyles, but he was no slouch. He spent most of his time in the archives or behind a computer, not in the gym. Sophia's breasts weren't large, but they were more than enough for his liking. Her hands were long and slender, perfect for circling his cock which was coming to life with each inch of skin she skimmed across. She circled behind him and traced the area where his wings were hidden beneath the surface. With Sophia being a half-blood, he didn't have to hide what he was with her. Her fingers dipped lower, finding their way beneath the band of his briefs. She slid her hands along his hips, pushing the cotton down, exposing his ass. She continued until they were pooled around his ankles. Instead of speaking, she tapped at his feet, and he stepped out of his underwear.

Sophia was still behind him, but he could feel her breath on his skin. She ran her hands up his calves, past his knees, up his thighs. She placed her palms on the globes of his ass as she kissed each cheek. Her thumbs traced the crease, and he held his breath. He'd been with some adventurous women over the years, so he knew what it felt like to have his pucker breached. It felt good having his prostate massaged, but it wasn't something he expected Sophia to do. She didn't explore the area further. Instead, she stood and pressed her small breasts to his back.

His dick was now hard as stone, and his beast was roaring inside his head. ***She is our mate. Take her.***

Nik wanted sex to be Sophia's idea. Her choice. He didn't sense turmoil from her spirit. He was pretty sure her body had not been abused while she was in prison. She placed open-mouth kisses on his back as she snaked her arms around his waist. Her left hand fondled his nipple while her right hand continued its journey south. Once she reached the hair below his navel, she didn't stop until she had his hard-on in her hand. Her quick intake of breath meant he was smaller than she was used to, or he was larger than she expected. Hopefully, she wasn't disappointed. Nik's cock wouldn't win any awards, but it wasn't anything to be ashamed of either.

Sophia explored his length, her hand sliding up and down with little friction. She was going to kill him. He could see it now… death by cock torture. "Sophia…" He needed more.

"Am I doing it wrong?" she asked.

Nik froze. Had his bunny never stroked a cock before? "No, not wrong at all. Just squeeze a little tighter." She did as instructed, and the pressure was perfect. A low moan escaped Nike's throat.

Sophia increased her speed as she said, "It's so soft, yet hard at the same time."

Even though most of his blood was in Nik's small head, he had just enough in the big one to realize his mate had never touched a dick. There was no way his beautiful female could still be a virgin. Could she?

"Baby, if you don't stop, I'm going to come. Not

that that's a bad thing, but the first time I get off, I want to be inside you. I'm not pressuring you. We'll wait until you're ready."

Sophia stopped stroking and stepped around to face him. "I'm ready. I've been ready for three years, Nik. If you want to wait because I'm on my period, I understand. But I want you. I've dreamed of this moment so many times."

"Are you sure? Because I'm afraid I won't be able to keep my beast at bay, not until we're fully mated. He's already pushing me to be with you."

"I'm sure. I think they're talking to each other again. Mine's telling me to hurry the hell up," she said and scrunched her nose.

That was all Nik needed to hear. When he took a step closer, she placed a hand on his chest. "Give me a second." She went into the bathroom and closed the door. Less than a minute later, the toilet flushed, and the sink turned on. When she returned, her hair was down, and her panties were gone.

She was stunning standing before him completely bare. He would take his time fulfilling her needs after they were mated, but right now, he was going to seal the deal. He closed the distance and grabbed her around the waist. She gasped, but then she grabbed his head and pulled him in for a kiss. For her to be a sexual novice, his mate knew what she was doing with her mouth. Nik couldn't wait until it was sucking his cock down her throat. He picked her up by her hips and tossed her backwards onto the bed. She scooted up until her head was at the pillows.

Nik climbed on top of her and licked his way up

her stomach, pausing to kiss her scar. He took a hard nipple in his mouth and sucked. Sophia moaned, wiggling her hips against his. The friction of her mound against his cock had him ready to lose his load. He gave equal attention to the other nipple before clamping his mouth down on hers. After he ravished her tongue with his own, he said, "Tell me one thing, Baby. Are you a virgin?" He pushed her thighs apart and slid his cock down between her legs. He could smell her arousal mixed with her monthly blood.

"Yes. I know it's going to hurt, but I'm ready, Nik. I want you to bite me when you penetrate me the first time. Please?"

"You're ready to be my mate then?" Nik continued sliding his erection through her slickness. "Ready to spend the rest of our lives together? For better and even better than that? In health and wealth? Giving me lots of beautiful little adventurous daughters and rowdy sons?"

"I'm ready," she husked as she pushed her hips into his, grabbing onto his shoulders. Her fangs were front and center, ready to give as well as receive the bond.

Nik moved his cockhead over her clit several times. Sophia groaned and closed her eyes. Her back arched and she begged, "Nikolas, please. Take me. Make me yours."

He placed the tip at her entrance. "Look at me." When she opened her eyes, he kissed her. Hard. He released her lips and dropped his fangs. When she nodded, he thrust into her wet core and latched onto her neck. She screamed his name right before she sank her own fangs into his shoulder. Her claws were scraping down his back, spurring him on. They released their fangs at the same time, but Nik didn't stop moving. Once he was balls deep in her pussy, he took up a steady rhythm, in and out. Her core was so tight, yet so slick. It was unlike anything he'd ever felt before.

"Baby, you are so godsdamn tight. You feel so fucking good." He searched her eyes for pain. He'd never been with a virgin before, but she was meeting him thrust for thrust. Her eyes were hazy with lust, and she was pulling at her nipples.

"And you're so big. I feel so full. Is it always this good?" she asked running her hands all over her chest, down to her pussy where she placed her fingers so she could feel him as he slid in and out.

"I imagine it will only get better for you. Me, however? I don't think it could ever be better than it is right now." And he was telling her the truth. He felt her core getting tighter. His mate was ready to get off, and he was going to be right there with her. "You ready to come for me, Baby?"

"Yes. Oh gods, Nik, harder. I'm… so… close…"

Nik kept his eyes on Sophia's face. He wanted to see what she looked like when she came apart. He whipped his hips faster, his cock deeper, hitting that spot that was going to do it for her. Her breathing became jagged, and she grabbed his biceps. Sophia hissed his name as her pussy shuddered around his cock. His own orgasm flowed through him as his lover squirmed beneath him. She was vocal and loud, and she was his. His bunny. His life. His love.

SOPHIA had died and gone to heaven. She was in bed with Nikolas Stone. He had not only taken her virginity, but he'd taken her blood. In more ways than one. She was now mated to the most gorgeous Gargoyle ever created. She closed her eyes and thanked the gods for creating him and the fates for choosing her to be his. She had waited for this moment for three long years. It had been worth the wait. Then again, if she hadn't listened to her grandfather, she could have been having wild monkey sex with this amazing creature all this time.

In the last few minutes, her future had taken a whole new direction. She had a life partner, and she was now part of the Stone Society. Having a Gargoyle family was one thing. Being part of the most powerful Clan in the States, possibly the world, was something totally different. Her family had just grown exponentially.

"Baby, are you okay?" Nik asked as he hovered over her, propped on his forearms. He kissed her nose, her cheeks, her eyelids.

"More than okay. I'm perfect," she purred.

"You sure are. Did I hurt you? I'm sure it had to hurt, being your first time, but I couldn't stop. You felt so fucking good, Baby."

"I might walk a little funny tomorrow, but no, you didn't hurt me. Can we do it again?" She didn't care how funny she walked. She was ready to have her mate filling her up, giving her more pleasure than she knew was possible.

"Already? You're going to kill me, woman." Nik laughed and rolled to the side. His cock was half-hard and all messy. She didn't care. That was their fluids mixed together. She couldn't think of anything more perfect than two beings fated to be together doing what they had only moments before. And if they got a little messy in the process? That's what showers were for.

"Oh, I thought with you being a big, bad Gargoyle, you'd be able to get it up again right away." She blinked at him and shrugged.

"I can, you little minx," he huffed. "I'm thinking of you and your fragile state."

Sophia laughed and ruffled his hair. "I don't think I've ever seen your hair this long."

"I've been a little busy, if you'll recall. Besides, I don't trust anyone here to give me a haircut. I'm afraid they'll mess it up and try to cover it up with a turban."

She laughed again. "I like it long. Gives me more to hold on to," she said as she grabbed a handful and used it to pull him to her. Nik growled and rolled on top of her, kissing her with lots of tongue. Sophia hadn't kissed a lot of men, but the few she had didn't come close to being as good as Nik. She could kiss him for days. When he rose up on his arms, he got a serious look on his face.

"What's wrong?" she asked as she pushed the hair back off his forehead. She really did like his hair longer.

"Was it good for you? Seriously. It was your first time, *and* we completed the bond."

"Oh, Nikolas. I already told you, I don't think it could be any better." Was her mate insecure? She knew this wasn't his first time, not that she really wanted to think about how experienced he was. Sophia had no problem stroking his ego. She would stroke his ego *and* his cock at the same time. He was one fine specimen of a Gargoyle. "Seriously," she mimicked, "if it gets any better for me, I'm not sure I can handle it."

"But you don't have anything to compare it to."

"No, but you do. Even if I did, I don't really want to compare past lovers. We're mated now, and like you said, for better and even better than that. If you thought I wasn't going to be better than past lovers, you shouldn't have mated with me."

"That isn't what I meant." Nik sat up and pulled her onto his lap. They really needed to take a shower. "I vow on my oath as a Gargoyle, that was the single best sexual experience of my life. The fates couldn't have chosen a better mate for me than you. This I swear." Nik fisted his heart and bowed his head to her.

She grabbed his fist and placed it over her own heart. "And I vow to you, Nikolas Stone, it was so much more than I expected, better than I dreamed. You are my perfect fit. My perfect mate."

CHAPTER TWENTY-FOUR

SOPHIA was sore, sleepy, and sated. After she assured Nikolas she was happy, they took a long, hot shower. While under the water, Nik lifted Sophia against the wall and had his way with her. It might have been at her request. After they bathed each other, they changed the sheets and talked. The last time Sophia glanced at the clock it had been almost three a.m. Now it was a few minutes past seven, and she was cocooned against her mate's chest. Not that she had a choice in where she slept. Nikolas had rolled her to her side and pulled her up against him, wrapping his arm around her. She woke up in the same position she'd fallen asleep in.

Sophia loved her grandfather dearly, but if she had only gone with her gut instead of his paranoid ravings, she could have been enjoying this type of sleeping arrangement for years. Now if she could find her parents, her life would be absolutely perfect. Nik's morning wood was nestled between her legs. If she wasn't on her period, she'd scoot herself back onto his erection and give him a proper good morning. Instead, she decided on a different type of wake-up call. She slid down the bed and rolled over so she was face to face with the object of her body's affection.

Sophia had read about blowjobs and watched them being given on videos. Being a virgin, she wanted to at least have some knowledge of how to please her mate. She was curious as to how a dick would feel on her tongue, but more specifically how the semen would taste. It couldn't be any worse than the slop she'd eaten in jail. The women in the videos didn't seem to mind it.

Instead of studying his erection any longer, Sophia decided to go for it. She stuck the tip of her tongue to the slit where liquid was glistening. It was a little salty, but kind of bland. She licked the tip again, and his cock jerked. When it did, she pulled her head back, waiting to see if it would happen again. When it stayed still, she decided to put the head in her mouth. She sucked on the end before sliding it farther back on her tongue. When she felt she was getting the hang of it, she remembered how she'd seen it done on videos and began emulating the pros.

Nik grabbed a handful of her hair and stopped her motion. She pulled off his cock and looked at her mate. "Good morning?" she tested. Maybe he didn't like being woken up that way.

"Morning, Baby. Let me turn over. Easier access to the goods." Nik rolled onto his back and bent one leg at the knee. He was right. She could get to him better this way. Sophia scooted closer and returned to sucking her mate. He didn't release his grip on her hair. If anything, it tightened. When she got comfortable with the depth, she tried to take him a little bit farther in. His cock hit the back of her throat, and she gagged a little. She tried it again, this time breathing in as it got close to her tonsils. Much better. The saliva was pooling in her mouth, so she swallowed around his dick. Nikolas moaned and grabbed her hair even tighter. Her mate liked that.

"Sophia, Baby..."

She didn't remove her mouth, but she did look up into his face. She raised her eyebrows and mumbled, "Hmm?"

"You are too fucking cute for your own good. And too good at sucking dick, too. I'm about three good swallows away from coming. If you don't want me shooting down your throat, you need to pull off now and finish with your hand."

"Mmm hmm," she replied and went back to work. She wanted him to shoot down her throat. This was her mate, and Sophia wanted to please him in every way possible. If that meant swallowing his little swimmers, she would. He was wrong, though. It only took her swallowing around his dick two more times before he lost it. When he was pulsing in her mouth, he held onto her head, keeping her from pulling off. She didn't mind it. She actually thought it was kind of hot in a caveman sort of way. When Nik was spent, he let go of her hair. She slid his dick out of her mouth, but not before she placed a kiss on the head. "There you go, little fella," she told his penis.

"Little fella? You trying to give me a complex, woman?" Nik put his arms behind his head and studied her.

Sophia wiped the slobber off her mouth before informing her mate, "He is little now. Deflated. Used up. Give me a minute, and I'll remedy that. Then he'll be big fella." She winked at him as she slid up his body. When he still didn't smile, she licked his nipple before biting at it. Nik squirmed beneath her and flipped her onto her back.

"Uh uh. No, ma'am. You've already had your wicked way with me. Now it's my turn."

Nikolas latched onto one of her nipples right as his phone rang. "Fuck, me."

"That's what I was going to do, but you so rudely fli... ahhhh," she screamed as he bit her nipple.

"Hello? You are? Shit, I'll open the gate. Hang on." Nik thumbed off his phone. "Julian's here," he said and rolled out of bed. He slid his jeans on commando and headed for the door. Before he got there, he came back, kissed her hard, and said, "Julian's here!"

Sophia pulled the covers up over her breasts and smiled. She had heard in Nik's voice how much he cared for his brother, but seeing the joy on his face made it perfectly clear how glad he was to have him there. Nik had told her how he and Julian spent all their time together. He also assured her that she was first in his life now. She promised him that she was happy he had someone so close.

She knew it was pointless to stay in bed, so Sophia went into the bathroom and freshened up. Once she was dressed, she made her way toward the sound of men talking and laughing.

As soon as she stepped foot into the living area, Nik's gaze found hers, and he held out his hand. Sophia went to him without delay. He kissed her on the temple before introducing her to his brother. "Julian, this is my mate, the troublemaker."

She slapped him on the stomach and laughed. "It's good to finally meet you."

Julian fisted his heart and bowed low. When he uncurled his body, he said, "On my honor. I'm sorry it took me so long to get here."

"But you're here now, Brother. Come on, I'll show you to your room." Nik was literally bouncing on the balls of his feet.

Sophia grinned at her mate. "I'll put some coffee on and see what we have for breakfast." By the time she had the coffee maker going, everyone else was awake and in the living room. Tessa stopped in the doorway, grinning.

"What?" Sophia asked.

"I know that look," Tessa said, crossing her arms over her chest.

"What look?" Sophia played innocent, although there was nothing innocent about what she wanted to do to her mate. She was ready to haul his gorgeous ass back to bed.

"The sated mate look. I see it every time I look in the mirror."

Sophia grinned. She couldn't deny it. Besides, everyone probably heard them when they made the bond official. Nikolas might have roared. "Yeah, but just think; we both could have been wearing these goofy grins for years now if we hadn't listened to JoJo."

"About that. Why didn't you tell me you had transitioned? I would have helped you through it."

Sophia didn't want to lie to her cousin, but she wasn't ready to tell her the truth either. "You were out of town when it happened. It took me a while to figure out who my mate was. When I finally did, I didn't mention it then because I couldn't go after Nik. At least not until the Gargoyles knew about us."

"Well now they know. I can't believe how you, Isabelle, and I are all mated to Di Pietros. Talk about the fates keeping it in the family."

"Speaking of Isabelle, how is she? I know firsthand about being kidnapped. It sucks."

"She's wearing the sated mate grin, too. And now, she has Connor with her full time. She'll be happier when Maria is up and around. It'll take some time to get over losing Rico, but she's tough. And she has Dante. He's like the Gargoyle whisperer. One touch and you're calm."

Nik and Julian returned from the back of the villa and poured themselves a cup of coffee. Sophia opened the fridge. The cool on her front was overridden by the heat on her back. Nik was behind her. Right behind her. She glanced over her shoulder and cocked an eyebrow. "Is there something I can assist you with?"

He bounced his hard-on against her ass and grinned. She shook her head and returned to the contents in front of her, pulling out stuff for omelets. She and Tessa set about making breakfast while the men talked about the photos. Sophia was glad to see Zeke fitting in with the full-bloods. They treated him as one of their own, because in truth, he now was. They all were whether JoJo liked it or not.

Once they finished eating, Zeke put the dishes in the dishwasher, and they all sat down with a laptop. Sophia grabbed the one she used most often. When she logged on, she noticed some of her folders were open. "What the hell?"

Nik grabbed her hand and rubbed his thumb across her knuckles. "I did that when you went missing. I was hoping I could find a clue as to where you'd gone. Please don't be mad."

"I'm not mad, Gorgeous, I'm just surprised you were able to get in, that's all. Nothing I have on here is a secret from you. You're the keeper of the gate for the

Gargoyles, so I would assume you want this information on the half-bloods. How did you get into my system?"

Nik thumbed over his shoulder at Julian. "He did it." She looked at Julian, and he shrugged.

"I'm impressed. Jonas can't even hack my system," she said as she put the folders back the way she had them.

"He's tried?" Julian asked.

"Yep. I had to have someone test it out. Who better than the mad genius?" Everyone laughed, because most of them knew she wasn't kidding.

"I do want to talk about all the information you have on the Clan, though," Nik whispered in her ear.

Sophia couldn't tell if he was mad or curious. She pulled back so she could see his eyes. He must have felt her uneasiness, because he kissed her on the nose and said, "Later."

Julian had numbered the photos so they could split them up. Sophia was trying not to cry as she studied the picture she was holding. It was hard not to focus on her parents, especially her dad. Theirs was a special relationship. She lit up around him much the same way Nik did around Julian. A thumb swept across her cheek. She blinked her eyes and kept the rest of the tears at bay. "I'm okay," she whispered. Nik smiled and returned to his own photo.

They had decided to order lunch when Zeke's phone rang. He looked at it and announced, "Xenia. Hello? You did? Okay, hang on. You're on speaker, go ahead."

Xenia's voice came over the small phone, but with

everyone in the room being a shifter, they could hear her with no trouble. "I think I found something. Look at photo seventeen. In the top left corner, there are several round glyphs. If I could get that blown up a little, I could be sure, but it looks like a drawing of the Cleopatra Disk."

While Julian began working frantically on his computer, Sophia looked closely at what her aunt was referring to. Julian said, "I have magnified the corner images and sent them to everyone's email. Xenia, yours, too."

"How did you get my email address?" she asked as a ding sounded over the phone.

Nik answered, "He's Julian. Just go with it."

Sophia studied the new version of the photo and said, "You're right, Auntie. It looks exactly like the artifact. But we still don't know what it means or where they are."

"Hold tight, little dove. I came across something in one of my father's journals that I'd never seen before. I've already scanned it in; I was waiting on an email address. Julian, I'll respond to the one you just sent, and if you would please, forward it on."

Within a minute everyone had the document she was referring to. "My father never mentioned anything about this particular expedition. After reading his notes, I think he was close to finding what he thought was Antony and Cleopatra's burial site. Sophia, I might know where your parents are."

CHAPTER TWENTY-FIVE

NIKOLAS prayed Xenia wasn't giving Sophia false hope. When they all calmed down, Xenia confirmed his suspicions. "Hold on everyone. I know the general area where my father was searching. The documents are dated 2035. That was twelve years ago. This same area has been used by rebels in recent years. It's a dangerous location. Probably one of the most dangerous in the country."

He interrupted her. "So what you're saying is this may not be where Sam and Monica are."

Sophia stood and walked over to the window. Nik followed her and wrapped his arms around her waist. She leaned her head back and said, "Something Xenia said stirred a memory... a map..." Nik didn't interrupt when she trailed off. He let her mind focus on what it was trying to recall.

Julian spoke up and told Xenia, "Thank you for this information. There is another matter we need to see to at the moment. If you don't mind, we'll call you back."

"Of course, I'll be waiting." The phone disconnected and the room was silent.

Nik said to the others, "I'm taking Sophia outside for a minute where she can concentrate." He led her out the front door onto the huge porch. They sat in one of the cushioned love seats, and he held her hands in his. "I want you to meditate."

"I don't know how."

"I'm going to give you a crash course. Now, get comfortable and close your eyes." Sophia leaned back, and he placed her hands in her lap. "I want you to pretend your mind is a filing cabinet. Separate the noises you hear and put them in the bottom drawer. Take your pain and put it in the middle drawer. Focus only on the memory from your past. I'm going to be quiet so you don't have to shove me somewhere."

Nik closed his own eyes and called his shifter to the front of his mind. *Can you sense her?*

Of course. But she doesn't need help. Sophia's mind is strong. Sharp.

Nik was still trying to wrap his head around the fact that he could communicate with the being inside. He'd always thought they were one and the same. He didn't mind it, though. Especially since it could speak to Sophia's shifter. Now that they were fully mated, they would be able to sense one another as well. He attempted something he'd never tried before; Nik concentrated on Sophia's mind. He did as he instructed her to do and focused only on his mate. At first, there was no connection. Then it was as if someone cracked a door to a theater. Nik was seeing snippets of something… a memory…

"Nik!" Sophia fussed. "I had it until you joined the party. How did you do that anyway?"

"You could feel me?"

"Of course. But you could have tiptoed instead of stomping around inside my head. Warn a girl next time."

"I wasn't sure it would work. I wasn't trying to invade your privacy, more like offering a boost of power."

Sophia grinned at him. "Gorgeous, I'm not mad. I

already told you, there is nothing I have to hide from you. Are we not partners now?"

"Yes, but—"

"No buts. You just surprised me is all. If you tell me you're going to join me in my thoughts, I'll try to open the door for you, if that's even possible."

Nikolas couldn't keep his hands to himself any longer. He pulled Sophia into his lap. She circled her arms around his neck and leaned in for a kiss. His dick thought it was play time and got hard. Sophia broke the kiss. "As much as I'd love to get naked with you right now, I need to look at a map."

"You remembered something, didn't you?" Nik kissed her nose and pushed her to her feet. He stood and grabbed hold of her biceps. He needed to touch her constantly. That was something he'd have to work on. Or not.

"I did. When I was sixteen, I confronted my mother about moving to New Atlanta with JoJo. She was looking at a map of Egypt. I didn't think too much about it at the time, but she had certain areas circled."

"And you think these areas have to do with where your parents are now?"

"I think if they don't, it's a pretty big coincidence, and I don't believe in coincidences."

"Neither do I. Let's go look at a map." He held the door open for his mate and asked Julian to pull up the map that corresponded to the area Xenia had referred to.

Sophia studied the map while Nik explained what was going on.

"Why would Monica have been studying a map of

Egypt? Tessa asked.

"Because, before she met Samuel, she was an archaeologist," Zeke replied.

Sophia stopped looking at the map. "How did I not know that?"

Zeke sighed. "This isn't my story to tell. When we find your parents, you need to ask them how they met."

Sophia stared at Zeke, but she was looking through him. Nik had a feeling when she found out what it was her uncle wouldn't tell her, it wasn't going to be pretty. "Sophia, the map?" he said, redirecting her thoughts.

"Julian, is there possibly an older map? The one my mother was looking at wasn't as modernized."

"Let me see what I can find." Julian tapped away and within a couple of minutes asked, "You mean like this one?"

Sophia stepped behind his chair and exclaimed, "That's it! That's exactly what my mother was looking at. She had this area here and this one here, circled," she said pointing at the screen.

Julian circled the areas on the map and saved it. "I'm emailing this to Xenia to see if it matches her father's documentations."

Nik didn't like the sound of the area they were discussing being overrun with rebels. He knew there was no way Sophia would stay behind when it came time to search. "If that is the area where we conclude your parents are being kept, I want to do a little recon before we all go traipsing over the sand and get shot at."

"I totally agree. While you males can fend for

yourselves, Tessa and I aren't equipped with that thick skin. Personally, I don't want to get shot. Being thrown in prison was bad enough," Sophia said.

Tessa nodded and said, "I like a good adventure as much as the next girl, but Sophia's right. We need to know what we're dealing with. We need to play this one by the book, so to speak. We can't go in fangs out, claws bared. We need to get our hands on some guns."

Gregor pulled Tessa to him and wrapped his arms around her. Nik knew what his cousin was feeling. The need to protect his mate was strong. Gregor said, "I hate to ask this since he's already in debt to his father, but could Keene get the guns from Brock?"

Julian stood from his chair and stretched. "Instead of Keene owing his father, why don't we just purchase the weapons? It's not like we don't have the money."

Nik agreed with his baby brother. "*If* it comes down to needing guns. The rebels might have moved on. We won't know until we scout the area."

"Zeke, what do you say about a little recon mission?" Julian asked. "I don't think Gregor and Nik will leave their females in our capable hands."

Nik laughed at his brother, but he was right. He loved Julian, and Zeke was Sophia's uncle, but there was no way he would trust her safety to anyone else right now.

"I say let's get ready."

While the two males were preparing for their trip, Xenia called and confirmed the circled areas on the map were indeed notated in her father's documents. "There's something else. I didn't think about it until now, but when my parents were killed, I was given access to a safety deposit box. The only item in the box was a slip of paper. On the paper were all sorts of numbers. Some looked like coordinates, but others were only random numbers."

"Did you ever look up the coordinates?" Nik asked.

"I did. They led to a location in the States. I was so distraught when I lost my father, I didn't pursue the information."

"Do you think those numbers are somehow connected to the location on the map?" Sophia asked.

"No, I don't think so, but I thought I'd mention them anyway."

"Why don't you send us the numbers, and we'll see what we come up with on our end," Tessa suggested. "We have some pretty powerful computer programs at our disposal."

"Is there any way to encrypt a photo? I don't want this getting into the wrong hands if it turns out to be something major."

Julian walked into the room and took over. "Xenia, this is Julian. I am going to email a program to you. Open it and install it on your laptop. When it's loaded, you will be able to send the photo to us."

Nik was the keeper of the archives for the Clan. It didn't take a genius to add names to a list. Julian was a different story. Nik was continually amazed at how intelligent his brother was. He had seen firsthand some of the things Julian had created, but to see him in action outside of the lab was always a joy to watch.

A few minutes later, Julian and Zeke were ready to go. The Stone Society jet was fueled and waiting for them at the airport. The flight to Luxor would get them close to where they needed to start. Julian and Zeke would scout the area and return as soon as possible. When Julian suggested he go ahead and search for Sam and Monica, Sophia emphatically said no. She needed to help search. Nik agreed, however reluctantly.

After the two men were on their way to the airport, the others opened up the email Xenia sent and studied the coordinates. There were several sets of numbers included. Sophia plugged the coordinates in the system while the others began deciphering the random digits.

"Holy shit. Holy fricking shit!" Sophia exclaimed.

Everyone in the room stopped what they were doing and came to her computer. "These coordinates? They're to my parents' place in New York. Why would Xenia's father have those in a safety deposit box?"

"Maybe he wanted her to find her biological family in the event something happened to him," Gregor offered.

"But why Dad? Why not JoJo or Caroline?"

"Well, your grandparents did give her up for adoption. And besides, Jonas is a little far out there sometimes," Tessa added.

"I thought the purpose of separating the siblings was for safety. Only Dad and Zeke knew about the others until you and I came along. I think there's more to it than that."

Nik kissed his mate on top of the head. "Don't worry about that now. Let's concentrate on these other numbers."

By the time Julian and Zeke had landed and checked into a hotel, Nik and the others were no closer to deciphering the numbers. They were tired of staring at a computer screen, so they decided to break for supper. "Do you think it's safe to go to a restaurant? I need to get out of here for a while," Sophia asked.

Nik couldn't imagine being stuck in a hole for weeks on end. Even though the villa was large, she still had to feel a little claustrophobic. "I think we can manage that. Between Gregor and me, nothing will happen to you."

The two couples showered and changed into more appropriate attire and headed downtown. They found a rooftop bistro where they could take in the crisp, fresh air while they ate. Nik kept an eye on Sophia's mood and heart rate. She was relaxed as she and Tessa swapped stories of being trained by Jonas. He and Gregor remained alert to their surroundings so the women could enjoy their evening out.

Once they finished their dessert, Nik stood and held his hand out to his mate. "May I have this dance?" Soft music floated across the air. Sophia grinned and placed her hand in his. He pulled her close and nuzzled her ear. "How many kids do you want?" he whispered.

"Fifteen," she replied without hesitation.

Nik pulled back and studied her face. When she laughed, he relaxed and pulled her close again. "I already owe you one spanking, woman. I do believe that calls for another."

Sophia continued to giggle. It was a sound he would never tire of hearing. "What is the first one for?"

"For running off to Egypt without me. For not telling me we're mates. For making me wait so long to sink my cock into your sweet…"

"Ahem," Tessa cleared her throat, smiling. "We can hear you."

Nik grinned and spun Sophia around, causing her to laugh louder. Gregor and Tessa joined them, and the two couples danced until the moon called to his spirit. He knew Gregor also felt it when his cousin closed his eyes and raised his face to the sky. Nikolas could not wait to get back to the States where he could spread his wings and soar.

Once back at the villa, the women went inside while Nik and Gregor lingered on the porch. Gregor clapped him on the shoulder and asked, "How is she?"

"Surprisingly, she's good. We talked at length last night about her ordeal, and she seems to be handling it really well. She's a tough one."

"It must run in their blood. Tessa's the same way. She almost died, and now she doesn't even mention it. The only thing that bothers her is she misses Tamian. She thought she saw him in Greece, and I almost wish she had. She pretends she's okay, but I can see the longing in her face when she glances at their picture."

"I can understand that. When we first came to the States and Jules and I lived apart, it was like part of my soul was missing."

Gregor nodded. "Same with me and Dante. Even though we've found our mates, we still talk to each other every day. I can't imagine if he up and moved with no contact whatsoever. Hopefully, Tamian will come back around. Tessa needs her brother."

After standing a few moments in silence, Nik was ready to get inside to his mate, but first he placed his hands on Gregor's shoulders. "I wanted to thank you for being here. It means a lot to me."

Gregor covered one of Nik's hand with his own and bowed his head. "Always, Brother."

Once inside, they went to their separate ends of the house. The women had already turned out the lights and gone to bed. Nik grinned the closer he got to their room. He was ready to give his mate that spanking.

CHAPTER TWENTY-SIX

NIKOLAS hung up from speaking with Julian. He and Zeke found the region Xenia sent them to. Rebels were still in the area, but it wasn't as heavily inhabited as it had been in times past. Julian suggested they contact Brock Tyson and purchase weapons. The Stone Society wasn't in the habit of doing business with arms dealers, but this was for their protection as well as keeping their true nature under wraps. It wouldn't do for the world to find out about the Gargoyles. Having Unholy running around was bad enough.

He returned to the bedroom where his beautiful bunny was sprawled out over the king-sized bed, taking her half in the middle. The shredded bedding was a glorious reminder of the way his mate reacted to him the night before. She admitted she had occasionally watched porn to learn what to do once they were finally together. To have been a virgin, Sophia was a quick learner. Nik was normally the aggressor in the bedroom, but with Sophia, he was enjoying lying back and watching his mate work him over. She had enjoyed receiving her spanking, but she hadn't hesitated in giving Nik a taste of his own medicine. At one point, his wings came out because she had him turned on so much. If they continued ruining the linens, he probably wouldn't get his security deposit back. Then again, he would buy stock in cotton if it meant they always had such an exciting sex life.

He hated to wake her up, but they had a rescue to plan. Julian wasn't able to get close enough to the hidden entrance to do any real recon, but the rebels were guarding something. The bed dipped as he sat next to Sophia. Nik ran his hand along her spine until it reached her panties. One more day, she assured him. Her periods only lasted three days at the most since she became a half-blood. He was ready for it to be over. As much as making love to her soothed his soul and fucking like rabbits soothed his beast, he couldn't wait to feast on her beautiful pussy. Speaking of rabbits, he remembered the gift he bought his first day there. He rose from the bed and opened the top dresser drawer.

"Soph, Baby, wake up." She rolled over onto her back, exposing her smooth, pale skin and her perky breasts. Nik adjusted his inflating cock and moved his eyes to her face. "I got you something."

She pushed her crazy bed hair out of her face and propped up on her elbows. "When did you go shopping?"

"When I first arrived, before I ran into Beatrice. I saw this in a shop, and it reminded me of you."

He placed the trinket in her hand. "It's not as cute as a bunny, but I thought it was pretty. Like you. Happy birthday, Baby."

Sophia's eyes misted as she stared at the figurine in her hand. "How did you know?"

"I have my ways," he said with a grin.

"Julian," Sophia muttered before she sat up and scooted into Nik's lap. "I don't care how you did it, I'll treasure it forever." Nik leaned in for a kiss, and she turned her cheek to him. "Ugh, let me brush my teeth."

"Nope. You're my woman, my mate. I don't care if you have morning breath, coffee breath, or cum breath. I'll always want to kiss you." He pushed her backwards onto the bed, took her gift from her hand and placed it on the nightstand. He slid his tongue into her mouth and gave her a proper good morning-birthday kiss.

"We'll celebrate your birthday the right way when we get home. For now, we have work to do."

After kissing her again, Nik left his mate to shower and dress while he whipped up a quick breakfast for everyone. When he heard the shower turn off, he waited four minutes before pouring a cup of coffee precisely the way Sophia liked it. As he was putting the milk back in the fridge, she padded into the kitchen. "Here you go," he said as he handed the mug to her. Sophia's eyes lit up like he'd given her another present.

"Happy birthday, Sophia," Tessa said as she and Gregor entered the room.

"Yes, happy birthday. Hopefully, we can give you a good present and get your parents back soon," Gregor added.

"Thank you. That would be a great present. When are Julian and Zeke getting back?"

Nik put everyone's plates on the table and said, "In a couple hours. They were getting ready to board the jet when I talked to Julian." Nik relayed the phone call, and he and Gregor talked about contacting Keene. The Gargoyles were used to their own appendages keeping them safe. In the past, they used swords against other Gargoyles, and in light of Alistair causing trouble for the Clan, they had recently taken up training again. Nik hadn't wielded a sword in a very long time, but he preferred it to an automatic weapon. He was old-fashioned that way.

By the time Julian and Zeke returned, Nik had reached out to Keene, who in turn contacted his father. Nik made it clear there was to be no favor owed by Keene; this was all on him. For the right amount of money, Brock agreed. He didn't ask questions about why they needed the weapons. Nik wouldn't have told him anyway. The fewer people who knew what they were up to, the better.

They spent the rest of the day going over maps and gathering supplies they would need for the trip. Each one would take a backpack with a flashlight, flares, a change of clothing, food, water, medical supplies, and a bedroll in case they needed to sleep. While the men were gathering supplies and retrieving the weapons, Sophia and Tessa put the food items together before cooking supper.

While they ate, Julian explained about the town right outside Luxor where they would begin their journey. He had already rented a small house there so they would have somewhere to convene should they get separated. They debated whether to go in during the daylight hours or wait until the cover of night. They all had advanced eyesight, and nighttime would give them the element of surprise. The only drawback was the noise the vehicles would make. Tessa argued the vehicles would be heard during the day as well. Either way, they were going to have to park and walk approximately a mile. They finally compromised and agreed on going in right before the sun came up. They would fly into Luxor during the early morning hours and begin before first light.

They called it an early night so they could attempt

to get some rest. Nikolas, however, got little sleep. He spent most of the night holding Sophia, watching her. Having his mate in his arms was a dream come true. The Gargoyles had all but given up hope on finding the one they would spend their lives with, but now that the fates had smiled on them, hope was restored. He thought back to all the women he'd bedded over his five hundred years, and he could no longer see any of their faces. They didn't matter. The only female who mattered was lying next to him.

What also mattered was how she was holding up mentally. Over the years, Nik had killed. Most of his victims were the Unholy who threatened the lives of humans. Unfortunately, he'd also had to take out humans who were just as bad as the Unholy. Humans without souls who were hell-bent on killing as many innocents as they could. He knew what it felt like to watch as the life bled out of someone, knowing he'd been the one to do it. Was Sophia really okay with the fact that she was responsible for ending someone's existence even if they'd tried to end hers? Or was she keeping it all bottled up inside, and one day it would come hurtling out when something triggered the memory? He would monitor her behavior without hovering. She probably wouldn't appreciate that.

He kissed Sophia on the cheek and rolled out of bed. Nik took his shower and headed to the kitchen to make coffee. Julian was standing at the counter, already sipping a cup. Nik said, "Good morning, Brother. I take it you couldn't sleep either?"

Julian shook his head. "No. I've been going over different scenarios and outcomes. The probabilities of this being the actual location where Sophia's parents are being kept are high. The likelihood of us getting them out with no casualties is low. My only concern is the women. Both of them have already been through a traumatic ordeal. I do not wish for this one to turn out the same, or worse."

Nik clapped his brother on the shoulder. "How well do you know Katherine?" Julian had spoken briefly to the female he now knew to be his mate before coming to Egypt.

"Not well, why?"

"I have a feeling she's going to be just as tough as Sophia and Tessa. She might not be a half-blood, but the fates are choosing females for us who are worthy of being our mates."

"Except for Frey. Abigail is a married, battered woman. I cannot wrap my head around that. Why would she be chosen for Frey? He's the toughest of us all, yet he was given someone he cannot have."

Nik refilled his coffee and sat down, cradling the cup between his hands. "Who says he can't have her? If she is being abused, he may be the one to save her. It might not be immediately, but I have a feeling they'll end up together. Somehow. We both know our brother has demons. Who better to help him face them than someone with demons of their own?"

"Truth. I hope it works out for them. All of them. Abbi's brother is caught in the middle of it as well."

"Frey will do the right thing," Gregor said as he entered the kitchen. He stuck his head in the refrigerator and came out with a carton of juice. He shook it then turned it up and drank it all down. He tossed the empty container in the trash bin before grabbing a coffee cup out of the cabinet. "As for our women, you know as well as I do there's no way either of them is going to stay behind. Sophia started this journey alone. She was willing to search for her parents with no help from anyone. Tessa was ready to come join her. Alone. They are tough and strong-willed, not to mention stubborn."

"You got that right," a sleepy Sophia said as she padded to where Nik was sitting. He turned his chair sideways, and she sat on his lap. She took a sip of his black coffee and scrunched up her nose as she swallowed. "This is my fight, and there's no way I'm not going."

Nik kissed her on her temple and said, "I wouldn't ask you to stay behind. I understand how important this is to you. Besides, if I left you behind, I wouldn't be able to concentrate. The last time we separated, things didn't turn out so well. Now, go take your shower, Baby. We need to leave soon." Nik urged Sophia out of his lap. If she sat there much longer, he would have to excuse himself to their bedroom. The amount of self-control it took to keep his dick in check around his mate was growing by the day.

He fixed her a cup of coffee the way she liked it and took it to her. Sophia was naked, adjusting the water temperature when he walked into the bathroom. He leaned against the door frame, admiring her body. He would never tell her she wasn't perfect, because she was, but if she gained a few pounds, it wouldn't hurt his feelings. She glanced over her shoulder and smiled when she saw the coffee.

"You are the best mate ever, Nikolas Stone." She took the mug from his hand and kissed him softly on the lips. "Thank you." She took a couple of sips before stepping into the shower. Nik left her to it and returned to the kitchen. He then filled both their backpacks so they'd be ready to go.

The men were gathered in the living area, drinking coffee and waiting on the women. Sophia and Tessa joined them a few minutes later. Both had their long hair French-braided and were dressed for an adventure. "Ready?" Julian asked.

They each grabbed a backpack and headed to the large SUV Julian had rented. Nik and Sophia climbed into the back seat, Gregor and Tessa took the middle row, and Julian slipped into the driver's seat. Zeke drove the van that contained their weapons. The trip to the airport was quiet. Nik put his arm around Sophia's shoulder and held her close. He wouldn't offer her false promises of bringing her parents home alive, but he did pray to the gods they found them safe and sound.

CHAPTER TWENTY-SEVEN

SOPHIA had never flown in a private jet before. Plush leather filled the cabin. Sofas lined the left side while fat captain's chairs filled the right. She couldn't imagine being rich enough to own something like this. Nik stepped up behind her and whispered, "It's pretty cool having our own jet, huh?" When she frowned at him, he said, "This is the Clan's jet. You are now part of the Clan, so technically this is yours, too." Sophia hadn't thought of it that way. She had her own money from working at the library, and as a watcher, she had her own account funded by the family.

Nik took her backpack and stowed it in the overhead bin with his. They took their seats so the pilot could take off. Once situated, Nik told her, "What's mine is yours."

"Even the Audi?" she asked, kidding.

"Baby, I'll buy you a brand new Audi or any other car you want."

Sophia didn't need a new car, but the idea of him buying her whatever she wanted made her heart swell. She had fairly simple tastes and didn't spend a lot of money on superfluous things other than books and good electronics. And bright shades of nail polish. One thing she was looking forward to was moving into his home with him. Her house wasn't small, but it wasn't suitable for a large family. She hadn't been kidding when she told him she wanted a bunch of kids. Sophia didn't want to start having babies just yet, but she didn't want to wait too long, either.

During the short flight, Julian asked questions

about their lives, but mostly, he was interested in Jonas. As a fellow genius, he was curious about the Gargoyle. Zeke spoke about his father, but was more guarded than Sophia and Tessa. They were forthcoming with stories of training with him and learning in his lab. Before she knew it, they were landing. Instead of stopping on the tarmac, the plane rolled into a private hangar so they could unload the weapons without bringing attention to what they were doing. Once they departed the plane, they transferred their equipment into a large van and climbed inside. It amazed Sophia how Julian had arranged everything so quickly in a foreign country.

As they drove to where the rebels were camped out, Julian pointed out the road that led to the house he'd rented. He gave them the address, told them what the house looked like, and informed them there was a security system in place. They each had the code to the alarm, and they knew where Julian had hidden a key. They had no need to stop there now, so he continued driving. When they were approximately a mile out from the rebel camp, they parked the van and got out. It was still dark out, but the moon was waning toward new and lent its light over the sand. The terrain was hilly which gave them an advantage. Everyone was dressed in khaki from head to toe. Their backpacks were military issue camouflage, so they also blended in with the area. The weapons were black, but hopefully by the time they were close enough to be seen, the rebels would already be taken out of action.

The plan was for the men to go in first while the women remained on a hill watching. Since the males were Gargoyles, they could disarm the rebels without getting harmed. Sophia and Tessa were equipped with both regular and night vision scopes even though they had excellent eyesight. On the off chance a rebel got away from the men, the women could shoot at them.

Sophia surprised them all when she checked and loaded her own rifle. Everyone except Tessa. They both had trained with numerous weapons over the years. As watchers, they never knew what kind of situation they'd be thrown into. Even Ezekiel had been impressed. Sophia smiled to herself as Nik watched her, his mouth agape. So far, he knew her to be the mousy librarian. He had seen a little of her adventurous side when she was disguised as Beatrice and Clara. Now, he was going to see what his mate was really made of. Gregor grinned at Tessa and rubbed his ass. What the hell was that about?

The hike to the rebel camp took about thirty minutes. They stopped several times to listen and make sure they were the only ones in the area. When Julian and Zeke did recon the day before, the two of them had been able to get close without being spotted. Once their group was about seventy-five yards out, Sophia and Tessa chose separate vantage points to watch the males from. Sophia kissed Nik, and without speaking aloud, told him to be careful with her eyes and her lips. He tugged the long braid hanging over her shoulder, then took off with the other males toward the caves.

Since Julian and Zeke hadn't ventured into the hole in the side of the hill, they didn't know who or what they would find inside. It could be the tombs Xenia had sent them to, or it could just be caves where the rebels were camping. Sophia settled into the sand on her stomach and waited. If Nikolas were a human, she would be scared. Since he was a Gargoyle, she was calm. Unless the rebels surprised the males with swords, they were safe. She glanced over at her cousin, who was also on her stomach. While the males were carrying automatic weapons, she and Tessa had chosen long range hunting rifles. Tessa was looking through the scope of her gun, finger tapping the trigger guard.

Sophia chose to watch through her binoculars so she could keep an eye on the surrounding area. She was quick enough that if one of the rebels was to get away, she would still be able to set her sights on him and take a shot. Scanning the area, she observed several dirt bikes and a couple of SUVs parked haphazardly away from where the rebels had made camp. A narrow road led away from the site. The four males separated and went in from different angles. There were seven rebels outside the entrance. The goal was to disable the rebels, not kill them, since they were at an extreme disadvantage.

Daylight was breaking, and the guards should be rousing soon. The Gargoyles didn't hesitate in making quick work of subduing the rebels. Only one of them woke before he was rendered unconscious, but Gregor had him in a choke hold that would make any professional wrestler proud. Unless someone deep inside the cave came outside, their group now had the advantage.

Nik motioned to the women, and they stood and made their way down the embankment to where the males were dragging the rebels away from the entrance. They quickly bound the guards' hands and feet before placing gags in their mouths. Julian had gone ahead into the cave to stand sentry. If there were more rebels inside, they didn't want to be caught unaware. Before following, Sophia strapped the rifle over her shoulder and removed a handgun from the holster at her hip. The rifle was good for long range, not close quarters.

They entered the mouth of the cave and met up with Julian. Torches were lit and placed in metal holders along the inside corridor. Sophia didn't have to be an archaeologist to know this was not some rough cave the rebels were using as a hideout. The inner walls were smooth, and the floor sloped much like those in the Valley of the Queens. The farther they walked into the tomb, the thinner the air became. The smell of urine and feces wafted through the hallway. Sophia prayed it was a good sign that the odor was strong.

In front of the group, Julian stopped, holding up a fist. The corridor split off into a tee. Julian pointed at Gregor, Tessa, and Zeke, indicating they should go right. She and Nik were to follow Julian to the left. Sophia was sandwiched between the two brothers, and she was okay with that. She wasn't of the mindset that everyone was created equal. The males had special skin and wings, thus making them virtually indestructible. She had enhanced senses, strength, and speed, but she could easily be killed. Sophia would gladly walk between her two protectors.

A low rumble of voices was coming from in front of them. They stopped and listened to guards yelling at each other. A loud whistle sounded, and one of the rebels yelled, "Get the prisoners out of here. We'll hold off the intruders." Julian barely had time to raise his weapon before shots were fired at them from around a corner. Nikolas put himself between Sophia and the gunfire, so she placed her back to his in case there was someone coming at them from behind.

Between shots, Nik asked, "Do you hear that?"

Sophia had to strain, but the sound of a vehicle starting caught her ears. "Shit! They're getting away." She didn't wait on Nik or Julian. She ran as fast as her shifter legs would take her, returning the way they'd come in. Tessa was right behind her. The rapid sound of automatic weapons blasted where she'd left Nikolas, but she didn't slow down. He could take care of himself. When she reached the mouth of the cave, she stopped and poked her head around the corner, Tessa at her back. The rear door of one of the SUVs was being shut. Right before the door closed, Sophia saw the silhouettes of two people on the back floor. The rebel who closed the door banged on the metal, indicating the driver should take off.

Sophia ran toward him, yelling at the car to stop. The rebel turned, gun raised. She didn't give him time to shoot first. She pulled the trigger on her already raised pistol. "They've got my parents," she yelled to Tessa. Sophia shoved the gun into the holster on her hip right as Nikolas and Gregor exited the cave.

"Sophia, what are you doing?" her mate yelled after her.

"Going after my parents. They're in that car," she yelled as she reached one of the parked dirt bikes. Thankful she had studied all kinds of motorcycles,

Sophia reached under the seat and turned the fuel switch on. Tessa was right beside her, slinging a leg over her own bike. Nik and Gregor had caught up with them.

"Dirt bikes?" Nik asked.

Sophia said, "It's more reliable than a camel." She smirked at him right before she kick-started the bike. She rolled on the throttle, getting impatient. "Are you coming?"

Nik shook his head and muttered, "Lara fucking Croft."

Gregor laughed and said, "Pretty fucking sexy, if you ask me."

Sophia let off the clutch and slung sand behind her as she took off after the SUV. The vehicle wasn't too far ahead of them. Instead of going out the way that led to the main road, the SUV took off across the narrow road she had spotted earlier. While the vehicle was four-wheel drive, the sand still proved to be a deterrent. The dirt bike only fared slightly better in the loose terrain. Tessa was more proficient at riding since she had a motorcycle she rode all the time. Sophia had only ridden a few times. Still, she was holding her own.

The road turned into dirt, and the SUV started going faster. Visibility was minimal with the dirt being kicked up from the vehicle they were chasing. Gunfire sounded, and bullets riddled the ground in front of Tessa. The rebel in the passenger seat was leaning out the window and firing. Tessa banked hard to the right to avoid being hit, and the loose terrain caused her to lose control. She leaned with the bike, kicking the back end around so that she slid with the bike instead of flying over the front of it. Gregor stopped to check on her, but she yelled out, "I'm fine, keep going."

Nik sped up and was soon in front of Sophia. They kept to the driver's side of the SUV and closed the gap. Her mate yelled, "Are you sure your parents are in that vehicle?"

"I saw two people. If it's not them, someone else needs rescuing."

Nik shook his head but gave her a smile, and Sophia took that as a good sign. When Gregor caught back up, Nik asked his cousin, "What do you say we have a little fun?" Gregor grinned, obviously knowing what his cousin had in mind. Nik told Sophia, "Back off a little. I don't want you getting shot."

When she nodded, Nik and Gregor opened the throttle and closed the gap between them and the SUV. Nik was on one side, Gregor the other. Nik let his wings unfurl and pointed the motorcycle toward the loose sand to the left. As he rose into the sky, the dirt bike teetered a couple of times before coming to a stop on its side. Gregor did the same thing on his side of the vehicle. By that time, Tessa had dusted herself off and caught up with Sophia.

The women kept their distance in case the SUV decided to make any sudden stops. Gregor didn't bother dodging the bullets coming from the rebel on the passenger side. They bounced off his thick skin as he pulled the man through the open window. He held the man in one hand while wrenching the rifle away with the other before tossing the rebel to the ground. As Gregor flew back to the SUV, he rendered the weapon useless, tossing it to the sand.

His wings disappeared right before he opened the door and got inside. On the driver's side, Nikolas was holding onto the door frame, punching the driver through his open window. Nik let go and hovered above the vehicle as the door flew open and the driver was sent flying across the sand. The SUV rolled to a stop. When Sophia and Tessa got close, they turned the bikes off and put the kickstands down. Gregor climbed out of the SUV smiling. Nik's wings disappeared behind him, leaving only a shredded shirt.

Sophia ran to the vehicle and opened the back door. Two unmoving bodies were on the floorboard, their heads covered with black cloths like the one she'd been forced to wear. She climbed in and removed the first hood. She sucked in a breath and cried out, "Dad!" Her father was unconscious, but he had a pulse. She removed the second hood, grateful to find her mother was also alive. "We need to get them medical attention." Tessa climbed in beside her and started checking them out.

Sophia laid her head on her father's chest and let the tears fall.

CHAPTER TWENTY-EIGHT

THE hum of tires turning over the ground alerted Nikolas to the fact that they had company. He and Gregor placed their bodies in front of the door, but relaxed when they saw it was Julian and Ezekiel. The two males exited their vehicle, Julian shaking his head. "I see I've missed the fun again," he said pointing to his brother's shredded shirt.

Nik grinned. "Hey, someone had to have our backs."

"Is that Sam and Monica?" Zeke asked, looking at the bodies in the back of the SUV.

"Yes. They're both alive, but we need to get them to a doctor," Tessa said as she climbed out of the back of the vehicle while Sophia remained inside with her parents.

"Are there any rebels left?" Nik asked Julian.

"No, we took care of the rest of them. Let's get Sophia's parents to the rental house. I'm going to call Brock Tyson and see if he knows of a doctor who makes house calls."

Zeke looked in on his brother and sister-in-law and squeezed Sophia's hand. "They're tough, just like you." He moved aside, and Nik climbed into the cramped back with Sophia, wishing the second row of seats wasn't there. Gregor angled into the driver's seat with Tessa riding shotgun. Julian and Zeke went back to the other SUV and led the way.

When they arrived at the point where they'd hidden the rental SUV, Julian and Zeke quickly swapped the rebel's car for their own. Before driving off, Julian handed the medical supplies over to Tessa who passed them to Sophia and Nik in the back. While they rode the rest of the way to the house, Sophia composed herself and began cleaning the dirt and blood off her parents' faces and arms. There were no cuts they could find on their skulls. The blood appeared to be from minor facial lacerations.

Nik took one of the wet wipes and used it on Sophia's sand-covered face. "You were amazing back there," he praised his mate. "Where did you learn to ride a motorcycle?"

"Yes, where did you learn that?" Tessa asked.

Sophia didn't look at her cousin. She kept her focus on her parents when she responded, "Did you never wonder why the mileage on your bike was off?"

Tessa gasped. "You didn't!"

Nik was gaining another level of appreciation for his mate. She was a sneaky little wench. Sophia glanced up at him and winked. "Oh, I did. But I always filled her back up. I even changed the oil once or twice." From the front of the SUV, Tessa let out a string of curses that would make the most seasoned sailor blush. Nik was now glad there was a row of seats between the two women.

When they arrived at the house, Nik helped Sophia down before reaching for her father. He carried Sam, and Zeke grabbed Monica. They took Sophia's parents into the house and placed them side by side on the master bed. Julian entered the room and informed them a doctor was on the way. "It's good to know an international criminal," he said seriously.

Sophia sat on the bed beside her father, holding his

hand. "Dad, it's me, Sophia. You're going to be fine. You and Mom are safe. We need to get you checked out and get some food in you."

Nik sat in the only chair in the room and prayed to the gods his mate was telling her father the truth. Considering they hadn't found Sam and Monica in the room where they were being held, Nik had no idea of the conditions they'd endured for the last month. Sam was a half-blood, so he would be stronger than his wife and able to withstand harsher circumstances, such as not being fed or given water. Monica was human. If she had not been given the proper sustenance, her body could be withering away inside. As Nik thought on these things, Julian entered the room accompanied by a man and woman.

"This is Dr. Ausar," Julian said, introducing the doctor, but the older man didn't speak. He placed his black leather bag on the bed and pulled out a stethoscope. He listened to both their hearts and checked their vitals. Nik could have told him what he would hear, but that would mean explaining to the foreigner how Nik knew it.

The woman remained off to the side of the room until he spoke to her. "Start both of them on an IV. Draw blood so I can determine if they have been drugged." The woman nodded and got busy. Sophia moved out of the way and came to stand beside Nik's chair. The doctor told her, "I will do everything I can for your parents. Until I get the bloodwork back, I will not be able to tell you if they are going to be okay."

"I understand. Thank you for coming out here," she said.

"Mr. Tyson is a friend of mine. When he calls, I do not say no."

Nik pulled Sophia down onto his lap. He needed to have his arms around her, to be touching her. He had told her the truth earlier when he said she was amazing. It didn't mean he hadn't been scared for her safety. She put the well-being of others before herself, even when she hadn't been one hundred percent sure the people they were rescuing were her parents. Her body was tense, but he couldn't blame her. Sam and Monica still weren't out of the woods.

Tessa stuck her head into the room. "Hey, Soph, why don't you take a shower?"

Nik agreed that a shower would feel good. They were both still covered in sand. She surprised him when she nodded. "Yeah, a shower would be nice." Zeke took their place sitting beside Sam.

When they stepped out into the hall, Sophia asked Tessa, "Are you going to throttle me?"

Tessa laughed. "No, since you changed the oil, I'll let it slide." Nik had a feeling Tessa wouldn't have been so lenient had Sophia's parents not been in bad shape.

Nik followed her to the other bedroom where their backpacks were waiting on them. Sophia unzipped her bag and stared inside at the contents. When she stood unmoving, Nik pulled her hands away and wrapped his arms around her. "Are you okay?" He already knew the answer, but he wanted her to be honest with him.

Sophia grabbed the front of his shredded shirt and buried her face in his chest. "No," she mumbled. Nik put his cheek to the top of her head and held his mate. "I'm here for you. No matter what happens, we'll get through this. Your parents are strong. They have their love for each other, and they have you. Love's a powerful thing, Baby." She leaned back and puckered her lips. Sophia looked like a silly fish, and Nik obliged with a pucker of his own. He loved how even in the face of possible adversity, she kept her sense of humor. Another reason she was his perfect match. "Come on; let's get cleaned up so we can get back to your parents. You go start the shower, and I'll get your clothes."

They didn't linger in the shower, not with a houseful of people and her unconscious parents in the next room. They worked quickly to wash the sand and grime from their bodies and hair. Once they were dried off and clothed, Nik detangled Sophia's hair for her. It was something he hoped to do for his mate every time she took a shower. "You need to teach me how to do that braid thing you did earlier."

"You want to braid my hair?" she asked, her eyes still closed. She didn't have to tell him she enjoyed what he was doing. The soft moans spoke volumes.

"Yes. I told you, I want to take care of you. Besides, when we have a little girl, I'm going to need to know how. Might as well get good at it before the time comes."

Nik didn't miss the smile that spread across Sophia's face when he mentioned a daughter. Of course, he wanted little boys too, but he couldn't wait to have a mini Sophia running around the house. Once Nik was finished with the comb, Sophia clipped her damp hair to the top of her head. They returned to the other bedroom where they found no change in her parents.

The rental house wasn't large enough to accommodate all of them, so Julian, Gregor, and Tessa planned to fly back to the villa. Zeke would stay with Sophia and Nikolas until there was a change in Sam and Monica. Julian left the SUV with them in case they needed to leave for any reason, and he and the others took a taxi to the airport. Sophia thanked them all for their part in getting her parents back. They assured her they were staying in Egypt until her parents were well enough to travel home.

Nik loved his family. He was blessed with a Clan full of brothers and cousins who always had each other's backs, no matter what. Speaking of brothers, he wondered how Frey was faring with his mate and her situation. He sent a quick text letting him know he was thinking about him. Nik didn't mention Sophia or her parents. He figured his big brother had enough going on in his own life without adding to it. He would be glad when all this was over and they were home together. Nik missed Sunday family day at the manor. He missed being around the others, the camaraderie they shared. He couldn't wait to get Sophia back to the States and share that part of his life with her. He was ready to share everything with her.

SOPHIA was thankful for Nikolas being by her side. He had no idea how much strength she was pulling from him. If her parents would wake up and talk to her, she would feel better about the situation. She and Zeke took turns sitting with them. The doctor returned the next morning to check their vitals and to give Sophia the good news. A drug was found in their system, but it was only something to knock them out temporarily. He suspected it was taking longer for them to wake up because of the lack of nutrition. Just as the doctor was readying his bag to leave, Sam started rousing.

Sophia rushed to his side. "Dad, can you hear me?"

"Sophia, where are we? Where's your…?" Sam saw Monica lying asleep next to him. "Oh, Monica." He grabbed her hand that didn't have the IV in it. "What happened? How did we get here?"

"Shh, Dad. Calm down, and I'll tell you what we know." She helped Sam slide up into a sitting position.

He pushed Monica's hair off her forehead before turning to his daughter. "Sophia, aren't you a sight for sore eyes. Zeke, Brother, what are you doing here? And that's…" Sam looked to where Nik was standing. "That's Nikolas Stone. Sophie, girl, you have some explaining to do."

"First off, Uncle Zeke is here because Tessa was in a pickle and couldn't come help me. Nik is here because he's my mate." Her dad started to protest, but she held up her hand. "Dad, stop. He's been my mate for three years; we've only made it official recently. Why don't you let the doctor look you over right quick? We have plenty of time to talk."

"No, I'm fine. Tell me what you know."

Sophia sighed, but relented. "I got a note telling me

you'd been taken, and if I wanted to see you again, I'd come to Egypt. So, I hopped a plane. When I arrived, I was given instructions to go to the zoo. I knew I was being followed, so while I was in disguise, I followed my followers. We ended up at the zoo earlier than planned, and I saw the clue being planted. When I was alone, I grabbed the clue; only it was an ancient artifact I needed help deciphering, so I went to see Xenia."

"Xenia, how's my girl?" Monica mumbled. Sophia was glad her mother was waking up, if somewhat groggily.

"Monica, Sweetheart, shh. It's okay. You're going to be okay. Get this IV out of me," Sam said as he began pulling at the catheter.

"Doctor! Dad, stop. Let the doctor do that." Sophia grabbed his hands as her mother continued to mumble. Her father was talking over her mother, trying to calm her.

The doctor entered the room and removed the IV. While he was working on Sam, Monica roused a little more.

"Mom, you're awake. Thank the gods," Sophia said as she rounded the bed.

"Sophia? What are you doing here? Where's Xenia?" Monica asked, clearly confused.

"Shh, Monica. You need to wake up, Sweetheart. Sophia's here. She found us."

Her mother blinked a few times. "Of course she did."

Sophia didn't miss the knowing look that passed between her parents. She waited until the doctor checked her mother over and removed the IV from her arm as well. When he was satisfied they both would be fine, he told them, "You both need rest and nourishment. The drug in your system will be completely gone in no time."

"Thank you, Dr. Ausar, for everything," Sophia said as she shook the doctor's hand.

Nik said, "I'll walk you out." She waited until her mate had the doctor out the front door before she confronted them.

"Mom, I was telling Dad how I found you, but I think that can wait until you're feeling better."

Her mother nodded and reached out for Sam's hand. "Ezekiel, what are you doing here?"

Zeke was leaning against the doorframe looking like he'd rather be anywhere but in that room. "Someone has to keep my brother in line," he said with a smile that didn't reach his eyes. Sophia could feel the tension building, and she was ready to know what the hell was going on in her family.

Chapter Twenty-Nine

THE rest of the morning was spent with Sam hovering over Monica. Sophia didn't remember her mother being such a delicate flower. Nik was outside talking to Julian on the phone. Zeke was at the stove stirring something that added a wonderful fragrance to the air. Sophia was studying the numbers Xenia had sent. Even though her parents were safe, Sophia still wanted to solve the mystery. She was tapping the eraser end of a pencil on the table and biting the thumb of her other hand.

"What do you have there?" Monica asked, looking over her shoulder. Her mom had showered and looked much more like herself. Her hair wasn't as long as Sophia's, but it was thick and wavy. She could let it air dry and still be beautiful.

"Something Aunt Xenia found in her safety deposit box. When her father died, he left this for her. It was a set of coordinates and some random numbers."

Monica sat down next to her daughter and asked, "May I see them, please?"

Her dad came into the kitchen but didn't sit down. He stood in the doorway with his arms crossed over his chest. Samuel Brooks was a handsome man. Most people mistook him and Sophia for brother and sister considering he looked to be in his thirties. Zeke stopped stirring and glanced over at his brother. Sam nodded.

Sophia knew this was it. She was going to find out what skeletons had rattled the closet door open. "Can we please wait on Nik?" she asked. Sophia needed her mate for strength.

"Wait on Nik for what?" he asked as he came in the front door.

"I have a feeling my world is fixing to tilt on its axis, and I need my rock. Sit, please?" She pulled out the chair next to her, and Nik sat. He took her hand in his and brought it to his lips.

Monica tapped her broken fingernail on the paper. "I know what these are. They aren't random numbers. They make up a cipher code."

"And you know this how?" Sophia asked.

"My brother, Mercer, was an archaeologist, as was I when I met your father. Mercer was a bit younger, but he was the brilliant one. In the beginning, we traveled all over, but once he got the slightest hint of where Cleopatra was buried, he couldn't focus on anything else. He begged me to continue the digs with him, but I was your father's mate, and as you know, that pull is stronger than any other. I left Egypt and Mercer and moved to the States with Samuel.

"Mercer was somewhat paranoid. He would make notations in his journals, but most of the time, only he could decipher them. He was the only one who knew what the numbers and symbols stood for. Even though he was younger, he taught me so much. One of the things he taught me was cipher codes. You take a set of letters and assign a particular set of numbers to those. Only the person with the numbers can read the message." She paused and wiped a tear from her face.

"Monica—"

"No, Sam. I'm okay. Anyway, it's not quite as simple as that, but you get the gist. These numbers are from the last cipher code he created before he died."

"But why would Xenia have these? She said her father gave them to her. That would mean Mercer is..."

"My brother. Mercer Carmichael, Xenia's adopted father, is my baby brother."

"But that would make you... almost a hundred. I thought you were in your mid-fifties."

"I'm so sorry, Sophia. When I got pregnant, Jonas had a fit. He insisted I give my baby up for adoption. There was no one I trusted more than Mercer and his wife. Xenia isn't your aunt. She's your older sister."

If Nikolas hadn't been holding on so tight, Sophia would have run out the door. "And you allowed JoJo to manipulate you into giving up your child? Do I have other brothers and sisters? What else have you been hiding from me?"

"We were weak. We let him convince us it was the best course of action. As for siblings, no. I refused to have another child until your father agreed we could keep you. I wanted to tell you; I did. But you know how Jonas is. The fewer people who know secrets, the less chance they have of being found out."

Sophia didn't know what to say. She was hurt. Felt betrayed. Then again, who was she to pass judgment? She had kept her own secret for three years. She didn't feel hers was as life-shattering, but again, what did she know?

"I guess you can understand why I didn't tell you about Nikolas. Were you ever going to tell Xenia? Now that's she's transitioned and knows about the family, I think you owe her the truth."

"And we'll tell her. Together," Sam said as he

finally sat down next to his mate.

Zeke turned off the eye of whatever he was cooking and said, "Now that you're safe, I'm going to see Cyrus. He's the only sibling left who hasn't transitioned. I'm going to tell him the truth. I'm going to stay close in case he needs me. Once that's done, I'll be taking a long vacation. Away from Jonas; away from the family." He left the room and walked out the door.

Sophia didn't blame her uncle. If the truth had been kept from her and she had to live without her mate the rest of her life, she'd be pissed, too. "Mom, right before I hopped the bus to New Atlanta, you were looking at a map of Egypt. Did it have anything to do with these codes?"

Monica nodded. "Yes. Your uncle was sure he'd found the burial place of Antony and Cleopatra. He was on a dig and unearthed a disk. Even though it was buried, it was pristine, as if it had been in a tomb all along. Mercer got the idea that there had been a possible underground shift and a new tomb was somewhere in the vicinity of the disk. His home was robbed, and the disk lost forever, but he still had his notes in his head. The only reason he ever put them to paper was in case something happened to him. He wanted Xenia to continue looking for the tomb. This note was his insurance that she would eventually come in contact with me. He knew I would recognize the numbers for what they were. Once the disk was stolen, he gave up his search for the tomb and went after the disk. He was killed before he could find it."

"What happened when you were taken?"

Sam answered, "We had just come home from

supper. I felt a charge in the air, like something was off. When we stepped into the house, the lights wouldn't come on. I went downstairs to check the fuse box, and as I got to the bottom of the stairs, I heard your mother screaming. Then silence. I forgot about the fuses, and before I could get to her, I was injected with something that knocked me out. When we woke up, we were in a dark tomb surrounded by rebels. We were told if we behaved, we would live. We complied. I knew being a half-blood I was stronger than they were, but there were too many of them. I couldn't risk them shooting your mother. So, we sat in that dank tomb for a month. We were fed stale bread and given a jug of water a day. Not too long ago, someone came to the tomb and told the rebels they were leaving the country, but they had someone else watching them. They were paid half their money and told they would receive the other half when the job was done. If you hadn't found us when you did…"

"Will you tell us your part of the story now?" Monica asked.

"Why don't you all fix a plate and begin eating. I need to talk to Zeke." Sophia kissed Nik and left him to talk to her parents. She found Zeke leaned against the SUV studying the sky. It was a cool, overcast autumn day.

"What do you see up there?" she asked as she mimicked his position.

"Escape, Sophie girl. I spend my time alone so I don't have to observe the love between Sam and Monica. Now I see that same love growing between you and Nikolas. Don't get me wrong; I'm happy for you. He's a good male. The fates chose well when they picked the two of you for one another. He comes from a strong Clan, and the more I'm around Julian, the more I realize you have been blessed beyond measure. I don't know what I did to deserve the hand I was dealt, but it's the only hand I have to play. I either continue bluffing my way through the game, or I fold. I don't have it in me to quit, so I will go take care of Cyrus. After that?" Zeke shrugged. Sophia's heart was breaking for him. It wasn't fair.

"I'm so sorry, Uncle. Seeing the tombs and knowing the Egyptians believed so strongly in reincarnation got me to thinking. I'm going to pray to the gods and ask that they intervene on your part. I pray the soul of Nefertari, or some other great queen, finds its way into this life and into the body of your new mate."

Zeke placed his arm around her shoulder and gave her a squeeze. "You do that. I won't hold my breath waiting, but you pray for me. If the gods listen to anyone, it would be you." He kissed her on top of her head and walked off. Sophia stood where she was until he was out of sight. The front door opened, and Nik said, "Soph? Baby?"

She wiped the tears from her eyes and sent up that prayer. "Coming."

Sophia returned to the kitchen where she explained to her parents everything that happened, from the time she received her note to the present. The only thing she left out was mating with Nik. They could imagine that part for themselves, if they were inclined to do so. Somehow, she doubted it.

The next morning, the Stone Society jet was waiting for them at the Luxor airport. Monica was still weak, but the more good food she ate, the stronger she got. Sam rebounded quickly; then again, he was part shifter. When they arrived at the villa, Zeke packed his bags and made arrangements to fly to Montana. Sophia was a little envious of her uncle. She had hoped to be the one to visit the wide-open land where Cyrus had hundreds of acres.

Since Monica was still recovering, Sam asked Sophia to call Xenia and request she come visit the villa. While they were in Egypt, they wanted to come clean with their daughter. Their other daughter. While Sophia had her on the phone, she suggested Keene accompany her. She knew firsthand how important it was to have the strength of your mate when you are blindsided with such a revelation.

When it was time for Xenia to arrive, Sophia asked Nikolas if they could go sightseeing. She didn't have to explain why. They had already talked at length about her having a sister and being kept in the dark all this time. Tessa piped up and said, "Gregor and I are coming with you. Might as well enjoy the city while we're here. Julian, do you want to come with us?"

Julian rose from where he was studying something on his laptop. "Yes. It will do me good to see something besides a computer screen for a while."

Monica stopped Sophia. "Don't you want to stay and talk to your sister?"

"I've talked to Xenia. I practically spilled my guts to her, thinking she was my aunt. You'll have to forgive me if I leave you and Dad to explain the situation by yourselves. I won't be a buffer for you." Sophia understood why they'd given Xenia up for adoption; it still didn't hurt any less that they kept it from her once she started training to be a watcher. "I came to Egypt to rescue the two of you. My work here is done. I'm pretty sure the threat is over; at least I hope it is. Now, I'm going to enjoy the sights while I can."

The five of them piled into the SUV and headed toward downtown. "What would you like to do?" Julian asked from the driver's seat.

Sophia answered, "I sure as hell don't want to go to the zoo." Everyone laughed including her. She could look back on the situation now that her parents were safe at the villa and Nik was by her side. "I would love to see the pyramids and the Sphynx while we're here."

"I'd like that, too," Tessa said.

"More sand it is," Gregor said. Both Sophia and Tessa had joked about carrying sand back to the States in their hair.

Sophia and Nik sat in the back seat of the vehicle, enjoying the banter between Tessa and Gregor. She knew her cousin was a handful, but spending so much time with the feisty redhead put a whole new perspective on the woman's wit and demeanor. She was strong and hardheaded, but she loved her mate fiercely. Gregor Stone was one badass shapeshifter, but Tessa wouldn't hesitate to put herself between him and someone or something who was trying to harm him. Sophia felt the same way about Nik; she just wasn't quite the hellion her cousin was.

They spent the rest of the day exploring the

Sphynx and touring the pyramids. Sophia and Nik walked with their fingers linked, always touching. Gregor and Tessa were just as bad. She didn't miss the wistful look on Julian's face when he watched couples together. He said he wasn't going to pursue his own mate until everyone else's were safe. Sophia had other plans, though. She was becoming quite fond of her new brother, and she was going to see to it he had the happiness he deserved.

CHAPTER THIRTY

NIKOLAS was ready to go home. Having your mate's parents sleeping down the hall put a damper on your sex life. He shouldn't care considering Sophia was a grown woman, but they did tend to get a little on the loud side. He wouldn't say he was content holding her while they slept. It was nice having her in his arms all night long, but his cock was aching to slide into the wet heat of his beautiful bunny. Sophia shifted, and her ass snuggled closer to his hard-on. She wiggled again, and Nik groaned. She was subconsciously trying to kill him. When she did it again, he slapped her on the ass, and she giggled.

"You naughty minx," he hissed.

Sophia snaked her top leg over his thigh and pushed back into him. "Nikolas Stone, do I have to spell it out for you?"

"But your parents," he reminded her.

"Are adults who may or may not remember what the mating pull felt like in the beginning. I really don't care. What I do care about is I have an itch and I prefer that you scratch it."

Well, alrighty then. Nik had been dying to get his face between her legs since he first saw her in the library, but he was going to wait until they were alone. When he assaulted her pussy with his mouth, he wasn't going to let up until she was shattering the windows with his name. He whispered in her ear, "Let the scratching commence," and bit her earlobe. Nik ran his hand down her leg and lifted it so he could reposition his cock at her entrance. He slid it through her slick folds. His woman was ready for him. With no warning, Nik thrust into her body, stopping when he was balls deep.

"Oh gods, Nik. Move, Gorgeous. Please move," she begged.

He kept a tight grip on her leg as he slid in and out of her slick core. This position was nice, but he needed more control. Nik pushed her over to her stomach and pulled her onto her knees. He took a moment to admire her perfect heart-shaped ass while stroking his cock. When she wiggled that ass, he smacked her on the cheek before rubbing the sting away. He gave the other side equal treatment and kissed the pale skin that was now pink. One day, he was going to turn both of those cheeks red. That, too, would have to wait until they were alone. He grabbed his length and put it where they both wanted it.

Sophia met him stroke for stroke, her ass rising higher with each thrust. Her moans were muffled by the pillow her face was hiding in. When her claws came out, he knew she was ready to come. He kept his own claws sheathed, but he did grip her hips tighter. It took all his power to keep his wings from unfurling when her pussy gripped his dick and pulsed with her orgasm. He pumped his hips through his own orgasm and squeezed his eyes tight when the blackness started to take over. He had never busted a nut so hard that he saw stars before he met Sophia.

She collapsed onto the bed with him top of her. Nik had to move her messy hair so he could get to her face. He loved her long, wavy hair, even when it got in the way. "Good morning, Baby."

"Morning, Gorgeous. I need a shower. And coffee. And food."

"In that order?" Nik asked as he rolled to the side so he wouldn't smash her. He wasn't a large male, but he had at least eighty pounds on his mate.

"Yes, in that order. I don't want to walk through the villa smelling like sex. Not that everyone doesn't know what we're doing. They all have excellent hearing. Everyone except my mother."

"Then let's get to it. I'm ready to get back to the States. We accomplished what we came for, and now we can go home."

They took a quick shower together, but Nik left Sophia in the bathroom so he could start breakfast. When he got to the kitchen, Julian was already at the stove. "You're going to make someone a good wife," he joked with his brother.

"If I had a female in my bed, I wouldn't have reason to get up so early. Listening to you and Gregor go at it with your mates is not easy. Besides, Dante called and woke me up."

Nik was pouring coffee when Gregor joined them. "Is everything okay back home?" he asked.

"I don't know if things are ever going to be okay again. First off, Jasper and Trevor are mates. Jasper's ex, Craig, was killed, and the evidence is pointing to Jasper. We know it wasn't him, because he was staking out Abbi's house. Someone sent Trevor some compromising photos of Jasper, so Trevor, feeling betrayed, took off. While he was gone, someone started following him. You'll never believe who it was."

"Who?" Nik asked.

"Theron. It seems Jasper and Theron have a past together."

"Theron's gay?" Tessa asked as she came into the room.

"From what Dante could get out of Jasper, Theron's a sadist. I doubt he has a preference of the gender he wants to inflict pain on. That's not the worst of it."

"The worst of what?" Sophia asked. She shooed Julian away from the stove and took over breakfast.

"Thank you. Remember I told you Frey's mate had an abusive husband? Well, he grabbed her from the community center and was going to kill her, but not before he tortured and raped her."

"What?" Tessa shrieked.

"Oh, gods!" Sophia cried.

"That motherfucker!" Everyone was talking at the same time.

Julian held up his hand. "Long story short… Frey found them right as Troy dumped Abbi over the bridge. Frey phased and caught her before she hit the ground. Jasper beat the hell out of Troy and was going to arrest him. Matthew confronted the man about abusing him and Abbi all these years. Troy shot at Matthew. Jasper phased, wrapping his wings around the boy. Trevor was there with Dante, and he ended up killing Troy. The good news in all that is Abbi's going to be okay."

"Holy shit. You were right, Julian. The fates are making it hard on all of you," Tessa said.

"This is why I'm not in such a hurry to be with Katherine." Julian filled them in on the rest of the story.

Nik was seriously ready to go home so he could support Frey.

"All this happened while we were fighting the rebels. Frey and Abbi are getting married in a couple of days. If we leave today, we can make it to the wedding."

"Wow, they didn't waste any time, did they?" Sophia asked.

"When you know it's right, why wait?" Nik asked her.

"Abbi is human, so Frey is honoring her way of doing things. I would marry her as quickly as I could, too, if I were in his shoes. Honestly, I know how he feels. When you come that close to losing your mate, you do whatever it takes to bind them to you," Gregor said as he pulled Tessa to him and held on tight.

"Such a romantic, Stone," Tessa said, but Nik could see the tears misting her eyes.

"Good morning, everyone," Monica said quietly. "I overheard your conversation, and I think it's wonderful you're going home. However, I have something I need to tell you."

Nik was glad to see his mate's mother happy. She was more than happy, though. She was excited.

"Sophia, I told you I knew what the numbers were. After your father and I explained to Xenia that we're her parents, we talked about Mercer. She forgave us, by the way. When we were reminiscing about my brother and his love for ciphers, she remembered another set of numbers she'd seen before. She went home and found a journal that she originally thought to be gibberish. Instead of it being nonsense, I explained to her what she had in her hands. It was the last code needed to decipher the numbers he left for her in the safety deposit box. Together, we cracked the code. Sophia, we know where Cleopatra and Antony are buried."

Nik thought Sophia would have been more excited at the bomb her mother dropped on her. If Monica truly knew the location of the tomb, this would put them all in the history books. While everyone in the room was whooping it up and congratulating Monica, Sophia stopped cooking and walked over to Nik. He was becoming accustomed to her movements. As strong a female as his mate was, whenever her parents were around, she needed to have him close. He chalked it up to the mate pull, until he reached out to check her vitals. Whenever her mother shared a secret, or in this case, some exciting news, Sophia's heart rate sped up and her shifter pushed for control.

Since Nik's shifter had a line to Sophia's, he pulled the beast forward and let it make the connection. All Nik had to do was hold his mate. Within seconds, she was calming down and back in control. He wanted to talk to Dante about how the calming effect worked. His cousin had a special ability none of the others seemed to have in that he could touch someone and ease their moods.

"This is great news, Mother. You and Xenia will be famous."

Monica stepped closer to Sophia, but Sam stopped her. He took his mate's hand and said, "No, sweetheart. Not only your mother and Xenia. This will include you, as well. You are the reason we were reunited. This is to be a family project. My three girls will make the discovery together."

Nik knew his mate was torn. He started to tell her it was okay, but Julian stepped up to her and took her hands in his. If this was anyone else, Nik's claws would be out. He knew whatever Julian had to say was important. "We all want to go home; no one more than me. Our big brother is getting married. He has been through a terrible ordeal, but he has come out the other side a victor. He is gaining a family. Not only does he have Matthew, but also a sweet little girl he's going to adopt. But you know what? Sixx can set up a live video feed, and we can be there with them in spirit. This discovery of Cleopatra and Antony's tomb will be nothing short of a miracle. This is history in the making, and as much as I want to be in New Atlanta with Geoffrey, I honestly want to be here just a little more.

"I want to be part of something that will go down in the history books. As Gargoyles, we have to hide our true natures, hide any good we do from the public. I have lived over five hundred years. The last fifty I've done so sitting back, looking at the world through a computer monitor. For once, I want to be part of something exciting. I want to be on the front lines when this discovery is made. I need to see it with my own eyes instead of going home and reading about it on a laptop. Sophia, think about it. You don't have to take credit if you don't want to, but if you miss out on this once in a six-million-lifetime chance, you'll regret it." Julian squeezed her hands before letting go.

"Six million, huh?" she asked.

Nik knew his brother had rounded the figure. Julian knew the exact percentage, but didn't want to show off.

"Give or take three hundred seventy-four," Julian added with a wink.

Sophia turned and looked up at Nik. "Are you okay with missing your brother's wedding? You and I can fly home if Julian wants to stay here."

"Baby, I think Frey would kick all our asses if we passed up this opportunity. As soon as we get home, we can visit him and his new family. Personally, I think you'll kick your own ass later if you miss out on this." Nik felt the same way Julian did. He wanted to be part of something extraordinary.

"If you're okay with it, let's do it."

"Yes!" Tessa yelled. "Lara fucking Croft, get your digging clothes on." Tessa had used the cover of being an archaeologist for years to travel the world visiting her cousins. Now, she was going to get to participate in a legitimate dig that could possibly change history.

Everyone laughed, including Sophia's parents. Sam wiped the tears off Monica's face and kissed her on the lips. Nik was glad Sophia agreed to stay. As badly as he wanted to be there for Frey, this was a story they could pass down for generations to come.

Chapter Thirty-One

XENIA arrived shortly after breakfast. Before the group began planning their expedition, Sophia asked to speak with her outside. Once alone, Sophia said, "I promise you I didn't know."

Xenia stepped closer and put her arm around Sophia's shoulder. "I know you didn't. Sam and Monica explained it all to me last night. Honestly? I'd rather have you as a sister than a niece."

"So, you're not upset?"

"Oh, I was mad as hell, but then I realized what good was being pissed going to do anyone? I could thumb my nose at them and cut them out of my life. Or, I could forgive them and have more family than only you, Keene, and Zeke. I might never call them mom and dad, especially considering I look old enough to be their parent."

"Stop it, you do not. You're beautiful."

"Just like my sister. When Monica started talking about her brother, I listened, because he meant the world to me. Mercer and Sadie couldn't have kids of their own. They tried for years. When Monica needed someone to take me in, she knew her brother was the one. It was a win-win for everyone."

"Everyone except you."

"No, including me." Xenia turned Sophia around to face her and placed her hands on Sophia's arms. "Little dove, I couldn't have hand-picked better parents. I had a life filled with adventure and knowledge. While Mercer was out digging, Sadie doted on me like you wouldn't believe. When I was old enough, Mercer began taking me with him. I have lived a life most people only dream about. I was raised in a loving home by parents I practically worshiped. I'm glad Monica allowed her brother to be my father. That might not make sense to you, but it's the truth. It does hurt that I was lied to all those years, but now I know the truth, and I have family when I thought I had none."

"Wow. You're really something, you know that?"

"Eh, it's in the genes. Now, let's go make history."

Sophia's heart healed in that moment. She had a sister whose spirit was as beautiful as her face.

Once inside, Xenia explained how the digging permits worked. She was a history professor at the University as well as experienced in archaeological digs. She would be allowed to lead the expedition with no trouble. Laws of the Council of Antiquities had become much more relaxed since the apocalypse. Julian produced documentation showing each of them to have a profession in a field relevant to the dig. If her father's notes were still accurate, they wouldn't have to do much digging to find the tomb. He believed it to be hiding in plain sight.

Keene was now in debt to his father even further. Brock was using his power to have the permit pushed through quickly. Instead of the approval taking a week or more, it should only take a couple days. While waiting on approval, they poured over maps, comparing recent copies to ones Mercer had stored among his things. The more they discussed the dig, the more Monica came to life. Sophia had never seen her mother so excited about anything. Ever. She had given up her life's work when she mated with Sam. Sophia knew she would do the same to be with Nikolas. Good thing their jobs within their families were closely related.

While the others were making plans and gathering tools, Sam pulled Sophia aside. "Can I talk to you?"

"Sure," she responded. She felt the same way about her father as Xenia had Mercer. Even when she was spending so much time with Jonas, Sam had been her hero. "What's up?"

"I want to make sure we're good. You haven't said much, and you won't look at me. Sophia, I'm so sorry. I know now keeping your sister from you was a mistake. Can you ever forgive me?"

"Xenia and I were talking earlier. When she described her love for Mercer, it was tangible. I could reach out and grab hold of it. That's how I feel about you, Daddy. You were always my hero, larger than life."

Sam blinked, tears shining in his eyes. "You said were. Am I not still your hero?"

"I think you know the answer to that. I couldn't ask for a better father, but now, I also have the perfect mate. I look back at you and Mom and the love you've shared. That, too, has been tangible. It's my turn to have that kind of love. That kind of life. The kind of life where I know my mate is going to stand beside me and protect me. Nikolas Stone is kind, caring, funny, sexy as hell, and strong. He's perfect. I just wish..."

"What do you wish?" Sam asked when Sophia got quiet.

"That Uncle Zeke could have that kind of life, too."

Sam pulled Sophia in for a hug. "Me, too, sweetheart. Me, too."

EZEKIEL would give anything if he was back on the Stone Society jet. He should have spent the extra money and booked his seat in first class. Instead, he was cramped between a large man who snored for ten hours straight and a teenaged girl who smacked her chewing gum. Not only that, but he felt nauseous the whole trip. If he wasn't part shifter, his blood pressure would be through the roof. He was headed home to California to unwind for a few days. He needed to swap out his clothes as well. The weather in Montana would be getting cold soon, and he didn't think his desert gear would work too well.

The plane landed on time, not that it mattered to Zeke. Rarely was he on a schedule, and today was no different. He had no one waiting at the end of the walkway welcoming him home. He had no time clock he had to punch. No real responsibility other than his brother Cyrus.

The customs line was extremely long, so Zeke mentally prepared to wait. "Ezekiel?" an older woman's voice asked. Standing several passengers ahead of him was a familiar face. The woman came backwards through the line and stopped in front of him. She was short, so he had to look down. "Are you Ezekiel Seymour?" she asked.

"Yes, ma'am." He racked his brain trying to

remember who she was. She was still pretty, and her eyes reminded him of someone.

"Good heavens, you haven't changed a bit. You look like you did when we dated."

"Dated?" He smiled all the while trying to remember her name.

She laughed. "You don't remember me, do you? I'm Sheila Varner. I was Sheila Bentley back then. You have to remember my daughter, Stella. Where'd she go?" Sheila looked around and grabbed a younger woman by the arm. "Here she is. This is my Stella, all grown up."

Zeke felt like he'd been punched in the gut. Stella was a younger, prettier version of her mother. His brain kicked in, and he remembered dating a woman a couple of times who had a toddler. Stella held out her hand, and against his better judgment, Zeke shook it. *Holy fucking shit.* He thought he was going to lose his lunch. Stella must have felt the pull, because she jerked her hand away.

"What the hell?" she murmured.

Zeke turned to Sheila and lied, "I'm not the man you dated; that must have been my father. I'm Ezekiel, Jr." There's no way Zeke was letting something as trivial as him dating Stella's mother thirty years ago drive her away.

Sheila laughed, cocking her head sideways as she studied him intently. "Well that sure makes a lot more sense. You're the spitting image of Zeke. I swear; you could pass for twins. You even have the same scar above your eye that he did." Sheila continued talking, asking questions about the senior Ezekiel Seymour, and Zeke answered her questions as vaguely as possible about someone who didn't exist. The line crept closer to the check-in point, and Zeke was trying to think of some way to get Stella alone later.

"So, Ezekiel, where are you coming from? We just got back from Egypt. Those pyramids were something else."

"You were in Egypt?" he asked Sheila, only he was looking at Stella. She had silky, straight black hair with dark eyes to match. She reminded him of an Egyptian queen. "You could pass for Nefertari," he whispered. Stella lowered her eyes, blushing.

"Sir, you're holding up the line," an airport worker chastised him. He made it through customs and waited on the other side for Sheila and Stella to come through. Thankfully, Stella was first, and she walked to where he was waiting.

"Your dad must have really been something. My mother still talks about him after all this time."

Zeke hated lying to her. If she was his mate, he'd eventually have to be honest with her, but until he knew for certain she could be his mate, he was going to avoid the topic. "Where are you off to?" he asked.

"Like mother said, we just got home from Egypt. I love her, but I need to put a little distance between us, if you know what I mean."

He sure did. "Stella, I'd love to see you again. After you get settled and jet lag has worn off, if you are interested, give me a call." He prayed she didn't have a boyfriend, or worse, a husband waiting on her at home.

"I think I'd like that," she said. "What's your

phone number?"

Zeke told her his number, and she programmed it into her phone. His phone buzzed in his pocket. As he pulled it out, she said, "There, now you have mine, too. Ezekiel Seymour, why do you seem so familiar to me?"

He couldn't tell her the truth. Not yet. He wanted to spend time together and be one hundred percent sure she could be his mate. So, he merely told her, "Sometimes the fates have a funny way about them."

She started to say something, but Sheila joined them. "Ezekiel, it was good meeting you. Please tell your father I said hello. Come on, Stella. I'm ready to be home."

Stella held out her hand again. Was she a glutton for punishment, or was she trying to see if there really was a strange connection between them? Zeke placed his hand in hers, and her eyes widened. Instead of letting go, he brought her knuckles to his lips and kissed them. "I'll be waiting," he said. Stella squeezed his hand before taking off after her mother.

Zeke knew they would more than likely be going to the same baggage carousel he was, but he didn't want to seem like a stalker. He ducked into one of the restaurants and ordered a drink. He sipped his whisky as he thought about the first time he saw Stella. He'd gone to pick Sheila up for their date. When she wasn't ready, he waited for her in the living room. The babysitter was already there, and a little girl toddled into the room. He remembered dark eyes staring up at him as she held onto his leg to steady herself. The little girl was babbling incoherently, and he'd been mesmerized. Zeke and Sheila had barely pulled out of the driveway when he felt sick to his stomach. He still took her out to eat, but he didn't gain his appetite back. A few days after their date, Ezekiel transitioned for the first time.

Zeke enjoyed two more glasses of whisky before paying his tab and retrieving his luggage. On the way home, he called Jonas. His father answered the phone, frantic. "Zeke? Where are you? Is Sam okay? Did you find them? How's Sophia?"

"Slow down, Father. Everyone's good. I'm back in the States, but I left everyone else in Egypt. They were having a family reunion of sorts. Xenia knows the truth."

"Huh. Listen, I'm glad you called. Your mother and I have something we'd like you to take care of."

"Huh? All you can say is huh?" It was just like Jonas to focus on his own needs.

"The truth is out, and Samuel will take care of it. It's out of my hands. Now, about that favor."

"I need to ask you something first. Is it possible to mate with a small child?"

"Are you crazy? Why would you even ask that?" Jonas said, incensed.

"Not that way! Gods, you really think I'd do that? What I meant was could being around a child cause the transition?"

"I suppose if the fates are willing to put someone through a test of sorts, it could be possible. Why are you asking?"

"I ran into someone I haven't seen since they were really young. I met her when I dated her mother. Soon after, I went through my transition. Back then, we didn't know the cause, but since we now do, I'm thinking she is the reason. I felt the mate pull strongly in her presence just now."

"Wait a second. How do you know the cause?"

"How we know isn't important. The fact that you hid it from us is. If you hadn't kept it a secret, I might be with my mate right now. All of your offspring have transitioned with the exception of Cyrus. I am on my way to Montana to rectify the situation. Back to my original question: is it possible?"

Jonas was silent for a moment, and if Zeke hadn't heard breathing on the other end of the line, he would've thought his father had hung up. Finally, Jonas responded, "It isn't something I've ever heard of, Son, but I would say it is possible. Now, about that favor…"

Zeke listened to his father drone on and on about some experiment he was currently working on. Since Tessa and Sam were out of the country, he wanted Zeke to help him. Zeke declined, reminding his father he was going to see Cyrus. He wouldn't put off the trip because Jonas had a wild hair up his ass. Maybe by the time he returned from Montana, Stella would be ready to see him.

He left the airport and headed toward his beach house. He had a feeling that one day very soon he would no longer need the soothing sound of the waves as a balm to his spirit.

CHAPTER THIRTY-TWO

SIXX set up a live video feed as promised, and they all watched as Frey and Abbi exchanged vows by the lake on Frey's property. Nik had to promise to take Sophia there as soon as they got settled.

The dig had been a success, even if it took longer to get the permits than expected. It was interesting to see Xenia and Monica working side by side. The others moved rocks and brushed stones, but more often than not, they watched the two women at work. Once the burial tomb of Antony and Cleopatra was unearthed, Xenia had her hands full with government and antiquities officials. They all agreed that Mercer would receive full credit since it was his notes that led them to the find. Keene was right there with her, making sure she kept her fangs in check.

Sophia's parents stayed in Egypt for a short vacation. Monica had been in her element, and she was considering going back into archaeology now that both her daughters had mates of their own.

Nikolas had never been so glad to see his house. Before he left for Egypt, it was a large, empty space filled with books and a hidden room where the Stone Society archives were located. As he carried Sophia over the threshold, it became a home. "Welcome home, Baby." He didn't stop to let her look around. Nik carried her straight to the bedroom and set her on her feet. "Clothes, off, now," he instructed as he pulled his shirt over his head. His cock was straining against his zipper, and he wasn't going to wait to slide into his mate's core.

Sophia was obviously in as much of a hurry since she was naked before he was. Nik stuck his thumbs between his jeans and his skin and pushed the material down his legs. Sophia didn't wait for him to get them all the way off before she was on her knees with his dick in her mouth. "Soph, Baby…"

"Hmm?" she asked, never slowing her mouth. He loved how she was so eager to please him, but he had waited long enough to get his mouth on her.

He pulled her up by the armpits. "I have an idea." Nik got on his back, his cock jutting straight up in the air. "Give me your legs," he instructed. He positioned her so her pussy was over his face, and right as she slid his cock back into her mouth, he licked her clit.

When she released him, she said, "Oh, gods, do that again."

Gladly. Sophia was getting really good at blowjobs. She was able to take him farther each time, but today she was having a hard time concentrating. Nik didn't care though. He knew her pussy would taste like heaven if he ever had the chance to get his mouth down there. He was right.

Her breasts were tapping his stomach as she bobbed up and down. Her enthusiasm at exploring his body grew each time they shed their clothes. She wasn't shy about experimenting, and she was open to each and every naughty suggestion Nik whispered in her ear while he was pounding her pussy. He stuck his finger between her folds, hitting that spongy spot just inside that would make her come apart if he hit it hard enough. He tucked that thought away for another time.

Right now, he was enjoying the taste of her mixed with the delicious way she smelled.

Nik concentrated on her clit, alternating between licking and sucking. Each time he pulled the bud between his teeth, she moaned. He bit her clit and smacked her ass at the same time. His bunny enjoyed her spankings. Sophia wiggled, her way of saying *thank you, sir, may I have another?* with her mouth full. He gladly obliged and smacked the other cheek. His fingers plunging into her core were already wet. He wanted her dripping before she came. He sucked her juices off his fingers, the taste better than the finest Scotch ever invented. "Gods, Baby, you taste so fucking good," he groaned.

Her hand was helping her mouth now, a sign she was getting tired. Instead of going back to finger-fucking her pussy, he teased her pucker. She pushed against his hand, and he took that as permission to breach her entrance. He slid his thumb into her pussy getting it slick before sliding it into her tight hole. He didn't push far since it was her first time. It didn't take more than that, because she pulled her mouth off his dick and started rocking against his face. "Nik, please..." She was ready. Nik flicked his tongue over her clit as he pulsed his thumb in her ass and his fingers in her pussy. Her core gripped his fingers as she screamed out his name.

When her pussy was no longer throbbing, he flipped her over onto her back and drove his cock deep. He crashed their mouths together, hoping her fangs weren't out. He enjoyed the taste of her juices on his tongue and wanted her to see how fucking good it was. Sophia wrapped her legs around his waist and licked at his lips. "Mmm, I taste good," she said as she plunged her tongue in for more.

Godsdamn his female was amazing. "I could fuck you forever," he husked when she stopped plundering his mouth.

"Then don't stop," she said as she grabbed onto his shoulders. Sophia dug her human nails into his skin. He barely felt it, but he knew the claws would be out soon. That tingling sensation started at the base of his spine. By the time it reached the top, his wings were out. His mate's fangs dropped, and she latched onto his neck. With a roar, he shot his load into her already soaked pussy. The feel of her fangs breaching his skin was his undoing every time.

After they showered, Nik brought in the luggage from their trip. They were both tired of sand and ready for the crisp air December was offering New Atlanta. Nik took Sophia on a grand tour of her new home. Her favorite room in the house was, of course, the library. "I feel like Belle in Beauty and the Beast," she joked.

"Ah, so I'm a beast, huh?" he growled in her ear as he spun her around the middle of the floor. Sophia giggled loudly, and he vowed to make her laugh every day of her life. "I've had dirty ideas about this hot librarian climbing the ladder over there with nothing on under her skirt."

"Is that so?"

Nik grinned and wagged his eyebrows. "Is this library large enough for you to quit your job?" he asked as he put her down on her feet.

She wrapped her arms around his neck. "Don't

you think I'll get bored, sitting here all day with nothing else to do?"

"What I think is you'll be busy rearranging the house when we bring all your things from your place. After that, I think you will be busy choosing which room will be the first nursery and picking the right color. I think, Sophia Brooks, that you are going to be so busy with little shifters running around this house you won't have time to be bored."

"You want kids now?" she asked with an eyebrow cocked. "But who will paint my toenails when I get fat?"

He swung her around again. "I will. Gladly," he added before he kissed her on the nose.

"Well, alrighty then," she responded with one of his favorite sayings.

Ready to see his big brother, Nik loaded Sophia in the Audi and headed over to Frey's. Julian was supposed to stop by as well. When they pulled up to the gate, Nik spoke Sophia's name into the security box. The gate swung open, and he drove on through. "Your passcode here is my name, too?"

Nik hadn't explained that the boxes were programmed with each of their voices, not specific words. "Actually, they're all voice activated. I could say Abracadabra and it would open. I just like saying your name," he said as they pulled up in front of the house. Frey and a teenage boy were shooting hoops. "That must be Matthew."

When they climbed out of the car, Frey came over and pulled Nik in for a big bear hug. "I missed you, Brother. I'm so glad you're home safe." Frey turned to

Sophia, fisted his heart, and bowed his head. "Sophia, on my honor. It's a pleasure to meet you. Nik, Sophia, this is my son, Matthew." They were shaking hands with the teen when a dark-haired little girl wearing a pink tutu ran out the door toward Frey.

"Daddy, Daddy, Daddy, Daddy!" she yelled as she launched herself at the tall Goyle. It was obviously something she did often, because he was ready for her.

"Yes, Amelia?" he replied. Frey's face softened as did his voice.

"We have company!" she exclaimed. Everyone laughed including a very pretty woman – Abbi. At first glance, she didn't look like a woman who had been abused, raped, and nearly murdered. Nik didn't want to look too closely, but there was a sadness floating right below the surface. She ruffled Matthew's hair before stepping into Frey's side. His arm circled her waist, and he introduced his mate.

Nik greeted her in the same way Frey had Sophia. They were vowing to honor and protect the other's mate at all cost. Amelia wiggled in Frey's grip and held her arms out to Nik. "You're my Uncle Nikky," she said matter-of-factly. Nik didn't hesitate to take her. He loved kids and couldn't wait until Sophia's belly was round with one. Amelia placed her hands on Nik's face and said, "She's really pretty. Is she your wife?"

Nik nodded. He doubted if Frey and Abbi had told the little girl about mates, so he fudged. "Yes, she is."

"Where's her ring?"

Nik laughed but quickly responded, "Sophia is perfect, and she deserves the perfect ring. I haven't found it yet."

Julian's Corvette rumbled down the drive, followed by a couple of Harleys. Deacon and Mason slid off their bikes, and Sophia stepped closer to them both.

"Don't even think about it, woman."

She turned and grinned, "But, Gorgeous, you said you would buy me anything I wanted. I want."

"No, I said I would buy you a brand-new car. *That* is not a car."

Deacon held the key out to Sophia, and Nik growled. Everyone laughed, including Amelia. "He's just joshing, Uncle Nikky. Aren't you, Uncle Deke?" Nik could see why Frey had adopted Amelia. She was adorable, and her nicknames were cute, too.

"Yes, munchkin, I'm kidding," Deacon said. As soon as he was close enough, Amelia held her arms out to him. "Don't feel bad," Deacon told Nik when he pouted. In about thirty seconds, Nik understood. Amelia reached for Mason. "It's a good thing we're tough. Her feet are just the right length to do some damage," Deacon said, cupping his balls.

"Are those steaks I smell?" Julian asked, sniffing the air.

"Yes. I figured once everyone got wind that Sophia was home safe and you were stopping by, we'd have a houseful." Frey no sooner got the words out of his mouth before Gregor and Tessa pulled up on their bikes, followed by Dante, Rafael, and their mates.

"Looks like we won't need to have family day tomorrow," Mason muttered.

"I dare you to say that to Rafael," Matthew said. If Nik remembered correctly, Abbi's brother and Mason were close to the same age, even though Mason already looked to be in his twenties.

"Connor!" Amelia squealed, and Mason put her down before she could make contact with her swinging foot.

"It's all over now," Frey said as his daughter ran toward Dante's new son. Even though Amelia was older than Connor by a year, he was obviously as smitten with her as she was him. He allowed her to take his hand and pull him toward the adults.

Once everyone was introduced to those who had yet to meet them, Connor surprised Nik. He fisted his heart, bowed his head, and said, "Sophia, it is an honor." He shook hands with Nik before allowing Amelia to drag him off toward the house.

"Wow, that was…" Sophia was choked up. Nik pulled her closer and kissed her temple.

"Impressive," Nik finished for her. "So, who are we missing? Where's Jasper?" Nik knew the latest member of their Clan was having mate issues, but he still hoped he would show up.

"He and Dane are working a case," Kaya said. Nik didn't miss his Queen's hand cradling her stomach. She wasn't showing, but she was carrying the heir to the throne.

"Congratulations, by the way," he said to Kaya.

"Thank you. Rafael has been waiting for you all to get home so he can pass out cigars. Since they make me sick, why don't we women head inside so the menfolk can smoke in peace?"

Nik wasn't ready to let go of his mate, but she kissed him on the cheek and said to Kaya, "Lead the way." He wasn't worried about Sophia. She already knew Tessa, and Isabelle was her aunt. The females all needed time to bond with each other, and Nik could go for a beer and a cigar.

"Who's watching the grill?" Rafael asked as he handed out the stogies.

"Urijah. Although, I'll probably have to put everyone's steaks back on. He likes 'em rare," Frey said.

The men headed to the deck where the Viking was indeed pulling the meat from the fire. Very few of the Clan were aware of Urijah's heritage. They also had no idea that Jasper fought for Ireland in the Nine Years War. As keeper of the archives for the Stone Society, Nik was privileged to everyone's background. Whether or not the Goyles shared where they came from was their prerogative. As his mate, Sophia would also have access to the information.

"If you, Mason, and Urijah are here, who's tending the gym?" Nik asked his brother.

Frey puffed on his cigar. When he exhaled, he said, "A new guy, Malakai Palamo. Kai came to us from the West Coast a couple weeks ago. Sin emailed his information; it should be sitting in your computer."

Nik was ready to get back into a routine, ready for a little normalcy. He was eager to start his new life with Sophia.

CHAPTER THIRTY-THREE

THE women were settled in Abbi's kitchen drinking sweet tea. Gods, Sophia had missed the sugary drink. After downing hers in one go, she refilled her glass and introduced herself to Isabelle. "I'm glad we finally get to meet."

Isabelle was a little standoffish at first, but Tessa loosened her up. "You're not gonna believe this shit, Belle. You have one less sibling than you thought. Turns out Xenia isn't your sister after all, but hers," she said, pointing at Sophia.

Sophia picked up the story. "It's true. JoJo isn't the only one keeping secrets. Seems it runs in the family." She explained how her parents kept the truth until recently.

Kaya said, "We already know the other stories. I'm interested to hear yours and Nik's."

Sophia grinned. "About that. I have a confession to make. I figure there's nowhere safer than here with you all."

Tessa asked, "What did you do now?"

Sophia scrunched up her nose and admitted the truth about the journal. The other women listened while she started at the beginning when she transitioned. Once she reached the end of her story, Tessa slapped her hand on the table. "I knew you planted that journal. I even asked you about it. Why lie?"

"I had a lot going on. My parents were missing, *and* you were still dodging Gregor. I figured once you were mated, you wouldn't feel the same about the Gargoyles finding out about us."

Kaya laughed. "I'm glad you planted the journal. I kind of like being mated to the King."

Isabelle nudged her shoulder. "You just like being Queen. Admit it."

The women laughed, including Abbi. Sophia didn't ask her about her ordeal. Instead, she held the other woman's hand in hers. They sat around the table, talking about their mates and the kids. Sophia felt a closeness with each of the women, even Isabelle. Once she and Isabelle had the chance to get to know one another better, she had a feeling they would be more than aunt and niece.

The sliding glass door opened, and the men came inside with steaks and potatoes. Abbi pulled salad out of the fridge while Matthew passed around plates and silverware. There wasn't enough room at the table, so the men either settled in the living room or returned to the deck. Sophia had witnessed a little of the camaraderie between Nik and his fellow Goyles, but to see it in full force between all these alpha shifters was truly a sight to behold. JoJo wanted to keep the half-bloods away from this? He didn't know what he was missing. Or maybe he did. Maybe he longed for the days of being part of a Clan but still felt the sting of being ostracized. That was another thing she planned to remedy.

"Izzy, Izzy, Izzy, Izzy! Come quick! Something's wrong with Connor," Amelia yelled as she ran into the kitchen then back to her room where she and Connor had been playing. Isabelle was behind the girl faster than Sophia could register. She wasn't faster than

Dante, though. The male was standing over his son by the time everyone else made it to the doorway. Sophia didn't see anything wrong with the boy; he looked like he was coloring.

"He's having a vision," Dante informed everyone. No one spoke while the boy drew a picture of what he was seeing in his mind. When he finished, Dante said, "By the gods." The men backed away from the door and ushered the women into the living room so they could see what Connor drew.

The boy held up the drawing, and Sophia gasped. "It's her. The woman who followed me in Egypt."

"That's Kallisto, Alistair's adopted daughter," Isabelle informed the ones who didn't know. "Connor, who else is in the picture?"

"That's Trevor, and the big guy is Kallisto's brother."

Dante cursed. "Theron. If both he and Trevor are in Connor's vision, this can't be good. Son, did you see where they were? Anything you can tell us?"

"No, Da. Just the people. I'm sorry."

Dante picked up his son. "Never be sorry for what you see. You have a special gift. *You* are special. This will help your Uncle Jasper keep his mate safe." Dante hugged his son close, and Connor placed his forehead to his father's. Something passed between the two, but nobody asked any questions. Dante lowered him to his feet, and Connor returned to Amelia's bedroom as if nothing extraordinary had happened.

"I'm calling Jasper," Rafael said. "I know he and Trevor aren't speaking, but he needs this information." Rafael and Kaya left the room together.

"I'm confused," Sophia admitted to the room.

Abbi stepped up and said, "It's time you heard my story."

Frey pulled her close. "You don't have to do this now, Sweetheart."

"I do. It's time." Abbi grabbed Frey's hand and pulled him to stand in front of the unlit fireplace. She situated herself directly in front of him, and he wrapped his large arms around her waist. She held onto his forearms and told her tale. Those who had been there when it happened were solemn. The others were crying. Even the males. "I told you what happened to me so you would understand what's going on with Jasper and Trevor. All of us in this room understand what it means to be someone's mate. We know those two are destined to be together, and it's up to us to help them find their way back to one another. Jasper's hurting, but so is Trevor. He feels betrayed. Defeated. I know that feeling, and I'm vowing now to help bring him around."

Frey buried his wet eyes in his mate's hair. When he pulled back, he said, "As we all are. Theron is in our territory, and if he's here, he might have brought his own Clan with him. We must continue to train. For now, let's finish our meal and celebrate the safety of every mate in this room."

Every woman had been through an ordeal before she was allowed to mate with her Gargoyle. Whoever said the fates were testing the couples had been right. Sophia glanced at Julian, who was talking with Mason and Matthew. She decided at that moment that playing matchmaker might not be the best idea. She would tend to her own business and allow Julian to make his own decisions regarding Katherine.

Nik and Dante were in deep discussion. Their voices were low, so she reached out to eavesdrop. Nik said, "I want you to read her. Make sure she's okay with everything that happened." Ah, her mate was worried about her. But how would Dante *read* her? She closed the distance to find out.

"Are you whispering about me?" she challenged him.

"Of course, Baby. I was telling Dante what a badass you were in the desert."

Sophia tilted her head as she studied Dante's face. He had a distant look in his eye for a mere second. When he focused on her, he smiled and said to Nik, "She's a tough one, your mate." Dante must have psychic abilities like Connor did. Nik pulled her close and nodded.

Sophia waited until Dante walked off and said, "Nikolas Stone, if you want to know how I am, just ask me. You don't need your cousin to use his voodoo mojo to gauge how I am. I killed a man. Maybe two. Both times were in self-defense. I am a half-blood who is mated to a Gargoyle. I am now a member of your Clan; a Clan that is being targeted by a deranged shifter. In all honesty, it probably won't be the last time I have to take a life. Because let me tell you, I will defend myself, you, our children, everyone in this room, and any other member of our Clan to the death."

"Hell yeah!" Tessa shouted and lifted her beer to Sophia. She didn't realize she had been speaking so loudly, but everyone was clapping and cheering.

Nik grinned at her and announced, "I think it's time to take my badass female home. Rafael, if we don't make it to family day tomorrow, I apologize."

Rafael clapped him on the shoulder and said, "Understood."

Nik picked Sophia up and threw her over his shoulder. "Nikolas Stone, put me down."

They exited his brother's house to wolf whistles and laughter. He set her on her feet so he could put her in the car. She didn't immediately get in. Instead, she pointed at the Harleys lined up in the driveway. "I want," she said and grinned.

Nik shook his head at her and laughed. "You can't ride a motorcycle pregnant."

"But I'm not pregnant yet."

Nik pulled her to him and placed his forehead to hers. "Are you sure about that?" He kissed her on the nose and helped her into the car.

When he was seated, she asked, "Do you know something I don't?"

Nik started the Audi and rolled down the driveway. "I think we should go home and practice."

Sophia liked that idea.

NIKOLAS pulled the Audi into the garage and helped Sophia get out of the car. They walked through the side door into the kitchen. "Do you want something to drink?" he asked.

"I'd love a glass of wine. Why don't you grab us

both a drink, and I'll change into something a little more… comfortable."

"Well, alrighty then."

Sophia giggled and headed toward the stairs. Nik hoped her idea of comfortable was naked, because he was going to take off anything she put on. He grabbed a bottle of red and two glasses from the cabinet. He wasn't a big wine drinker, but tonight he was ready to toast his mate and their new life together. When he got to the bedroom, he was surprised to find it empty. "Sophia?" When he received no answer, he looked in the bathroom. Nope, not there either. "Where did you go, you little minx?"

Music floated through the air from down the stairs. Nik grinned and retreated to the library. When he got through the door, he froze. Sophia was on the ladder looking at books. He placed the wine and glasses on an end table and walked over to where she was reaching for something on the next shelf up. His mate was wearing a negligee and no panties. It wasn't the skirt he'd pictured in his mind, but it'd do. His mouth watered, and his dick sprang to life at the sight of her bare ass.

"Get your fine ass down here now, woman," he instructed. Sophia looked down at him and cocked an eyebrow. "Now," he ordered. She obeyed, but she did so slowly. His mate was giving him a show as she lowered herself to him one rung at a time. When her ass was eye level, he placed his hands on her waist to stop her. He pushed the flimsy material aside and kissed both perfect cheeks. Sophia pushed her ass closer to his face. When the negligee fell back down,

Nik ripped the offending garment from her body.

Sophia gasped, but she stayed where she was. "You've been a bad girl, Baby. What do you think I should do about that?"

She wiggled her ass and said, "You should spank me."

Nik unbuttoned his jeans and lower his zipper to relieve the pressure. His cock was begging to be inside her delicious body, but he wanted to play first. He smacked her right cheek, and she moaned. He popped the left one, leaving a handprint. "More," she pleaded breathily. He didn't want to disappoint her, so he smacked both sides again, her skin growing redder with each strike. Before he gave her more of what she wanted, Nik kissed and licked where his hands had been. When his tongue neared her crack, Sophia pushed back into his face once again.

He placed his hands on her cheeks and pulled them apart. He licked her pucker, and her body dipped down. Nik didn't want her to fall off the ladder, so he wrapped his arms around her waist and carried her to the sofa. He placed her knees on the cushions and pushed her chest over the back. He knelt behind her and went back to licking her hole. His thumbs caressed the inside of her legs and came away wet with her juices. "You like this, Baby. You're ready for my cock, aren't you?"

"Yes, Nik. Stop teasing me and fuck me."

Those dirty words coming from her pretty mouth had Nik's dick leaking. She was going to make him come without touching him. He stood so he could remove his clothes before getting back on his knees. He pushed her legs wider so he had better access. Nik slid his tongue from her clit up to her pucker.

"Nik, dammit, fuck me. I need to feel you buried deep."

He couldn't stand her begging. He wanted to please his mate, give her exactly what she wanted. Nik smacked her ass hard as he stood and stroked his length. He placed one foot on the sofa and angled his cock at her entrance. His mate didn't wait on him. Sophia pushed her ass back and impaled her core with his dick. She placed her hands on the back of the sofa and began thrusting hard. He had fucked some wanton women in his time, but to see his mate using his body for her pleasure had his beast roaring.

Nik normally kept his wilder side at bay during sex, but deep down he knew what Sophia needed. He grabbed her hips before handing over control to that voice inside begging to be turned loose. His fangs dropped as he pounded his cock into his mate's willing body. Sophia's claws came out, finding purchase in the leather of the sofa. The primality of their mating was palpable as Sophia growled at him.

Nik found himself lifting Sophia from the sofa. He picked her up and turned her so she was straddling his waist, and his dick was again pounding her core. He slammed her body into the bookcase, her claws digging into his shoulders. Her eyes were dark, and her hair was wild. She licked her lips and demanded, "Harder." He was pretty sure her shifter was front and center as well.

The music in the background could no longer be heard over the slapping of skin, the grunts as he thrust into her hot pussy, or her jagged breathing. Her fangs were now cutting into her lip. Nik leaned in and licked the blood running down her chin. She grabbed her hair and pulled it to one side, exposing her neck. He took the invitation and sank his fangs into the skin where her shoulder and neck met. As soon as he punctured the surface, Sophia's body jerked, her pussy clenching his cock. They came together, yelling out as their orgasms overtook them.

Nik held on tightly to his mate, pulling her back away from the wrecked rows of books that were now scattered on the floor. Sophia dropped her head to his shoulder and whimpered.

"Baby, are you okay? Did I hurt you?" He sat down on the already ruined sofa with her straddling his lap. He pushed her hair away from her face so he could see her eyes.

"I'm… perfect," she assured him, scrunching her nose.

Nik laughed. "Yes, you are." He pulled her to him and wrapped his arms around her waist. Her breasts squashed against his chest had his dick coming back to life.

Sophia pressed their mouths together, her tongue finding his. His mate loved to kiss. She rose up on her knees and placed his erection at her entrance. She lowered herself onto his cock and set a slow rhythm that matched the music. Their beasts sated, Nik and Sophia made love until they could barely move.

As they were walking up the stairs to the bedroom, Sophia said, "We keep that up and we'll be needing a nursery in no time."

Nik couldn't keep quiet any longer. "Dante did mention the color pink."

Sophia stopped walking and stared at her mate. Nik grabbed her hands and kissed her knuckles. "What do you think about the name Lydia?"

EPILOGUE

2057

SOPHIA said goodbye to the children at the library where she volunteered once a week, reading to kids who were left in a mother's day out program. Even though she had a child of her own and another on the way, she had room in her heart for those whose family lives were less than perfect.

She was on her way to meet Isabelle at the diner where Dane had first met Marley. The sky was growing darker with every step she took. She could take the bus, but the diner was close enough she could walk. She hoped the rain held off until she was safely inside. When she was less than a block away, her phone rang. Amelia.

"Hello, sweet girl."

"Aunt So, where are you?"

"I'm headed to the diner to see Izzy, why?"

"I need you. I remembered you went to the library on Wednesdays. You're the closest one to me."

"Slow down. Where are you?"

"I'm at the bus terminal. Some creep is following me, and I don't have time to wait on Dad."

"I'll be right there. Don't go outside. Stay near other people."

Sophia's mind drifted back to when she was sixteen and she encountered a similar situation. The bus depot was three blocks from the diner. She took off running in that direction, calling her shifter forward. When she arrived at the terminal, it was like déjà vu.

Her sixteen-year-old self was sitting, waiting on JoJo to come rescue her from the man who had exposed himself to her on the darkened bus.

Only Amelia wasn't waiting for her. Sophia opened her senses and heard Amelia's voice coming from the men's restroom. When Sophia pushed open the door, a nasty man had her niece cornered. He had his cock in his hand, stroking it. "You want some of this?" he asked, shaking his dick in her direction.

Before he could shake it again, Sophia shoved his body against the wall holding him in place with her claws. "Get out of here, sweet girl. Go wait for me in the lobby." Amelia nodded and ran out the door. The man struggled with Sophia and managed to twist around facing her. Her mind flashed back, recognizing his black eyes. He was older, but the same man who exposed himself to her all those years ago had been ready to assault her family. Her claws were digging into his neck as she seethed, "You filthy bastard. I should have let my grandfather kill you." With her free hand, Sophia pushed the man's hand out of the way and latched onto his penis. She raked her claws down the length of his shaft, leaving it attached by a sliver of skin.

Sophia clamped her hand down over the man's mouth, smothering his scream. She pressed his nose together, restricting his oxygen until he passed out. When he slumped onto the floor, Sophia washed her hands and exited the restroom. She found Amelia and hauled the girl out of the terminal. "What did you do, Aunt So?"

"What should have been done a long time ago."

"Did you kill him?" the girl whispered.

"No. But I guarantee he'll never molest another young girl." She wrapped her arm around her niece's shoulders and hugged her tight. When they arrived at the diner, she told Amelia, "Go on in and tell Aunt Izzy to order me some tea. I have to make a phone call."

Once the girl was inside, Sophia called Nik. "Hey, Gorgeous. I need a favor."

"Anything for you, Baby."

"First, I need to you to hack into the security monitors at the bus terminal, if there are any. If they actually have some, I need you to wipe the feed from the last half hour."

"Okay, then what?"

"I need you to call Dane. There's a man in need of medical assistance in the restroom."

"Soph, Baby. What did you do?"

"I took care of our family. I promise I'm okay, but I need to get inside and check on Amelia before I call Abbi."

"I'm on it. But Soph, please come home so I can see with my own eyes you're all right."

"I will, just as soon as I have tea with Isabelle. Love you." Sophia hung up and headed into the diner. Her unborn baby was wild enough without her drinking coffee, so she settled for hot tea. Sophia slid into the booth next to an animated teenager.

"I'm telling you, Aunt Izzy, the man was a creep."

Isabelle cocked an eyebrow at Sophia. "I swear, I don't know who's worse... you or Tessa.

"Tessa," she and Amelia answered at the same time.

"Why were you on the bus anyway?" Sophia asked Amelia. "You're too young to be wandering around alone."

"One of mom's favorite ballet dancers is performing at the civic center to raise charity. I wanted to surprise her with tickets."

"You do know there's this thing called the internet? You could have bought them online."

"I don't have a credit card. I had to go to the box office to pay cash."

"Oh, sweet girl. Next time, call me, and I'll get the tickets for you."

"Thanks, Aunt So." Amelia kissed her on the cheek before diving into her hot chocolate.

Once the waitress was out of earshot, Isabelle asked, "What exactly did you do?"

Sophia plunged her tea bag up and down in the hot water. "I need to tell you a story. You were already in Greece, and I was sixteen..."

Nikolas and Lydia were standing beside the garage, waiting for her. Lydia, mimicking Nik's stance, was her father's child in every way. Sophia didn't bother hitting the garage door opener. She knew she had some explaining to do. She wouldn't do it in front of Lydia, though. The girl was only nine.

Nik opened the car door and held out his hand. Sophia had been blessed with her mate. He was still as loving and attentive as when they first mated. The sex hadn't gotten less in frequency, but they did have to be quieter now that they had a child in the house. "Hey, Gorgeous," she greeted him with a kiss. "Hello, my beautiful girl." She placed a kiss on her daughter's head before closing the door. "What's going on? You both act like I've been gone for weeks, not hours."

Lydia folded her arms over her chest. "Daddy was cussing a blue streak. I want to know what you did to make him mad."

Nik laughed and covered Lydia's mouth. "You're not supposed to tell my secrets."

She wiggled away and scowled at Sophia. For a nine-year-old, she was wise beyond her years. "Mo-om," she sang.

"Lydia," she sang in return. "I didn't do anything your father wouldn't have done." She tapped her daughter on the nose and headed toward the house. Once inside, Sophia decided to turn the interrogation tables. "I ran into Mrs. Mitchell at the library. She said you got another detention. Would you like to explain that?"

"Chip Abernathy was picking on Tabitha."

"Where was her brother?" Sophia couldn't believe Anthony would leave his twin alone long enough for someone to pick on her.

"In the principal's office. He got in trouble for punching Chip before lunch. Chip went after her again, so I stepped in."

Sophia couldn't get mad at her daughter when she had just taken up for someone, too. Nik remained quiet, having a pretty good idea of what happened at the bus terminal. He allowed her to be the disciplinarian, anyway.

"I can't believe Tabby didn't smack him herself," Sophia said.

"Nah, she has me and Anthony watching her six."

"Her six? You've been hanging out with your Aunt Tessa too much."

"Did you at least get a good shot in?" Nik asked. Sophia smacked him on the chest, and he rubbed the spot as if she actually hurt him. The only time she inflicted real pain was in the bedroom.

"Well, did you?" Sophia smirked.

"Of course I did. Uncle Frey would kick my butt if I didn't use good form."

Sophia and Nik laughed at their daughter even though she was not wrong. Until the kids were old enough to transition, Frey was teaching them martial arts.

"Besides, you've told me forever that family is everything, and we defend our family."

"That we do, sweet girl."

"So, am I in trouble?" Lydia batted her eyelashes at her father. Nik looked to Sophia who shook her head.

"No ma'am. Now, please go to your room so I can have a chat with your mom."

Lydia hugged them both before running up the stairs.

"Now, it's your turn, Mrs. Stone." Sophia had legally changed her name when she found out she was pregnant with Lydia. She was mated to Nik, and as shifters, that was all they needed to commit themselves to one another. Still, she liked the sound of it.

"Were there video cameras?"

"Yes. Who was the man?" Nik asked.

"Remember the story I told you of my bus trip to New Atlanta?"

Nik nodded. "Yeah. I still want to find that

sonofabitch and kill him."

"Put it this way. He won't be shaking his shit at girls anymore."

"That was him? Soph, did you kill him?"

"No, but I did render his dick useless from now until eternity," she said with a gleam in her eye.

"How is Amelia?"

"She's Frey's kid; she's fine. I'm telling you, Gorgeous, this bunch we're raising is going to be hell on wheels when they transition."

"They're already giving me ulcers."

"This is true. Ow, speaking of ulcers..." Sophia grabbed her stomach.

"You did not just call my son a stomach affliction," Nik chastised her.

"I'm the one carrying his big ass around. I have a right to call him what I want."

"I'd call him lucky. Lucky to have the best mother in the entire world." Nik pulled her as close as he could for a hug. "I'm proud of you, you know. For taking down the man in the bus terminal. I wish you would have called me and let me handle it, though."

"You'd have killed him. Besides, I'm glad to know that I was able to defend my family and get the creep off the street."

Nik kissed her. "Family is everything."

Sophia nodded. "And we defend our family."

A Note from the Author

I hope you enjoyed Nikolas and Sophia's adventure. They'll be back in upcoming books. If you enjoyed their story, please leave a review. It doesn't have to be long, just honest and heartfelt. Jasper and Trevor are next, and Jasper has to deal with a ghost from his past. I have tried to get you ready for Jasper and Trevor; make you fall in love with them enough to want to know their story. Some people don't read MM books, but I wrote theirs in a way you can read the book but skip over the sexy times. You'll know when they're coming. I hope you give them a chance, because love really is love.

About the Author

Faith Gibson is a multi-genre author who lives outside Nashville, Tennessee with the love of her life, and her four-legged best friend. She strongly believes that love is love, and there's not enough love in the world.

She began writing in high school and over the years, penned many stories and poems. When her dreams continued to get crazier than the one before, she decided to keep a dream journal. Many of these night-time escapades have led to a line, a chapter, and even a complete story. You won't find her books in only one genre, but they will all have one thing in common: a happy ending.

When asked what her purpose in life is, she will say to entertain the masses. Even if it's one person at a time. When Faith isn't hard at work on her next story, she can be found playing trivia while enjoying craft beer, listing to hard rock music (preferably live), reading, or playing with her pit bull pup.

Made in the USA
Monee, IL
10 October 2020